About the Author

Firstly, Mary Barr would like to thank you for reading her book. She has been wanting to write a 'chick flick' for quite some time. Ms. Barr knows this book is really not one because she enjoys divulging into the characters just a little too much. She knows only too well there is always another side to the page and a second or even a third meaning to everything. Ms. Barr loved writing this book, it was fun. She also loved all the characters, in their own ways. She's sorry about the rather unexpected ending, but life does have a way of biting back, when least expected!

How to Buy a Husband

Mary Barr

How to Buy a Husband

Vanguard Press

VANGUARD PAPERBACK

© Copyright 2024
Mary Barr

The right of Mary Barr to be identified as author of
this work has been asserted by her in accordance with the
Copyright, Designs and Patents Act 1988.

All Rights Reserved

No reproduction, copy or transmission of this publication
may be made without written permission.
No paragraph of this publication may be reproduced,
copied or transmitted save with the written permission of the publisher, or in
accordance with the provisions
of the Copyright Act 1956 (as amended).

Any person who commits any unauthorised act in relation to this publication
may be liable to criminal prosecution and civil claims for damages.

A CIP catalogue record for this title is available from the British Library.

ISBN 978-1-83794-248-0

This is a work of fiction. Names, characters, businesses, places, events and
incidents are either the products of the author's imagination or used in a
fictitious manner. Any resemblance to actual persons, living or dead, or actual
events is purely coincidental.

Vanguard Press is an imprint of
Pegasus Elliot Mackenzie Publishers Ltd.
www.pegasuspublishers.com

First Published in 2024

Vanguard Press
Sheraton House Castle Park
Cambridge England

Printed & Bound in Great Britain

Dedication

To all the girls who didn't know –
'Love is given – not taken'.

To my daughter, Veronica.

Contents

Chapter 1	Lyme Harrington-Lynch	13
Chapter 2	Chased on the Ocean	25
Chapter 3	He Drives an Aston Martin	38
Chapter 4	Madam Roderic ~ 1	55
Chapter 5	Another Date	58
Chapter 6	Love Above the Clouds	67
Chapter 7	Madam Roderic ~ 2	95
Chapter 8	Feather Brookston	99
Chapter 9	The First Date	111
Chapter 10	Granny Harry	137
Chapter 11	The Date	153
Chapter 12	Madam Roderic ~ 3	166
Chapter 13	Brook and Morris	171
Chapter 14	Daddy Takes Charge	192
Chapter 15	How to Buy a Husband – The Plan	206
Chapter 16	How to Buy a Husband	221
Chapter 17	Madam Roderic ~ 4	233
Chapter 18	The Soft Power of Conrad Lynch	238
Chapter 19	Holt Visser	253
Chapter 20	Engaged at Last	256
Chapter 21	The Wedding of Brook and Morris	264
Chapter 22	Madam Roderic ~ 5	275
Chapter 23	Lyme and Holt's Wedding Day	283
Chapter 24	An Ending or just the Beginning?	301

Chapter 1
Lyme Harrington-Lynch

My name is Lyme Harrington-Lynch. I'm thirty-five years old. I have straight brown hair, large alert violet eyes under long dark lashes, my best feature so I'm told, are my good teeth. I know I'm not pretty and I'm certainly no beauty, but I really have no desire to be beautiful. I see all the work it takes. Although, when I'm pushed to make an effort on my appearance, I will do so provided it doesn't take up too much of my time.

This is my story. You may think it's slightly unusual, or you may not. But growing up, I didn't know my life was not like everyone else's – it was all I knew. As you may have guessed by the title of this book, I bought my husband. Yes, I did, and to a point it worked! I will tell you how it happened and how it ended but first a little more about me.

As you know my name is Lyme. There is only my father and myself; our main residence is in the affluent city of Westlake in Texas. Although, my daddy has many homes around the world, along with two private jets in which to travel. One jet is solely for business use for himself and his executives, while the other is for our personal use. As you may have guessed, I am an only child. I don't mind, I have never known it any other way. Although, as you can imagine it does put all the responsibilities and expectations squarely on my shoulders. And with a father – who is one of the richest oil barons in America – it is a lot of responsibility.

My mother was the beautiful socialite, Jennifer Harrington. She was a petite, auburn haired, beauty. To me, she was the most beautiful lady I had ever seen. I know it took her a lot of time to remain beautiful, but she was dedicated to her beauty. I'd watch everyone stop when she entered a room. I saw the way the men looked at her. But always Daddy would shine with more admiration than them all. He would glow with pride when she was around.

You may have noticed I sadly speak of her in the past tense. I was just twelve years old when she died. It was a most unfortunate age for any girl to lose her mother. It was unexpected, sudden and tragic as most deaths are. My father never spoke of what actually caused her death. He shut himself away in his suite of rooms for almost two months – no one saw him or spoke to him. I was left on my own to grieve, however I could. I'd often sit outside his closed double doors crying, and I believed I could hear him sobbing inside his rooms as well, or maybe I just wanted to think that. He was not a man to show weakness of any sort but like me, I know her passing hit him hard. For the next several years my Granny Harry would stay over, she would hold me close while I sobbed and just remain in my presence. I could never have got through this terrible time without her.

So, I grew into a teenager. When I needed guidance, I would remember all the things she'd told me. Many of those things, which at the time didn't seem important, but in my teenage years I'd look back and try to remember her words; they suddenly seemed vitally important! By the time I entered my twenties, I realized that being a beauty was hard work and maybe I didn't want to be one after all. I possessed neither her good looks nor persistent motivation. The constant criticism from my father was also a major reason why I decided to just be, me.

My life unfolded like an empty diary, something you held dear and keep close but upon opening it, you realize the pages are almost blank. Each day or so there is an entry, something superficial about where I went or what I did, who I met or the parties I attended, but each page contained a lot of blank empty space, on which there was no words, no thoughts and no emotions shared. The emptiness of my diary was indeed like the emptiness of my heart. I didn't want my innermost thoughts to be felt, seen or written. I didn't want to show the depth of my emptiness, my despair, anguish, desperation or depression.

Late at night, I would lay alone in my huge bed safely in my bedroom in the dark. There was only me, me alone by myself with my thoughts and dreams. Alone, wrapped in my raw desperation, solitude and fear. My need was so deep. I never wanted to allow it out; I never wanted to meet it – to feel it. So, I focused instead on the blank and empty solitude inside of me, it was a familiar place. That place was my only true friend. A place, I happily receded to.

There was nothing there. It was a void. A deep, dark, heavy hole of nothing, but I guarded that place. It was precious to me, more precious than anything I possessed. It was my deep, dark solitary void of nothing and with it I could do whatever I choose, create anything I wished and in my world I could be anyone I wanted to be. As I lay in my bed at night, I felt safe and secure. It was a time that was mine, all mine and I treasured every minute.

But time was not my friend and right now it was proving so more than any other time in my life. My clock was ticking and had from the moment I was born. Judgment day was looming and it was getting very close.

Over time things change, and these changes had been sneaking up on me for years. I knew they were lurking, but suddenly my time had run out. I was thirty-five years old and my time had run out. Maybe I sound melodramatic, but it's how I'm feeling. That awful feeling when your life is closing in and you know without a doubt changes are afoot. Daddy's deadline was upon me and what Daddy wanted, he got. Several weeks before my thirty-fifth birthday, which was another reason for him to throw a gigantic party, another social event here in Texas, to which all the rich and famous people were invited. I confronted him, I asked, begged and cajoled him for more time to find a husband. He wanted an heir. It was the one requirement of me he had made very plain over the years and it was the one thing he would never back down on. My whole adult life, he had told me that he wanted a grandson or perhaps, now he'd even settle for grand-daughter. He wanted this child to be presented to him before I was thirty-five. He would choose my husband after that time, if I could not. And my time was up. The ticking of the clock had proved my enemy and now my time had run out.

But before I continue on, let me tell you about my father. He is the reason I need an empty void – a place of safety to recede into at night.

Conrad Lynch, or Lyn to his friends; is a force to be reckoned with. He stands over six foot tall, but he looks shorter due to his stocky build. With shoulders as wide as a barn door and legs the size of tree trunks. He has a solid muscular body. It has always been so; I don't know why because since I've known him, he's never done any manual work and lifting a whisky glass to his lips is the entire extent of his daily exercise. However, at sixty years of age he is strong, very strong physically and mentally. He built his empire from nothing. Nothing but sweat and luck that is. He is single-minded in all he wants and nothing gets in his way. His empire is built on oil. He is a genuine oil baron and one of the richest. Forget the old oil barons like J. D. Rockefeller or J. Paul Getty. Conrad Lynch is even richer and more successful than the legendary Haroldson Lafayette who died in 1974. Conrad Lynch's riches have long surpassed Rex Tillerson of ExxonMobil and James Mulva of ConocoPhillips.

Conrad Lynch sits at the very top of the ladder and at present he is slightly richer than Harold Hamm – the founder and CEO of Oklahoma Resources. Harold Hamm like Conrad Lynch holds the reins of his company tightly while he retains ownership of over seventy-five percent of company stock. At sixty-four years of age, Harold Hamm is four years older than Daddy, but in power and dollars. They are well-matched.

However, I don't know how Harold Hamm reached such heights of success nor do I know him well, but I know Daddy well and he is devious, cunning, street smart and single minded. Lynch Oil is almost entirely owned by him. I hold a few shares, of course, as do some of his top executives, but he keeps control by retaining a high percentage of shares. He also holds full ownership of Lynch Transport, Lynch Media and shares a fifty-one percent ownership to my forty-nine percent of Lyme Hotels and Resorts. Supposedly, Lyme Hotels and Resorts is my baby to run as I please. Although on closer inspection, you would see he handles and oversees everything concerning the resorts and I am merely told what to do and when. He plays his hand well and uses me as the front person, so I appeared to be the power behind the wealth and success of the Lyme Resorts and Hotels – when in fact no one but Daddy holds the power. I know no one ever will, not while he lives.

I mentioned he is devious, and one of the ways he controls others is to know a dirty little secret or two about them. Usually, the secret contains something sordid, immoral, improper or illegal, something that will instantly destroy them, if ever the world gets to hear about it. He holds the power. The power to destroy lives. For this purpose, Daddy employs Newton, a big thug of a man. He says little and does what he's told, without question. He is a kind of a bodyguard, private eye and hit man all rolled into one. He's seldom seen but never moves far away. Newton, no doubt, is kept constantly busy with my father's requests and orders of one sort or another.

My father is extremely charismatic and has a huge presence; you don't even need to look up when he enters a room to know he's there. You feel him, magnetic and powerful. He is unmistakably. Soon his booming voice, authority, arrogance and dominance leave no doubt that Conrad Lynch has arrived and is in control. I have never seen anyone remain unaffected by a meeting. Furthermore, it goes without saying that he is in command. I often wonder, if I am the only one who dares stand up to him. However, I do that seldom, it is always rather daunting and emotionally draining for me. Daddy appears to thrive on conflict, he feeds on it. He finds it entertaining that anyone should challenge his authority and like most people who know him, I hate him for it.

My father, Conrad Lynch, is cold, hard, and always in control. He stands tall and he stands alone, isolated and uncompromising. I sometimes wonder, if that is where he wants to be. You may wonder why there was never another Mrs. Lynch. Well, there were many ladies; they would arrive late at night under Newton's supervision and leave early in the morning in Newton's car. I seldom met them and was glad I didn't. At social functions he would always have a young, beautiful woman on his arm, usually a different one each week. He'd treat her well. Although, I'd observed the coldness in his eyes never faded. He would be happy and laughing and the center of attention like he always is, but the coldness behind his eyes remained. I saw it and I knew everyone else did also. Was it there when my mother was alive? – I don't know – I guess I wasn't old enough to understand. Sometimes, should he require a partner, I would be called upon or else, Amber Buxton – the CEO of Lyme Resorts and Hotels. Amber Buxton also oversees Lynch Media and she is maybe the only other woman he respects apart from me; if he does indeed respect anyone.

Amber Buxton is forty-five years old and beautiful in a classy elegant kind of way. She has used a good cosmetic surgeon over the years and it shows. She had shiny brown hair, green eyes; sparkling personalities, dazzling smile and fast wit. However, her skills as CEO of Lyme Hotels and Resorts are what set her apart from the rest. She is a sharp, astute businesswoman. My daddy trusts her as much as he can trust anyone. He also likes and maybe trusts Padbury Prentice – the CEO of Lynch Oil, and Lynch Transport and trucking. These are his two wingmen and along with Newton completed his inner circle. To be included is a rare honor indeed.

Conrad Lynch has a square jaw, a rugged complexion with deep lines furrowing his face down either side of a firm mouth, and a mass of curly, sandy hair streaked with gray and small steel blue eyes. Around his eyes, you see evidence of laugh lines where the sun hasn't ventured, but these lines happened long ago – now perhaps, just a shadow of forgotten happiness. Should he dislike you? His steel blue eyes will search your soul and cut through you like a knife. When he is angry – which is often – his pupils almost disappear. They contract until they are tiny black granite dots in the center of his blazing blue eyes – he will stare at you without blinking and you will see so much hatred and venom even the toughest of men fall weak at the knees. Needless to say, I challenged him rarely and chose my battles well.

Now, I must introduce my two ditzy friends. Firstly, Janice Pansy, we call her 'Pan' as in Peter Pan. Actually, she is my only ditzy friend and such a girly girl. I have known Pan forever. She may not be my first choice of friends today if I had a choice, but I went to grade school with Pan and she lives not far from me. Pan's family is also extremely wealthy except hers is old money, while ours is new – usually the two don't mix.

The best way to describe Pan is ditzy. She giggles all the time over anything; she is a plastic blonde and has everything in all the right places. I seldom see her eat actual food, but she drinks anything and often. Her days are spent staying beautiful and her nights partying. Her name is found on the 'whose who' of society. Pan is very rich but not very smart; in fact, she would go along with most anything so long as it didn't require any kind of exertion and didn't chip her nails. She's very pretty, and she had been married and divorced twice by the age of thirty-five. Her parents ensured, she married well and, on each occasion, and with each husband she becomes richer than the last. Because Pan is truly ditzy, she allows Madam Roderic – a well-known and not so well-liked clairvoyant – to run her life.

Madam Roderic appears at the gates of the Pan's mansion at least three times a week. Whether Pan calls her or she just arrives, I do not know, but one thing I do know is that Pan never denies her entry and hangs on her every word. This strange woman who I have only met on a couple of occasions appears to run Pan's life. She tells her what to wear, what functions to attend, which ones not to attend, and who she should keep company with. Madam Roderic's words not mine. Apparently, according to Pan, Madam Roderic predicted each of Pan's marriages and then their demise. Brook and I joked that it was probably Madam Roderic who scared Pan's husbands away. She gives both Brook and I the creeps. We agree that fortune-tellers are fun but this woman is anything but fun. She stands about six feet tall and is as thin as a spring breeze. Her hair, when I saw her last was wispy and bright purple.

Her face, I liken to a hungry hawk. She has beady brown eyes that constantly dart around, thin lips and a long hooked nose. She wears too much makeup that doesn't match her skin – instead leaves a line where it stops and her natural shallow skin color begins. Under her multi-colored flowing dresses or robes, as she prefers they are called, it is hard to tell if she is actually a woman at all. Her voice is deep, yet quiet. Her long nails and boney hands are cold to the touch. Collectively, she is rather scary. Although Pan seemed enamored by her and believes emphatically everything she has to tell, Madam Roderic comes at a cost. Pan once told me she charges two thousand dollars a visit but defended Madam Roderic's astronomical fees by letting me know – this covers her for as long as she stays. Pan ended her statement with a giggle as only Pan can.

Then there is Feather Brookston, we call her; 'Brook' deeming Feather too weird a name plus I never thought it did anything to enhance my unusual name either. We would be known as Lyme and Feather – no, no, no! Her family may not be rich, but they are certainly not poor; however, they don't live in Westlake like Pan and I. Brook is a smart girl. She went to university and studied law; she's into adventure, and I've had lots of fun with her and I've also learned a lot by being with her. Brook's tall and willowy with auburn brown hair and big brown eyes. She shows all her emotions in her eyes and there are many as her moods change often. Brook is often unhappy, and she blames her string of boyfriends. I think it is mainly because she prefers bad boys to gentlemen. She thinks of herself as streetwise and a little crazy, and I think her assessment is almost correct.

I go to the shooting range and play tennis with Brook. We got our pilot's license together and took to yachting and piloting boats at the same time. Brook is the one I share my adventures with. Brook is the one who will be screwing the captain while we are having our first lesson on boating. Then, I must somehow manage to steer the boat, so I learn fast. I had to with Brook because her mind is never far from sex and her next conquest.

Brook just purchased her own house – I feel proud of her as she did it on her own. I know she gets an allowance from her family's trust fund, and I know she is a partner in several law firms – she has helped to set up. But the fact that she saved enough money to purchase a house on her own is impressive; what is more impressive is that she wanted to own her own house at all. I know how easy it is to live off your rich parents; I do it and have never really thought about it until now. I guess I could purchase my own home, but why would I when Daddy has comfortable homes all over the world?

Does Brook have my back? I don't know… But maybe more than Pan who wouldn't even know what I was talking about…

Now you have a small insight into my two best friends, I will share with you some of my life.

Chapter 2
Chased on the Ocean

The hot breeze snapped at my hair whipping it across my face. Casually, I reached behind my head and braided it with my fingers. It would stay that way for a while and remain out of my eyes. The sun glistened on the blue water, it felt warm and welcoming. After my earlier confrontation with Daddy about giving me some more time to find a husband, I decided not to stay around him during the weekend. I knew it would be tense, should I cross paths with him in our huge house? It was actually Fox, our housekeeper – the woman who had tried to take the place of my mother – who suggested it.

"Lyme, I know he's upset you yet again, I can see it in your eyes. Go somewhere this weekend, you're only going to mope if you stay around here. I do believe you had a little win. It's something big for Mr. Lyn to give you more time. It's indeed something. Have some fun, and things will look different when you return, I promise they will!"

'Maybe I shall Fox, I know you're usually right. I'll call the girls.' And half an hour later Pan, Brook and I were on the phone making plans to fly to L.A. for the weekend and take the boat to Catalina Island. Daddy owned a beautiful twelve thousand square feet oceanfront home on Newport Beach. The house came complete with its own mooring. Our boat was an Azimut 48 and was, of course, named 'The Harrington'. It didn't spend its entire life moored by the house, but instead it was usually birthed in a secure dockyard not far away. I called the pilot of our jet to check it was available and then the house in Newport Beach. They would contact Captain Chipper Lopez. He would have our Azimut 48 stocked, fueled and ready to go. She was a sleek, modern marvel, and I was looking forward to piloting her, after we left the coast.

Once the steward poured us each a glass of crisp cool champagne, we settled in for the flight.

'Do you like the color?' Pan asked, waving her newly-painted nails in front of our faces. They had little flowers on each nail with gold sparkles in the center. Certainly, a work of art and they did look pretty, but not practical.

'You know we're going on the boat, Pan,' I commented, holding her hand to the light of the jets window as I inspected them more closely. Maybe I should get my nails done one day; not nearly as long as Pans, of course, but they did look girly.

'I know. Well, everyone can do everything for me. I can lift a glass, so what else could I possibly need to do? So long as my hair isn't messy because I can't hold the comb and I wouldn't know what to do with it anyway. I have so many extensions.' Pan giggled, flashing her pink gold and diamond iPhone, which sparkled brilliantly as the light caught it. She then proceeded to take yet another selfie of her nails.

'Pan, we haven't any staff on the boat, just the captain.'

'Well, what's his job anyway if he can't wait on us?' She giggled before turning the phone toward her perfectly made-up face and smiling into it.

'He's supposed to be piloting the boat, Pan,' I said, laughing at her dumbness as I often did.

'Hope he loads up the water skis,' Brook added and when no one answered she continued, 'Is this the same captain as last time or do you have a new guy now?'

'Sorry, Brook, same guy. He's at least fifty and married,' I replied.

'So, I gave up a weekend of wicked sex with Ric Jameson for a weekend of no sex with two girls on a boat with an old married captain? I guess I'll just have to find someone new elsewhere then. Ric is getting on my nerves, actually,' Brook added, looking down. I caught her look and knew there was more.

'Forget him, Brook, he's a bad boy. He's not worth it.'

'I know he's trouble; so heavily into drugs he can hardly keep it together lately. He kinda scares me. I'm glad we're getting away. Although, he was really angry with me for breaking our date. Says he'll follow me as he needs more powder and apparently, I'm going to get it for him.'

'Brook, be careful. That's a dangerous game,' I added quietly, not liking what I was hearing,

'Yeah, even I know that. Drugs never make you beautiful – they just get you wasted. Remember what happened to Weston.' Pan surprised us; she seldom joined in on anything serious. We briefly thought of her brother who was in rehab again after another overdose. We were driven from the jet to the boat and in no time, we were leaving solid land behind us...

The sun glistened off the blue ocean as we boarded the long sleek boat. Once the captain had greeted us, he wasted no time getting underway. Soon we had changed into our bikinis and were seated on the deck up the front.

'More champagne? I hate pouring, but I guess there's no one else,' Brook said jumping up and heading to galley to retrieve the half-empty bottle of champagne. We lounged on the deck, sunning our limbs and watching the world fly by. The calm blue ocean and the company of the girls made me feel alive again, and no doubt the champagne helped. I usually only had two glasses, but today, I was on my fourth.

Brook came up from below deck with the bottle in her hand as she flopped down beside us into the deeply cushioned loungers, then she whispered,

'Hope you bought your gun with you Brooke?'

'Why?' inquired Brooke lazily half closing her eyes,

'Just in case, Brook, You know I usually bring mine with me.'

'I know, me to. I had a feeling, so I bought enough ammo to kill a small army. Don't know why, but I guess Ric's getting to me more than I care to admit.'

'Brook here, pour,' Pan ordered holding out her glass.

'Chipper will never let you take the wheel if you have much more to drink Lyme.'

'Who cares? I'm really glad, I decided to get away. Look at that boat, Brook, it's moving toward us way too fast. It's been following us for a while, and now it seems to be closing in.' I said, turning fully toward the rear of the boat and shielding my eyes from the sun. I stared at the boat rapidly approaching in our wake.

'Maybe, we're going to be attacked by pirates.' Pan giggled raising her iPhone and taking several photos of the boat behind us.

Brook hadn't looked behind as she was facing us on the cushion and unlike Pan and I, she had her back toward the rear of the boat.

'Miss Lyme, can you come, please?' Chipper, the captain called over the intercom. I jumped to my feet thinking Chipper was happy for me to take the wheel. The Azimut 48 had the bridge on the second deck at the top of the boat, so the captain had a wide unobtrusive view of everything around him. I raced up the stairs and was soon standing beside Chipper. In front of me, the controls, computer screen, and many gadgets moved and jostled on the boat's brightly lit dashboard. The Azimut 48 was equipped with the latest of everything, and Chipper often said it was his favorite of all the boats, he piloted.

'I'm ready,' I said eagerly standing at his shoulder.

'Miss Lyme, there's a boat following us. It's a Sabre 42 salon express. It joined us just after we left the marina.

It appeared to be waiting for us to leave.' Chipper zoomed in on the boat with the powerful camera mounted inside the rear of the boat. Together, we clearly saw two men; one looked vaguely familiar, but I thought no more of it.

Then Chipper continued, 'I'm not liking the look of this. I've radioed the coast guard and forwarded to him photos of the boat and its occupants.' Chipper hadn't finished speaking when he stopped talking and wound in still closer on the closed-circuit TV monitor. To our astonishment, one of the men seemed to be loading a rifle. As we watched, he moved up onto the front deck of the speeding boat, while the second man remained at the wheel. The boat was so close now it was tossing in the water from our bow wave. Although our boat cut through the water with little movement, we still left a white, foamy wave in our wake.

'He's loading a Remington Versa Max Sportsman, it has auto load and could easily take us out from there.' My last words were almost a whisper as suddenly, I realized what was about to go down.

'Pan, get below deck now. Brook, get the guns; seems like we're under attack, hurry!' I screamed into the intercom. I saw Pan stay where she was and giggled at my urgency, while Brook jumped into action almost diving below in her haste. Chipper again radioed the coast guard explaining our predicament and giving him coordinates of our location. He was still talking on the radio when the first ping hit the side of the boat just below where we were standing on the bridge. I looked down to see Pan turn her head in the direction of the shots, she still hadn't moved. I lay on the deck while Chipper moved further down his seat. Again, I called for Pan to get below.

Brook emerged with our guns; together we had purchased the same type. We each owned a 45-caliber automatic Remington 1911 handgun. The main reason we liked them was because they were finished in black with bright red grip. So, we can tell them apart we have our initials printed on the red barrel – mine was in gold and Brooks in silver.

Brook crawled out of the galley on her stomach, a gun in each hand; she was now wearing a green camouflage t-shirt over her tiny orange bikini. She slithered along the deck as the first full round of gunfire hit the boat. Soon another round quickly followed, somewhere a window shattered. Brook grabbed Pan and almost dragged her toward the galley before pushing her to safety. I knew she never would have made it herself. I knew Brook loved this stuff; she would be seeing it as a huge adventure and Brook was fearless. I really needed my gun. Brook fired off a few rounds directly at the boat behind. It was no more than twenty feet to our rear and beginning to move toward our right side.

Her first round fell short, but Brook was a good marksman and soon she had blown out the windscreen of the boat. Still on my belly, I crawled to the edge of the deck above her. I leaned out over the side and she instinctively knew what I wanted; in a single motion she threw my gun up to me. Her aim was good and reaching out, I caught it in mid-air. Our attackers took instant advantage of this and hit us with another burst of gunfire. I saw holes in the deck all around me, and then I heard Chipper groan loudly. He had been hit. Blood oozed from his right arm as he tried desperately to hold the boat on course and keep her moving at maximum speed.

I wondered, why we couldn't out run the Sabre? we were newer and faster, but now I could see the problem. I saw Chipper lose his grip on the wheel as all around us gunfire ricocheted off every surface. The beautiful dashboard of the boat was smashed and the TV screens were completely shot out.

'Chipper's been shot, Brook, I need to steer,' I yelled to Brook who had by now managed to crawl behind the engine hole and was perfectly positioned to attack the enemy. The boat was careering around wildly in the ocean. Chipper still held the throttle open and kept us moving fast. Our speed was the only thing stopping the Sabre from coming along side, that and our erratic movements. Chipper was slowly sinking to floor – the look of pain and sweat on his face openly apparent.

The Sabre seemed intent on boarding us, and at one point when the gunfire lapsed, I saw Brook quickly reload and throw up another cartridge to me; it landed some distance away, but I didn't need it yet anyway. Then a man's voice yelled to us over the noise.

'Give up, you bitch, we're coming aboard, you know you've lost. You know what we want…' That was what I thought he said, I know he had tried to say things before, but each time Brook opened fire upon him and his words were lost. It was scary having another large boat so close that we could yell to each other and be heard. We had no satellite, no radio and the steering seemed to be getting heavier. The moment I heard the voice, I slowed the engine and whirled around. This had to end. In an instant, I hide behind the captain's chair and focused on the enemy. Until now, I hadn't really been trying to hit anyone, even though I thought I had, but now I was intent on doing so. I had inherited Daddy's single-mindedness. I was aiming for the driver of the boat. Their windscreen was long shattered and they had kicked a small hole in the center from which to see through. It was at this hole that I aimed as our boat began to career forward unaided by human hands. The second I had him in my sight, I fired a heavy round directly at his chest.

The reaction was instant. I had a hit. The boat swerved hard to the right away from the back end of our boat, as it did so, the shooter who was lying on the deck, flew up in the air. Brook fired heavily at him. I knew I must grab the wheel but before I did, I aimed at the rear of the boat; it appeared to be now half out of the water. I thought it might flip completely, but I know the Sabre was solidly designed. I aimed a round into the gas tank. I assumed it was located at the back. I fired. My shots sunk deep into the fiberglass hull. I waited, but nothing happened.

Then the shooter, who had been flung from the boat high up in the air, swiveled his body toward us and raised his gun. He fired directly at me from his upright position, and I felt my hair tugged out of my scalp. Then seconds before he hit the water, he again fired; this time around, it hit our boat just below the water line. He disappeared under the surface as his boat circled wildly in the water. Some distance away I saw the water turn slightly red as the driver of the boat surfaced. In the distance the coast guard approached. On the floor at my feet, Chipper moaned with pain; he must have been hit by another ricocheting bullet and now blood oozed from his left thigh, also.

I knew we'd been hit where it hurt most, I knew water must now be pouring into the hold; I understood I must act before we sunk. I grabbed the wheel and turned sharply for the coast. I missed the guy in the water by inches and the look on his face was worth it.

'Harrington, this is the coast guard you've taken a hit to the right side of your hull and you are not responding to our radio calls. What can we do?' the coast guard called. I didn't want to slow the engine, but I had to answer him, so I came close to the coast guard's vessel and as I slowed, I felt the boat was already beginning to lean as water raced into our hull.

'I'm going to try and make a run for the shore, we're badly damaged. Please, arrest the bandits that attacked us.' and before they had time to answer I roared off, leaving a trail of foaming white bow waves in my wake. Moments later, Brook was on the bridge, she had the first aid kit and was kneeling down next to Chipper. The boat felt heavy as I steered, it was exhausting trying to keep it straight.

'Lyme, we're taking in water.'

'I know, Brook, we've taken a hit below the waterline; the bastard was professional. If I can plane the boat, it will lift out of the water, and maybe go fast enough that the holes remain above the waterline and we can make it to shore.'

'You'll never make it, it'll never work.' Chipper groaned, becoming semi-conscious briefly as Brook tried to bandage his wounds and stop the blood. He groaned loudly with pain and then slipped again into unconsciousness.

'Where we headed, Lyme, the marina is that way?' Brook added, pointing up the coast.

'I'm going to run the boat onto the beach, it's our only chance; otherwise, we'll sink.'

'I'm bored. Can I come out now? The carpets beginning to get wet and the boat seemed to be tilting. Although I finished the champagne, so maybe it's me who's tilting.' Pan giggled emerging from the galley, still holding the empty bottle. Brook looked at me and said nothing, she just rolled her eyes and I did the same. Soon Pan asked,

'What happened to the captain? He looks sick and the boat is so untidy.'

'Have some more champagne, Pan, and get us a glass too,' I called.

'Well, Madam Roderic told me not to get on a boat with you too; she said it could be dangerous and thought that I would maybe get bored, and I think she was right. No, Brook, I will not pour you a glass of champagne, I've just had a fresh manicure.' Pan said giggling as she examined her nails; no one was listening.

Brook was looking over the side of our boat, it was leaning heavily, and from the smoke trail behind us and the sound of the engine laboring; we could soon be in serious trouble. We were only about half a mile from shore, and I was beginning to see people playing on the edge of the beaches.

'You know it's illegal, Lyme,' Brook said, and I knew she was referring to beaching a boat this size on a public beach. I nodded and asked her to check for rocks as we drew closer. I knew there was a small area of private beach enclosed in some rocks, and that was where I was headed. Daddy knew the owners, and if I had to pay them off for using their beach, I would, without hesitation.

'Get on your cell phone, Brook, we should have service now; call 911, get an ambulance, get help.' I ordered realizing I sounded like Daddy. Brook hung over the side; the back of our boat was almost in the water.

'We're not going to make Lyme, forget the rocks, move faster.' I doubted if there would be any rock anyway, so I hit the throttle. Chipper groaned with the sudden movement of the boat, and she lurched forward, wounded and desperate.

I headed straight for the shore as the ocean invaded the deck. We hit the sand with speed to spare. Bang, we made it; we were safely on dry land.

'You're a rough driver, Lyme, the captain's better at it than you,' Pan called – she still had the champagne bottle in hand. Then she added, 'Why are we here?' as she slowly looked over the side at the deserted beach under our boat. However, Pan quickly adapted as she always did. She posed in several places on the boat and began taking selfies of herself and then posted them online.

While we waited for help, I looked at Brook and wondered,

'Who the hell were they? I guess they were pirates. Although it was a nice boat for pirates to have, probably stolen, and we must have been a random target!'

Brook's face was white, I thought she was gutsier than that, but as I stared at her I knew it was something else.

'What's up, Brook, what are you hiding?' Just as we heard the siren from the ambulance approaching, Brook whispered,

'It was Ric…' It took me moment to comprehend just whom Ric was, and when I understood, I didn't reply.

Pan and Brook returned to Texas on the jet, while I stayed behind to sort things out. I knew Pan had another important social engagement that night to which both Brook, and I were invited. I hoped Brook attended. I'd never seen her so unnerved by any man but something about Ric scared her.

I emailed Daddy and apologized for making him angry. I knew he wouldn't acknowledge it, and I had never tried this before, but somehow, I felt weakened by the time on the boat. Then I said, 'I am ordering this year's model of the Azimut 48.' Then I asked, 'What did he want to call her?' In moments his reply came through, straight forward and simply.

It read, 'Harrington 2 – glad you're having fun.'

Chapter 3
He Drives an Aston Martin

There was a lot to organize before I returned to Texas. I checked on Chipper, the moment I took the girls to the jet. He was conscious after coming out of surgery. His wife by his side, he seemed in less pain. She was a short chubby Mexican woman with kind eyes and unkempt hair. She set upon me, the moment I entered the room. I didn't think the sound of her loud voice would help Chipper recover any faster, but perhaps he was used to it; she clearly wore the pants in the relationship. She was worried about the bills, while he wasn't working and recovering.

'…we have our son's tuition at university and my daughter's car payments, this has come at such a bad time. When Chipper recovers a little, I will ask him if I must sell the house; I think it's the only way…'

'Mrs. Lopez…'

'…and he will lose lot of his regular clients also, and this is his busy season. It promised to be his best year ever. Chipper is living his dream…'

'Mrs. Lopez,' I said for the second time hoping to get her attention. I understood she was in shock and assumed her constant talking was the result. I was relieved to see Chipper again had some color in his face and appeared more comfortable. Although his wife was not doing anything to create a calm atmosphere. Finally, she stopped and looked at me,

'I am sorry for your husband's condition...' I began.

But she cut me off again. 'You cannot imagine how this will bring us down, life is such a struggle...'

'Mrs. Lopez, please listen to me.'

'Yes, yes, all right, who are you?'

'I am Lyme Harrington-Lynch.' At the sound of my name she dropped Chippers hand, leaped out of her chair, and looked like she was about to attacked me,

'You, you are the reason my Chipper is laying here? You are...'

'Is everything all right in here? Another five minutes only then Mr. Lopez must rest,' the nurse said briskly, poking her head around the glass door. Mrs. Lopez quickly calmed down, smiled and nodded. I took this as my chance to continue.

'Mrs. Lopez, I am trying to make this right. Your husband is fully covered by our insurance policy – both medical and physically. You will not need to sell your home—' I began.

She cut me off again. 'You don't understand you're a rich bitch. How could you know, you think a bit of insurance will make this go away? You think you can make this right...'

Just then Chipper moaned, opened his eyes, looked directly at his wife and said, 'Listen, my dear, listen to Lyme.' And his eyelids closed again. I was getting increasing annoyed with Mrs. Lopez. I wanted to leave and come back to check on Chipper later, once she was gone.

'Mrs. Lopez, you are clearly not in any state of mind to listen to what I have to say, or to the offer I am trying to present to you.' She opened her mouth to speak, but I kept on talking. As I spoke, I handed to her a small brown overnight bag that was partly full. 'In here is two hundred thousand dollars in cash; it is yours free and clear and will help you pay your bills until Chipper is well again. Sorry for your troubles and also what happened to Chipper; he is a good man.' With that, I got to my feet and walked swiftly out of the room. Mrs. Lopez's voice began again immediately. She was incorrigible!

Both Brook and I had sustained some minor glass cuts and bruises from the attack, and once back at the house we needed to use the first aid kit on each other, so now I looked a fright. The bruising was starting to appear darker, and I had several Band-Aids on my neck, cheeks and hands to cover the cuts I had sustained. I had a meeting with Amber Buxton and the architect for Lyme Resorts and Hotels early next week, so I hoped I healed before then. We were just completing another resort and when the talk turns to color schemes and decorating, Daddy hands things over to me. I had decided to stay on at Newport Beach until after the meeting; I knew I would enjoy the change of scenery.

I also wanted to oversee the purchase of our new boat along with the old one being taken away. It would be restored and sold. I watched as they managed with difficulty to get the forty-eight feet luxury cruiser onto the boat trailer from the sand where I'd beached it. They had first tried to fix the holes in the hull and pump the water but it proved too time consuming, and the owners of the beach wanted the boat moved. I thought their request reasonable, considering. I knew I should offer them money, but they didn't accept it and said they just wanted the boat gone. I believe they saw this as getting into Daddy's good books in some way. Apparently, the property owner imported large trucks and had previously supplied some for Daddy's trucking fleet; I believe he hoped to do so again.

The next day I spent with my old college friend, Vaughn Holt. Vaughn had married into a novo rich and well-respected Newport Beach family. She now had two delightful children. I knew after the conversation changed from her children; it would move onto my state as a single woman. We'd recently had a brief telephone conversation, so I knew she intending again to introduce me to another man whom I didn't know and didn't care to know. Another blind date! Nothing inspired me less. Sure, they were all nice guys; sometimes they were even good looking, but the thought of spending my life with them and my bed. No, I just couldn't do it.

Although, I will meet whoever she asked me to meet this time, mainly because she knows of Daddy's deadline, and she also knows that I hadn't any other potential suitors. Vaughn is doing this because she wants to help me, and at present I could do with some help in the dating area. So, I will have an open mind this time around unlike the previous times. I had already decided I didn't like him, and they only liked me because I was rich or because I was the daughter of Conrad Lynch, or maybe both. I knew I'd never really given them a chance.

Vaughn and I hugged as we took a seat in a booth in the small intimate restaurant, she had selected. It was in a ritzy neighborhood, and the food smelt delicious. Vaughn was slightly taken aback by my battered appearance, so I knew I must tell her what had happened. After I finished the story about the attack on the boat, she asked much the same questions as I had,

'But who were they?'

'I think one of them was Brook's boyfriend,' I replied.

'He must have gotten here fast. I thought you said he was in Texas when you left, and he was annoyed at her for breaking their date.'

'I did, and yes, he must have moved fast. But I guess we got here fast also, so I'm sure he could have done the same.'

'But why would he want to harm Brook? It sounds like he was trying to kill you, too. What haven't you told me, Lyme?' Vaughn was sharp; she had always thought of me as a squeaky-clean 'girl next-door' kinda girl. Although having Brook as a friend, I could never remain so for long.

'I believe he's heavily into drugs, Vaughn, and he wanted money.'

'Now that's scary, Lyme. I always thought you said you would never get involved in that stuff.'

'I'm not involved, Vaughn; he's Brook's boyfriend not mine.' I said indignantly.

'You were in the boat, it was your boat, so you're involved, Lyme. Be careful, scumbags like him can get irrational quickly. What does your father say?' Vaughn surprised me with her question. I couldn't imagine why he would even need to know, and I didn't know why Vaughn would ask such a thing; she knew how my relationship was with him. She had seen his temper many times first hand and also been on the end of his sharp tongue; she of all people should understand.

'He doesn't know. I told him I was upgrading the boat, and that's all I'll tell him.' It was time to change the subject, but after a short silence when I watched Vaughn's mind working overtime, she smiled slightly and said,

'Well, now all this business is over with, I'm taking you to the spa this afternoon; no excuses, you need some TLC, a new haircut and color and certainly a facial, maybe eyelash extensions and…' This was too much, and I stopped her saying more before she got entirely carried away.

'No eyelash extensions, maybe just an eyelash tint. I hate all the girly stuff, Vaughn, you know I do. Pan's always trying to get me to go to her hairdresser or buy an expensive designer outfit that I don't like and won't wear.'

'All right, Lyme, but after I spoke to you, I organized the four of us to go to a restaurant that's just opened. It's supposed to be chic and understated, just your type of place.' I heard her words but was stuck on the four of us part.

'Who is he this time, Vaughn?'

'Don't pout, Lyme, your situation is desperate. You know your father will pick someone he likes and you can't stand.' I had to nod my agreement, because she was right.

'His name is Clive Broadbench; he's six feet tall, has dirty blond hair and green eyes. He's kinda handsome or at least I think he's almost handsome. He's like an abandoned kitten. He has a cute face, sparkling eyes, and he's high energy and sort of quirky.'

'So, how old is he, and why is he single, and where did you meet him?' I asked all at once knowing I must show some interest in a potential future husband. Suddenly, as I listened to Vaughn, I realized that maybe this one would just have to do.

'Alvin met him through work, I think he's a bit older than us but not yet forty. He's a reluctant junior partner in his father's law firm. But all he really wants to do is surf, play tennis and hung out with his friends; you could be a perfect match.' Vaughn finished flashing me one of her brilliant smiles. I was not sure just why she thought him, a perfect match from what she told me about him; we have nothing in common at all, maybe I was missing something.

Soon she whisked me off to the spa, a luxurious place, tastefully decorated with soft relaxing music playing and dimly lit rooms with plenty of ambience. My girl was a short Mexican girl, and I knew immediately she would be asking a lot of questions. All thoughts of a few restful hours left my mind. She poked at the cuts and bruises that were once fresh on my face, and I decided it was time to put a stop to it.

'I am here to enjoy your services and relax. I don't want to discuss what happened to my face. If you want a client who will chatter I'm not it, so maybe I should have another girl,' I said calmly, as she rolled her eyes and left the room. Soon a tall blonde girl entered.

'Hi, I'm Lori, I'll be looking after you today. I understand you will feel more comfortable with a caucasian girl as you don't like Mexicans.' Lori commented. Her words annoyed me, but I didn't let it show as I tried to correct her understanding of what I wanted.

'It was not about her being a Mexican, it was more about the amount she chattered, and all the questions she asked.'

'Oh yes, Chico is a talker, a lot of our clients enjoy a good chat when they're here.' And with that Lori got to work. I had to admit it felt good and the silence was restful. I must have slept through the facial and massage. Gradually, the soft music drifted again into my ears, and I became aware of her smooth hands working their magic. I had forgotten Daddy's anger, my pending blind date and the meeting with Amber Buxton. Suddenly, they didn't seem so important. I decided Vaughn was trying to help, and I would just go with the flow just as Fox always told me to do.

Vaughn, then took me to a designer store that specialized in cocktail wear. Soon we settled on a black strapless chiffon dress; I've never liked strapless. But it was tasteful and clinched in under the bust with a single row of sequins. It did not cling to my body but flared out and sat just above my knees. I was not a small petite girl and my body shape favored that of Daddy's rather than my mother's perfect size zero figure. I wore a dress size eight and liked to remain mainly covered. I told Vaughn, I already had several suitable cocktail dresses in the closet at Newport Beach, but she would have none of it. I guess she wanted to shop. She said once I was pregnant a few times, I would enjoy the power of shopping and the designers that flattered my body and made me look good. It was after four p.m. by the time we exited the store, so I made a quick dash home to get changed and ready for my date with Clive.

Standing in front of the long mirror in my dressing room, I decided that I liked what they had done to my hair. It had been cut shorter by about five inches and now glowed a subtle, deep red under the light. A few highlights had been placed closer to my face. My makeup was understated also and highlighted my cheekbones and eyes. I was feeling good about my date night and spending it with Vaughn and Alvin. Once I put the black cocktail dress on, again I decided I didn't like it. It didn't look nearly as good as Vaugh said it did in the store. I was feeling a little more confident with my looks after all the pampering at the spa, and I thought I could venture into the dark green

Oscar de la Renta. It would be a nod to one of my favorite fashion designers. I had met him on several occasions, and he had dined at our house in Texas. I felt it was a great loss to the world when he passed, he was so alive and creative, I liked him a lot and loved his fashion label.

My green dress was nothing like the black one. I had lots of little black dresses, but this was my only green one. The green dress fitted me snugly showing off my curves in all the right places. It fell just below the knee and had a sheer panel covering me from neck to bust line. I thought it looked sexy, and as I turned, it shimmered seductively in the light. I added high lacy pumps and a small clutch and called down for the limo. It was twenty minutes to six. I should make it to Alvin and Vaughn's on time.

My car pulled to the curb several minutes after six, and as I alighted, a metallic blue Aston Martin screamed to a stop at the curb missing contact with the back of the limo by only a few inches.

'Well, the dress is green and you look like Lyme.' I was taken aback by the man with the large grin leaving his car; he had so much energy, it simply burst out of him. In two bounds, he was at my side, quickly shaking my hand before taking it and placing it through his arm. I couldn't help but giggle – then walking much too fast, he almost dragged me toward the front door.

'I'm wearing heels so you'll have to slow down.'

'Sorry, never worn any myself. Yes, I guess they are rather difficult to walk in, nice though.' He suddenly untangled my hand from his arm and held me at arm's length before turning me around and whistling under his breath. I knew I blushed. I had never met anyone like him. He was handsome in a sort of lost kitten kinda way. He wore brown shoes that desperately needed polish on the toes, grey flannel pants and a black t-shirt under a crumpled dark green sport jacket. The jacket looked like it had been left on back seat of his car for a while, and had seen many things dumped on top of it.

'Okay, no need to walk. Those shoes look good, but I can make the journey easier.' He didn't wait for an answer, but quickly scooped me into his arms before resuming his fast pace lanky walk to the large double front doors. With a huge grin, he deposited me gently back on the ground. What just happened, I had no clue. He hadn't even properly introduced himself, and already I was in his arms, and my life was upside down. What kind of a man carries me in his arms when he doesn't even know me? I thought I'd tease him a little before he rang the doorbell. He stood grinning at me, and I was again reminded of Vaughn's words. Yes, I thought he does look like an abandoned kitten wanting a home. Maybe, I could reach out and scratch behind his ears and expect him to purr in return.

'So, what makes you think I'm this Lyme person?'

'What?' he said looking perplexed as his grin momentarily left his face, only to quickly return before he replied, 'You must be. I even wore a Lyme colored jacket – don't say I carried you here, and I have the wrong girl?' he said the grin disappearing. It was quickly replaced with a sad crestfallen face. He looked at the ground, and I thought he might cry. He played it well. I knew I didn't have the heart to continue it on.

'Okay, I'm Lyme.' At my confession, I saw his huge grin return. It lit up his face, and he looked mischievous and happy again – the lost kitten was back. He pressed the doorbell before looking slyly at me from the corner of his eye and adding,

'I knew it all along; I can read you know – strange as that may seem. I'm actually quite smart. But it was really the name "Lynch #7" on the back of your limo that gave you away. However, if you're really an impostor, I won't tell anyone, and I wouldn't mind a bit.'

Of course, I remembered the number plate on the rear of the limo. Daddy numbered all his cars, and they all had the name 'Lynch' personalized on each of them. So, I'd been caught out – well, he was funny anyway. Before I could utter another word, the door opened, and we were inside. Everyone was greeting everyone. Vaughn scolded me for not wearing the black dress. She, of course, looked amazing. Alvin was a six feet tall ex-NFL player. I'd always thought him very handsome. He was down to earth; adored Vaughn, and from what she told me he was a great father to the children. Whatever money he had made during his career, he'd used wisely and was always proud to say that he never touched a cent of his trust fund.

'Well, Lyme, I think you look amazing, and green is great choice of color. Don't you agree, Clive?' Alvin said hugging me tightly and kissing me on the cheek.

'Already said so. I'm happy to admire a beautiful woman whether it's from a far or close up,' Clive added winking at me as he complimented Vaughn, and we walked through the house and out to the huge deck where drinks and hors d'oeuvres waited for us.

Clive was easy company. He got on well with everyone. I couldn't imagine him being a lawyer, and at no time did he mention his career. He spoke a lot about surfing and occasionally about the last game of tennis he'd played with Alvin. Once I was alone with Alvin, he asked, 'So, what do you think? He's a catch, isn't he?'

'He certainly seems nice.'

'Nice, Lyme, is that all?'

'Well, I don't know if he's husband material.'

'Lyme you could do far worse, and it's not forever.'

'What do you mean?' I asked. Alvin surprised by his comment as we stared out over his neatly manicured lawn, swimming pool and gardens beyond.

'Marriage is not forever these days, Lyme. Why, you can change your husband or wife like you change your socks – you only need to marry and keep him for however long he entertains you, or in your case, as long as it takes to have a child and keep your father happy. It's not forever, Lyme; this is twenty first century after all!'

Alvin's words about divorce worried me, or maybe it was the fact, he even thought about it. I knew Vaughn assumed when she'd married him, they would be together forever. Was there a deeper meaning behind his words? They truly seemed to adore each other, so maybe he was just saying that to make me feel better. Anyway, what did I know about romance? Apparently, no more than what I read in a book. I was not the one who should be speculating about the state of anyone's marriage or even about romance.

Alvin took my arm, and together we walked toward the waiting limo that would take us to dinner. The rest of the evening flew by. Clive was, as promised; charming, entertaining and attentive. As the night drew to a close, and we said good night to Vaughn and Alvin. To my amazement, Clive scooped me in his arms yet again and carried me to my waiting limo. Once we were near the car, I looked closely into his face; it was only inches from mine. For the first time ever, my heart fluttered.

'I'm not putting you down, until you agree to see me again tomorrow, nothing formal like this. In fact, I'll take you to the animal petting zoo. You can't say no, Lyme, really you can't,' he said; still holding me tightly in his arms. I thought he would kiss me, and I knew I was defenseless if he did. I thought of all the reasons to say no to him, but he still held me tightly; I obviously didn't seem heavy at all.

His eyes never left mine, as I said, 'Sure, sounds like fun.' With that he kissed me lightly on my lips and stood me gently on the ground before my driver appeared and opened the rear door.

'No heels tomorrow; otherwise, I'll have to go to the gym some more.' He teased, leaping into his car and roaring away into the darkness. I still had a smile on my lips as his taillights disappeared, and we drove sedately home.

That night as I lay in my bed alone, I closed my eyes and drifted to my lonely place. Slowly, I entered the void that beckoned me there. However, several minutes before I felt nothing, I saw Clive's face grinning at me in the darkness.

'Get out of my space,' I yelled, but he just seemed to grin more before the image of his face slowly faded, and I was alone again. Darkness closed in, I searched for my void in my mind. I felt my desperation, solitude and need engulf me. The loneliness came savage and raw, clawing its way toward me. No one cares, no one loves; no one needed me as my desire for my empty void increased. I fought desperately the impending depression, despair and emptiness, and suddenly I could feel the void of nothing begin to engulf me, I was almost there.

Then from somewhere in my mind, I heard Alvin words, words he had spoken to me just this evening, 'Marriage is not forever.' I could clearly see his face and hear his words going over and over in my head. In the darkness of my room, I sat upright, I reached for the light, and I smiled. Maybe I had been sent the answer after all. Marriage was not forever. Why had I thought it was?

I searched my mind for the answer I remembered it was something my mother had once said to me when I was a little girl. 'You must always make your husband happy, Lyme. Because once you're married, marriage is forever. There's no going back. You cannot change your mind or say you've made a mistake. And when you bring children into the world you must ensure you have a happy life and marriage to bring them into. A happy husband is a happy life and a happy wife is also a happy life. Keep your husband happy, and he will keep you happy and give you everything you desire. Remember that, Lyme, remember my words for when you are older you will understand. Marriage is forever.' Then I heard my little girl voice ask,

'But, Mommy, how could Daddy not be happy with you? You're the most beautiful lady in the whole wide world?'

'Beauty is important, of course, but there's way more to a marriage than being beautiful. Beauty comes in many forms, Lyme. You're the most beautiful girl in the world so go to sleep now, you're our little princess, and we love you.'

Yes, I remembered her words, how often my mother's words had saved me. I replayed her words again in my head. There was so much more meaning to her words now. I wondered, if maybe she thought Daddy wasn't happy with her. Maybe, she wasn't happy with him? Then I thought of Alvin's words again, so in contrast to Mommy's.

'Marriage is not forever.' Well, of course, it's not, not any more. I thought of Pan and her two marriages, it was her choice when she wanted to be married, and when she didn't. I turned the light off again. I now understood my confusion I heard Mommy's words of all those years ago, and somewhere I had always thought marriage is forever. Now, I realized marriage wasn't forever and that made everything more possible, more attractive. Suddenly, I turned on the light again and bolted upright in bed. I knew I could do this. I could do it without the deep, lasting, all-consuming love I had never felt. I could do it without giving too much of myself to someone I didn't love…

Yes, I could do it, and I could have it all. Perhaps Clive was the perfect husband, he was fun, and kinda cute. Could I ask for anything more? I would marry him, have some babies and then cut him free with a large settlement, of course. Daddy would have his heir and me my freedom.

Turning off the light again, I lay in the dark, with my loneliness all around me, my solitude, just me by myself. I closed my eyes and searched for the void; the void that was my safety blanket the void that was mine, alone. I smiled suddenly thinking of Clive; as I slipped into sleep, I realized I didn't need my void tonight.

Chapter 4
Madam Roderic ~ 1

'You shall allow madam to speak of other things on occasions. Miss Janice only wishes to hear about her wardrobe changes, her social life and her beauty.'

'Yes, yes, I do,' Pan replied giggling as she clapped her hands together thinking again how clever and accurate the older lady's predictions proved to be.

'Things you may not wish to hear.'

'But, madam, I just want to know about me. That is what makes me happy. Please do not concern yourself with anything else.'

'Madam Roderic will always tell you, what she sees as important for Miss Janice and her life. Maybe, this is not always what Miss Janice wishes to hear.'

'You can tell me if my next beauty treatment will be a success?'

'You are a very beautiful woman, Miss Janice. I see your surgery as a success, but beware the press are lurking outside the clinic as you exit. I see you needing another way to get to the limo. You have exited the same way too many times, so please be warned this time they shall be waiting.'

'Madam, such good advice. Of course, I shall take care. Now, what social functions should I attend this week?' Pan asked giggling as she sat in her bedroom with her many invitations spread in front of her and her social secretary standing in the back ground holding a notepad and pen, awaiting the answers.

'I must tell you what I see.'

'Of course, you must, madam,' Pan said, giggling thinking madam Roderic was about to talk of her upcoming weekly engagements.

'Madam, she sees your fruity friend, the very rich one whose father likes to bathe in oil.'

'You mean Lyme,' Pan said, giggling from madam Roderic's description.

'I cannot imagine why you wish to speak to me about my friend, Lyme; nothing exciting ever happens in her life.'

'It may be exciting if she stays with a man with the initials "R", but I see her in dangerous hands, another man she sees and falls heavily for. He is tall, he is blond. He is married and dangerous you must warn her to stay away, there is danger in her future if she pursues him, danger, danger and death.'

'Really, madam, you cannot mean Lyme? You surely mean Brook. Lyme would not go after a bad boy, or probably any boy, although she needs to take her father's wishes seriously. Let's get back to these invitations, madam.' Pan giggled at the thought of Lyme going out with a bad boy, but she made a mental note to call her soon; they usually talked or texted every day anyway.

'Lyme, has danger all around; her father does not treat her well. He is a wicked man. She may subconsciously attract another wicked man to be her husband. Beware of her future; you must warn her, Miss Janice.' Pan laughed at madam's dramatic expressions as she waved her arms in the air and closed her eyes to prove her point. Pan found her most entertaining.

'You entertain me well, madam, but I am only interested in my life. I have told you this before. I know you are wrong about Lyme. I think you have her confused with Brook.'

'There is no confusion in madam's vision; all comes to me clear and concise. It is you, Miss Janice, that shows confusion as to what is important.' Madam concluded her deep monotone voice never changing pitch, only raising slightly in volume as she made her point. Her arms moved through the air in a dramatic manner that Pan found most entertaining. Pan found her fun to watch and knew Madam Roderic was worth every cent she paid her. But not for one moment did she listen to any of madam's warnings.

'Can we return to my social engagements now, madam?' Pan asked, and with a sigh Madam Roderic picked up the first invitation from the table, she held it firmly between her palms and closed her eyes.

'No, you are not to attend this function.' She responded dropping it, before repeating the progress with next invitation. Pan giggled as she watched Madam Roderic closely. This was the type of thing she expected from madam Roderic, this was the reason she paid her. All was right in Pan's world.

Chapter 5
Another Date

My optimism kicked into top gear the next afternoon as I prepared for my date with Clive. Something inside had shifted. A change in the way I thought, or maybe my perception and understanding of life and myself. I didn't know exactly what it was, but I knew it was real, because I felt it. I guess it was due to Alvin and his brief talk with me, or was it due to my mother's words of so long ago. But why did I now have such clarity and understanding, after all these years? I couldn't help thinking there was still more hidden in my mother's words. Again, I wondered if her marriage to Daddy had been a happy union and had bought her lasting love. I knew it had given him everything he'd ever desired. But I questioned for the first time her feelings about her side of the marriage.

I was dressed in Calvin Kline flats, true religion jeans and a bright pink designer T-shirt. I thought this was the appropriate way to dress but just in case, I threw into my bag a lightweight black crepe dress and some high pumps that were so soft they almost folded in half. I also packed perfume, lipstick and a comb for my hair. Surely, I wouldn't need anything else.

Clive was early, way early. I heard his car zoom up the circular driveway and screech to a stop. Instinctively, I knew it was him, who else was such a fast and reckless driver? Just as well I was ready. I raced through the huge house and down the stairs just as the doorbell chimed. Still slightly out of breath I threw open the doors as I called to the staff that I had answered it. The least people who knew about my date the better.

'Hey Clive, you're early,' I greeted him as he grinned his huge grin and sauntered inside without being asked,

'Nice place, quietly classy,' he muttered looking around and whistling under his breath, before turning to me and adding, 'Ready to go?' he asked gallantly offering me his arm.

'Sure,' I said grabbing my bag.

Just as we were about to exit, he added, 'Hope you're up for tennis? Thought we'd play a few games. If you can't play, I'll teach you,' he added winking,

'Hold on. I forgot something.' I quickly said disengaging my arm from his as I raced back up the stairs, leaving him standing in the huge entranceway. As I reached the top, I briefly glanced down. He stood alone in a strange house, and I saw suddenly how small he looked and not so confident after all, or did I just want to imagine it.

Tennis, oh! I had packed quite the wrong things. To my bag, I added my tennis shoes and tiny lacy white tennis dress with the built-in shorts, and of course, my tennis racket. Did Clive assume I couldn't play tennis? Well, we shall see about that!

He was still standing where I'd left him a few minutes earlier; the huge front doors remained ajar. He turned as I raced down the stairs. Only this time he didn't offer me his arm; quickly, he swung the doors wider, so I could pass. I carried a different tote bag – as the last one was not nearly large enough. I now carried a taupe leather tote, its wide straps so long the bag almost trailed on the ground. Once outside, Clive grabbed my bag before, to my utter amazement, he grabbed me. I thought he was about to kiss me, but instead he lifted me easily into his arms.

'Been working out,' he said, his generous mouth breaking into a huge grin. His hair looked unkempt and his clothes were again wrinkled but smelt clean and fresh as I was wrapped in his strong arms.

He held me firmly and I couldn't help giggling, as I asked, 'Why are you carrying me? I'm not wearing heels.'

'So, you don't race back inside. I can't let you get away a second time; I have the court booked.'

'Oh, I thought you just liked keeping me close.' I teased.

'Yeah, I guess I do, even though it means extra workouts.'

'Yeah,' I said punching him lightly on the shoulders. His grin increased as he deposited me beside his car, swung open the door, throw several coke cans, pizza boxes and hamburger wrappers onto the back seat, and helped me in.

He drove like the wind. I thought Daddy's driving crazy and erratic, but this guy was completely wild. They say you can tell how a man will make love by his driving; if that was correct, I decided I never needed to find out!

I held on for dear life as the car careered around bends through yellow lights, almost stopped at a stop sign before rocketed on at full speed. All the while Clive chatted to me; about what I haven't a clue. He spoke calmly almost as if we were sitting opposite each other having coffee. I knew I had several new bruises by the time we arrived at the petting zoo. Clive showed no consideration for his passenger and stopped by jamming his foot hard onto the brake. The car pulled to a screeching halt, and the moment it did so, Clive dived out the driver's door raced around to my side of the car and yanked open my door before grabbing me and pulling me out, his actions reminded me of a dentist extracting a reluctant tooth. I was still regaining my composure as I stood somewhat bewildered on the sidewalk. Unexpectedly, he grabbed my hand. Clive walked at the pace of a fast jog to the gates of the animal petting zoo. A tour guide Clive must have organized earlier promptly greeted us.

'Hi, my name is Dollar, I will be your guide today. Animal lovers, are we?' she asked, her nose ring wobbled as she spoke and her black and pink hair spiked high on her head. Unlike her nose ring, her hair didn't move, not even when the warm breeze teased my skin.

'Well, I don't have anything against them so long as they don't piss on me – I hate doing laundry, so if they do,

Dollar, you're washing my clothes,' Clive responded laughing. Dollar walked to the first enclosure and ushered us in through the gate.

'These little creatures are called bandicoot possums; they like to sleep during the day and are native to Australia they are commonly found in the Northern Territory of Australia. Yes, you can stroke him,' Dollar offered the tiny sleepy possum to me, and I was astounded at the softness of its fur. He was sleeping but appeared quite used to people touching him. His coat was light brownish grey and surprisingly silky. Clive also petted him, and it appeared he enjoyed interacting with animals.

Clive put his arm around me as we continued on another slow walk, this time coming to an enclosure we couldn't enter.

'Inside here, you see the sleeping spectacled flying foxes; they come from the Megabat family…' and so she continued on telling us all about the sleeping bats inside the enclosure.

I sneaked a peek at Clive who seemed to be enjoying himself that is until we began to walk again and Clive asked, 'Must we walk so slow? We have a court booked in half an hour for tennis, Dollar, so can we speed this up?' I could feel he was getting annoyed, although it didn't show on his face.

'I don't need to pet them all, so maybe, you can just tell us about the interesting ones.' I offered and with my words Clive scooped me into his arms kissed me hard on the mouth before quickly depositing me down again as he said,

'My kinda girl.' Then he pumped me with a high five. I hadn't been ready for any of it and was astonished by his behavior.

I spent the next fifteen minutes racing around behind Dollar. Clive took the lead. I listened briefly as Clive asked, 'So what's in here?' or 'Where do these animals come from?' He was interested in a sort of hurried way. I would have been happy to linger most of the day and pet everything, but I was okay with our fast journey through the petting zoo.

Now, we were whizzing around corners and along the highway cutting in and out of almost every car in our path. I clung to the handle above my door and often closed my eyes. Driving in Clive's car was anything but restful and as far as sitting back and enjoying the scenery that was never going to happen. He drove so fast; almost everything was a blur. By the time we slowed to enter the "members only" tennis club, I was shaking with anxiety. We'd had no accidents, and on closer observation Clive did seem to be in total control of the car and his driving, regardless of the erratic way he threw the car around every corner.

Again, he raced to my door and simply scooped me out. This time, I related his actions more to an oyster being pulled unwillingly from its shell.

'Guess, you don't have tennis clothes because you've never played before. They'll make allowances, and if they don't I'll just tell them who you are.' Clive said, grinning and winking at me as he said the last part. I didn't respond. He raced toward the men's change room before telling me to stay where I was. Well, I had no intention of being made to look like an amateur, so I hightailed it to the women's changing room the moment he was out of sight. I assumed he would change his clothes just as fast as he did everything else. So, I needed to hurry. There was no one else inside the changing room, so I opted for a booth, quickly opened my bag on the nearest seat, and in moments I was dressed, had my head and wristbands on and was putting on my tennis shoes.

Then, I raced out to where I was supposed to be waiting for him. I expected him to be looking for me by now, but to my surprise, he was nowhere to be seen. I stood where I was for a few minutes longer, turning around to see if I could spot him. I thought he might have gone straight to the courts.

Then a low whistle came from behind, and turning I saw him walk toward me. Dressed casually in his tennis whites. The tennis dress I had chosen was sexy, not only because it was short but also because it was sheer lace and fitted me to perfection. I had been having tennis lessons nearly my whole life and my instructors included many world-class professional players. I wasn't crazy about the game like Clive, but I enjoyed playing and did so often. I had inherited Daddy's competitiveness in all sports, so I liked to win.

'Wow, did you just go to the pro shop and purchase some clothes? Well, good move, and yes, I approve.' Clive slowly walked around me. I knew he had noticed the glances of the other guys as they walked past, and it felt good. Then he saw my nine hundred and fifty dollar pair of Jimmy Choo's tennis shoes; he seemed to recognize them immediately. For a few seconds, a perplexed look crossed his face, and then his grin returned before he noticed my very expensive Chanel tennis racket. He said nothing but didn't bound onto the court as I was expecting him to do. Clive had forgotten his balls, so he retreated to the clubhouse; I knew the set was already mine.

'Shall I show you how to hold the racket?' he asked coyly, and I could tell he was slightly unsure whether he should be asking me or not.

'Yes please, I'm looking forward to learning the game; don't let the racket and shoes fool you,' I said being coy but also covering my bases in case he proved a better player than me, although somehow, I doubted it. Slowly, he took my racket from my hand and we walked onto the court. Then he moved close behind me and wrapped his arms tightly around me before positioning my fingers on the racket and showing me very carefully just how to swing. He then turned my face to his and softly kissed me. The kiss lasted several seconds and it was the first time he had kissed me seductively, and I responded for the first time in my life and kissed him back. Together, our temperatures rose. But sadly, I didn't feel the flutter of my heart as I thought I would. I had briefly felt something for him on our first meeting. I wanted the feeling so badly. I wanted him to be the one, I needed it desperately, I could taste it, I wanted all 'the feelings' and I wanted him to be 'my special man'.

He was nice enough, and I could probably bear him around quite easily. We certainly shared some kind of chemistry, but he wasn't the one to make my heart flutter, and my knees go weak. I couldn't make it happen.

Several years ago, I'd started reading romance novels, it had opened up a new world for me and taken me places I didn't know existed, or at least in my mind. Until then, I had always read adventure stories; I could never get enough of them. In comparison, the romances were shallow as far as purpose and storyline went but taught me a great deal about love. Whereas I didn't believe everything they said, I knew for sure there was a lot missing in the two brief affairs I'd had and the many blind dates I'd been on. In some of the stories the heroin managed to fall in love before she had even spoken to the man. I thought this was a little exaggerated but the thought made for an emotional story. I wanted and needed these feelings, but for me time was running out, and I knew Daddy was probably planning and plotting my marriage at this very moment. Even though Clive couldn't beat me at tennis, I knew he would have to do, and somehow, I must encourage and play up to him. It would be better if I really felt something deeper for him, but I didn't and I mustn't let him know. I needed this man, I needed to marry him, so I must do what every good girl does – fake it!

Chapter 6
Love Above the Clouds

I found myself thinking of Clive quite a lot. It surprised me. They weren't romantic thoughts so much as the need for someone to marry, so I can get Daddy off my back. Clive would make a great husband. All I needed to do was convince Clive. I knew I must be subtle, loving and attentive. However, I had no real urgency to see him again. I knew Clive found me to be most attractive; this feeling was not new to me. I often felt bad that so many of my blind dates tried so hard, and I didn't. I guess I thought I had everything in life I could possibly want. The next morning before I woke, Clive had sent flowers and a note asking when he could see me again. I had put him off the night before using the need of readying myself for my return to Texas in the next couple of days, as my excuse. Although I could tell by the look in his eyes, he was not to be put off.

I had spoken to both Brook and Pan and told them about him. Several times during our conversation, Brook said she'd heard his name before but couldn't remember where. So, I knew Brook would be doing her usual sleuthing on my behalf. Pan was true to who she was and wanted to know what he looked like; what sort of car he drove, how much money he made, and when I would be marrying him. Then the conversation arrived at Pan's favorite topic; what I would be wearing to my wedding. Or rather the name of the designer I had chosen to make my gown. Of course, I hadn't given it a moment's thought. So, Pan chastised me heavily and said she guessed it would have to all be left up to her as usual. She assumed she would be a bridesmaid and wanted to know my colors for the wedding. So, I managed to frustrate both my best friends with my lack of answers in just two conversations.

That evening, Clive sent a second enormous bouquet of roses, jasmine and several other sweet-smelling flowers. He had heard me well when I said how I loved pretty flowers that also smelt good. Although the roses didn't smell, the other flowers did, and I had them placed in my bedroom. I put the card with his cell number printed on it beside my bed. It was the third time he had handed me his card with his private cell number on the back. I called Clive that evening as I lay in bed and tried to have a cozy intimate conversation with him, or it was what I thought a cozy intimate conversation should be. We didn't actually speak of sex but Clive hinted quite heavily that he was ready to move our friendship onto a relationship just as soon as I was ready. I wasn't sure where this should go, so I avoided answering his innuendos and suggestions until the last. I didn't want to seem too desperate, but I wanted to encourage him and give him reason to believe I, too, am very interested in having him in my life.

'So, when are we going to get down and dirty Lyme? I haven't been able to get the image of you in your sexy tennis dress out of mind. Who would have known you were hiding such a body under those frumpy clothes you wear?' Clive chuckled at his own back handed compliment, and I could feel him grinning with mischief over the phone. I was a little taken aback that he was calling my wardrobe frumpy. I know I wasn't always dressed in the latest fashions like Pan, but I usually wore designer, and I usually thought I looked pretty good.

I know he needed some reason to keep chasing me, so I merely said, 'I'm guessing you're a guy who appreciates a girl in a sheer lacy negligee? What's the color that does it for you, big boy?' I heard him chuckle again after concealing his intake of breath. I thought I had said enough, I had him thinking now. He didn't answer right away, and we chatted on about our next date. I said we could go cruising on one of Daddy's boats.

'Yachting is okay, but I'm a guy who likes speed.'

'Who said anything about a yacht? Clive. Maybe, my father likes speed also?' I teased. He was laughing, and I liked the sound of his laughter, but I immediately thought of his driving and wondered again if I wanted to get between the sheets with him. I could feel myself mentally backing away. Just as the conversation came to an end, he said, 'Penny for your dreams, Lyme; I hope I'm in them. And by the way, I'd prefer you with no negligee or anything else. I'm a skin-on-skin guy – just for the record. Sleep tight.' And he was gone.

My meeting with Amber Buxton and the interior designers for the newest resort in the Lyme Resort and Hotel chain, proved long and exhausting. I had decided to try a new interior design firm, and they sent us their top people, two well-dressed men and one woman. They had a huge selection of layouts and swatches, along with many charts of suitable color combinations. The woman never stopped talking, and she appeared to be more of a pushy sales person than the designer. The quieter of the two men was the most knowledgeable, and the only one I listened to. Amber, and I had done this on several other occasions, and it was our choice to have the same color interior throughout the entire chain of resorts. But the woman designer would have none of it; she wanted this resort to stand alone. Finally, Amber asked them to leave us alone for a while so we could discuss our options and decide. The woman was reluctant to leave, and when she finally did, Amber let out a long, slow breath as she said, 'Well, we won't be using that firm again, she's exhausting. She never stops talking, where on earth did you find them?'

'I agree on both counts, it was a mistake to try someone new, but I understand how she sold herself. I think she would be better suited as a door-to-door salesman or saleswoman, although she could easily talk anyone under the table,' I added. We both laughed as a soft knock came from the door and our very late lunch was served to us on the farthest corner of the boardroom table. It was the only space that remained uncluttered with fabric and layouts.

'I believe we should stay true to our color scheme, this one must match the other hotels and resorts. It will standalone anyway, because the interior is so clean and modern, it will portray a subtle new elegance. I think the colors are the one thing that will keep them all unified, so they are recognizable as part of the same chain. This is the one I think we should go with,' I said holding up the one with the closest colors to other resorts.

'I agree, Lyme, in fact I like it better than some of the others, it's both vivid and subtle together the contrast is most attractive.'

'We could have completed this hours ago if we'd had a chance to discuss our requirements, Amber.'

'Certainly, we could have. Lyme, I must move on to my next meeting. I know you can wrap this up on your own. Or leave it until tomorrow, if you prefer,' Amber offered.

'I'm hoping to fly home tonight, so I'll call them back in now. Can you instruct your secretary to call my pilot and have the plane ready for takeoff around ten tonight?'

'Consider it done, Lyme.' And with that she left the room. I soon had the interior designers return and much to the redheaded woman's annoyance the colors were confirmed. Once they left to my amazement, Amber's secretary informed me the jet was not able to stop over and take me home tonight. Apparently, the pilots were in a simulation session while the plane was in for an overhaul and maintenance.

The other jet was solely for Daddy's use and the executives of Lynch Oil, and he had it booked for the next three days. 'Shall I book you on a commercial flight Miss Lyme?' The secretary asked, and I nodded my reply. I had never flown any other way other than on our private jet, this would be a new adventure. Then, I thought of all those strangers sitting next to me at such close proximity. I knew we would be sitting shoulder to shoulder, perhaps even touching... *eeeek*, maybe this was not an adventure after all. I would try this new experience of traveling first class on a commercial flight, just this once; I felt a need to go home. I needed to talk to Granny Harry, my grandma. She was Mom's mother and the woman I felt closest to in the world. I needed to talk to her about Clive.

The noise and bustle of the huge airport, the porters, the people, and the rude check-in clerks were exhausting to me. After the long walk to the gate, we were herded onto the waiting plane like cattle on the ranch. I was booked on an Air Canada long haul flight that had just arrived from London, England. So, I am told it was larger than most commercial planes. The seats were reasonable, comfortable, and I was even given help placing my bags in the overhead lockers. Once seated, I waited as the long plane gradually filled up. To me, it was a shocking sight with everyone jostling and complaining. There was hardly any room to move, and I watched in amazement as a large fat man tried desperately to squeeze by a young blonde girl in his haste to get to his seat. Chaos followed as he managed to get himself, and the girl wedged firmly between two seats. They had completely blocked the aisle, so everyone waited. The young girl had a look of distaste and horror on her face at the sweaty, smelly stranger she didn't know who was pressed up against her, so tightly. I admired her for keeping her cool; I knew I couldn't. The fat man on the other hand yelled and abused the airline staff as he complained about the width of the aisle, the tardiness of the staff, the slowness of the passengers etc.

Many of the passengers were softly giggling, and I had to admit it was a funny sight. Soon, I forgot the commotion around me and opened my book to read. It was a heavy read, and it took me some moments to get fully into it. I was reading the old classic "The Lady in White" by Wilkie Collins. I had so far, only read several chapters. As I often do, I took the book in my other hand but just as I did, a large woman with an even larger handbag jostled by me and knocked the book from my hand across the aisle.

'Ooops,' she muttered and with no intentions of retrieving it, she kept walking. Or as I looked after her, she kept wobbling onwards; her enormous rear filled the aisle from side to side completely. She simply wobbled like a bowl of Jello. As soon as the aisle was clear of passengers, I put my head out and searched for my book. There it was on the opposite side of the aisle, two seats in front of me in the hands of a tall blond man. He was reading the back cover. I could only see the back of his head, the way his blond hair curled around the smooth skin of his neck. Something stirred inside me as I stared, I was unable to speak or move my eyes from the back of his head. As if he felt me staring, he slowly put the book down and turned toward me…

His blue-violet eyes met mine. I couldn't help but stare; how could I not stare. I heard no sound; I saw nothing but his large blue eyes. The world stopped. He was the most handsome man I had ever seen.

And just like that – I was in love.

I kept on staring. In those eyes I saw, my life, my children, my world. This is the man, the one man I have been waiting for – forever. I couldn't take my eyes from his until finally, I was aware he was waving his hand between our gaze. I blinked, and he held the book toward me. 'Yours?' he simply asked and all I could do was nod my head. He made no movement that said he was about to bring the book to me, so I kept staring. Until another nod of his head, and he again raised the book in my direction. I now understood that he wanted me to get it. Slowly, as if in a dream, or some old slow motion movie, I undid my seat belt and got up from my seat. For the first time ever, I was conscious of the way I looked, how my hair was falling, the fact I had again forgotten to apply lipstick. I wondered if I had on any perfume, and if so, was it still working. Was it too late to get it from my bag along with the lipstick, mascara, foundation and anything else I happen to have on me.

Just then, the hostess came by and asked if there was anything I wanted. Nothing she could give me I thought, but I replied 'no', then she asked me to take my seat for departure. What was I to do? My book was clearly visible on the arm of his seat. Like him, it was waiting for me. I called softly to him, but he didn't look up. Again, the blonde stewardess asked if there was anything I required, and again I replied 'no.' My eyes still hadn't left the back of his head. What was he, a celebrity of some kind, a movie star, singer or royalty? He was certainly handsome enough to be any or all of these things.

The blonde stewardess hovered around him, I could see she was flirting; she was a gorgeous, tall, slim, blonde with pouty full lips and opaque greenish eyes. She kept leaning into him and laughing softly… it was killing me. He's mine, mine, go away. I screamed in my mind. Then another first-class passenger asked for champagne. A moment later, she had the chilled bottle in her hand wrapped in a cloth. She held several long-stemmed champagne glasses in her other hand. She gave one to him and slowly filled it, moving as close as she could get. Then she reluctantly moved toward the other passenger, whom I couldn't see, and filled their glass. We were now moving down the runway. Finally, I took my eyes from the back of his neck. I lay back in my seat and closed my eyes. My heart was beating so fast, my palms were sweating, and I knew my cheeks were flushed. How could I quiet my heart, still my racing pulse? Everyone must be able to hear my heart as it beats out of my chest. I must gain control of myself. Daddy always said he who loses control, loses the game, and this was a game, a game of love and a game of life and this was one game I had no intentions of losing.

Once we were in the air, I quickly searched my bag, inside I found lip gloss, mascara, perfume and blush, neither of which had been used much before. I applied them as best I could and ran a comb through my hair; I had to admit I did look better, fresher, even prettier, somehow. My eyes seemed to come alive under the black mascara, just as Pan always said they did, and my lips seemed fuller somehow. I wish I'd listened more closely to Pan when she'd explained how to flirt. I had never needed to flirt before but now I knew I did.

Why didn't the stranger with my book turn around? Why didn't he look at me again? He must feel what I'm feeling, surely, he must, he too must know! Then I remembered Brook's words about how dumb men are sometimes when it comes to woman and attraction. Perhaps she was right; maybe he didn't know. Along with the many things that tumbled out of my bag as I searched, came my cell phone. I quickly sent a message to both Brook and Pan and said I'd found him; they'd know what I meant. I had no time to say more as the stewardess had returned, she was again flirting with him. Now she was lifting my book, scanning the back cover, shaking her head, she turned to look at me after something he said. She was about to return my book when someone up ahead called to her, and she replaced it on the arm of his seat and walked away. I felt my cheeks burn as she looked in my direction and giggled. I thought he may turn to me also, but he didn't, he never moved, other than to refill his champagne from the bottle she had left him. Soon our meal was served. I had been hungry previously but no longer wanted food.

My heart kept pounding as my eyes burned into the back of his head, willing him to turn toward me, just a glance, a look, a nod. I would take any of it. I had to get myself under control. I needed a plan. I needed to get nearer to him, to talk to him, touch him. But how? We were already well on our way to Texas. What would I do if we landed before I had his name. The thought scared me beyond words.

Then, as I watched he rose from his seat, and without so much as a backward look, he headed toward the front of the plane and the toilets. Like me, he had an empty seat beside him – should I move forward and occupy it before he returned? He may think I'm a little strange, but he did have my book, and it was still sitting on the arm of his seat, right beside the aisle. As if in a trance I moved the few seats forward and slowly moved past his seat to the empty one beside the window I took my book as I passed, after all it was my reason for being there. I sat waiting. My heart beating too fast, and my nerves tingling. I wondered yet again how a complete stranger could have this effect on me?

Without looking up from the book, I was aware of movement up ahead, and then he sat beside me and dropped his tray in front of him. Lying on his tray was a purple folder; I knew the color immediately. Clearly printed on the front, I saw the words 'Lynch Oil' stamped across it and in heavy red ink the word 'confidential'. How could this be? I stared at the folder. I knew his eyes were focused on me – inquiring…? Inquiring what? Why I was sitting beside him? Who was I? Why wasn't I saying anything? My cheeks burned, my palms sweated, and I took a very deep breath before saying, 'Thanks for catching my book.'

'Yeah, not something I'd ever read,' he replied his voice smooth like satin.

"Hi, I', Lyme Harrington – Lyn…' I was about to say Lynch when I thought better of it. 'I'm Lyme Harrington.'

'Strange name, Lyme,' was all he said.

'Your name?' I asked sounding more authoritative than I felt.

'I wasn't aware we needed to trade names because I retrieved your book?'

'Sorry, I didn't mean it to come out that way. I just wanted to know who you are and thank you for saving my book from being trampled,' I replied with my best smile. I felt him relax slightly.

'Holt Visser,' he replied as if the conversation was now at an end.

'Do you live in Texas or just passing through?' I asked hoping to sound casual as the stewardess passed by and gave me a look that could kill an elephant at sixty paces.

'You have a lot of questions,' he answered still not looking at me, he was filling his glass – he didn't offer to fill mine. His nearness had a huge effect on me; I was thinking thoughts I had never thought I would be thinking. I wanted to tear his clothes from his body; I wanted to get close to him. I wanted to feel his lips on mine, to run my fingers over his skin. I wanted him to make love to me. I had moved my arm closer and now we were almost touching, it felt like he was giving me an electric shock. Surely, he must feel it also. Then I was aware of his voice; he was speaking to me. '...so, you don't know if you live here or not?' he was saying with a smirk. Whatever he had just asked me, I hadn't heard it. 'I live in Texas, in Westlake actually.'

'Fancy suburb, actually,' his reply mimicked me.

'So, are you staying over in Texas for a while?' I ventured not knowing if he would answer this time or not,

'I will be moving into the company apartment tomorrow. Then I have several free days before I fly out and report for work. Any further questions you'd like answering?' His words dripped sarcasm. His eyes flashed deeply challenging and moody. The effect of those eyes looking into mine was immediate.

Before I knew just what I was saying I said, 'How about I take you out for dinner? As a thank you for rescuing my book. I'll pick you up, and we can go anywhere you chose.'

'That's one important book, young lady,' he said looking directly at me again. His look unnerved me and his nearness excited me. Every part of my body felt alive like it never had, it felt like I was vibrating. I must answer; I could tell he was waiting,

'Yes, I always like to finish what I start, books I mean.'

'Well, if it leads to a free meal, then I'm glad I rescued your book. How does a girl like you afford to fly first class and take a stranger to dinner at the restaurant of his choice? I warn you I have expensive taste. So, do you always travel first class?' he persisted.

Fortunately, I was able to answer honestly, 'No, this is the first time.'

'Excuse me ma'am, we are preparing for landing. Would you please return to your seat and fasten your seatbelt?' the stewardess interrupted.

'I am perfectly capable of fastening my seat belt, here,' I replied annoyed, but by this time Holt had already stood up to let me out. As I moved past him, he told me where he was staying and he said he'd see me at 8.00pm that evening. It was already after midnight. I heard the words but couldn't reply, his body was so close to mine it was more than I could bear. I moved past him slowly, lingering as long as I dared. I felt his body heat and smelt his subtle cologne; my pulse raced.

As I sat down in my own seat, I heard the stewardess reply to something he said, 'Rich bitches they're all the same, think they can have anything they want.' I decided this would be my last time flying on a commercial plane. I now held a new and greater appreciation for Daddy's private jet.

It seemed like forever before we landed and coasted slowly into the gate, and even longer before we disembarked. Sitting looking at the back of his head was pure torture when moments before, I had been so close to the object of my desire. The moment we could turn on our cell phones, I sent a text to both Pan and Brook saying I was dining with the man of my dreams, tonight. Then I sent another text saying I was sorry; I couldn't make the opening of the new restaurant tonight as I had more important things to do. Pan responded immediately saying that no matter how wonderful he is, having your photo taken on the red carpet at one of the most prestigious and popular restaurants in Texas, is definitely more important than anything, and she couldn't understand how my priorities were so mixed up. She informed me she was already thinking about her hair and makeup for tonight's event and that I should be too. I could tell she was annoyed with me for letting her down, but I assumed Brook was still going and would be her plus one.

Brook's reply was somewhat shorter it simply read *'Really? Call me.'* I looked up from my phone in time to see Holt getting up from his seat. He was leaving. My heart raced even faster, I was panicking; there were people in front of me, between him and I. I pushed quickly through and asked him if he had a business card, just in case I needed to call him.

'Do you always ask strangers for things? Here you're the first to get one, these just arrived from the printer before I left home, gotta go, see you later.' Passengers were moving forward as one, and I was almost swept along and out of the plane, but I pushed my way through many people behind me who were all complaining that I was going the wrong way. It was only three seats back, but it seemed like it took me forever. Quickly, I retrieved my bags and turned with the crowd, hoping that Holt would be waiting for me somewhere up ahead. He was tall and blond, but I couldn't see him anywhere. Perhaps, he was waiting outside. I felt sure he would be waiting to carry my bags; I'd always had someone to carry my bags.

I moved forward with the other passengers, who I felt were all too close to me and crowded my space. As I moved forward, I searched the crowd ahead, checked everyone beside me, but as yet I couldn't see him. Finally, after a long walk I entered the terminal. I searched the crowd and spotted my driver but Holt was nowhere to be seen. Why hadn't he waited for me?

On the drive home, I decided what I would wear. Several outfits sprang to mind, but finally I settled on the black lace off the shoulder dress. It was subtle, sexy, and comfortable and fitted my body snuggly.

Upon entering the house, Fox greeted me at the door. Over the years, it had become our routine to share a cup of tea in the kitchen on my return from a trip. Fox worried about me and wanted to hear all I had done and my plans for the next few days, mainly where I was going and with whom. She was the only one who cared, so I didn't feel her questions to be an intrusion on my life. Today, I didn't feel like I had the time or the inclination to share tea with Fox. I asked her to book my hairdresser and makeup artist immediately for this evening. If they were already booked, I told her to offer them more money until they agreed to attend to me.

Fox looked perplexed, as I knew she would; this was not a request she was used to hearing from me. She waited, staring at me inquiringly, until she was sure I wasn't about to offer an explanation. Only then did she finally say she would attend to my request before bringing our tea to my room. I knew she really wanted to hear what had changed in my absence. I needed a few hour's sleep but really all I wanted to do was sit and daydream; I could still feel the tingling of my body when my arm brushed against his. It was a magically feeling that seemed to power me to life with an intensity I had never known.

Brook was the first to call me; I had hardly sat on my bed to dream when my cell chimed for attention,

'Lyme, what the hell – can you mean you've met a man? Have you suddenly lost your mind or changed it, and now you think you are in love with Clive? Why girlfriend, I thought you said the feeling just wasn't there with him, although he was a fun guy. Have you become so desperate that your now delusional?' Brook spoke in her usual hurried manner without taking a breath. Just when I thought she'd stopped speaking she quickly added,

'I almost forgot I've been doing some checking on Clive, I knew I remembered the name. I met him at a law function several years ago. I believe he's a lawyer or something. But Lyme, this maybe a shock to you but, I'm sure he was there with his wife!' I heard her words and I knew she was waiting for a reaction from me, but I merely said,

'Brook, it's not Clive, although we had fun. I wish it was, I really did like him,' I replied honestly.

'Well, if he's single now make it him. Love is vastly over rated. I should know I'm always falling in and out of it. Speaking of love, I need to talk to you about something…' her tone changed as her voice trailed off,

'Is everything all right, Brook? You sound…' before I had finished my question, the line went dead. I immediately redialed several times, but each time it rang only twice before going to voice mail. I guessed she'd call back; Brook had me worried this was not like her at all.

'Brook, call me back, what happened?' I left another voicemail just as Fox entered the room, she wasn't carrying the tea tray as I expected,

'Lyme, Mr. Lyn wants to see you right away,' she said, her face telling me this wasn't for anything good. 'I wanted to talk to you first,' Fox continued. 'Mr. Lyn, he's been busy in your absence, busy finding you a husband; he says your time is up. I don't know what triggered it, but he had an appointment with Doc Masterton, after the Doc persisted for months, and when he arrived home his mood was foul. We all got the worst end of his tongue and abuse. When he was done with us, he seemed to change his focus on you. Sorry, Lyme, I was going to tell you…' We heard his voice bellowing from the distance of his study. I could tell his door was shut, but he had a voice like a raging bull, especially when he wanted something.

'LYME – WHERE THE HELL ARE YOU? CAN'T MY OWN DAUGHTER COME WHEN SHE'S

CALLED. LYME. GET THE HELL IN HERE,' he bellowed. I looked at Fox, and we both understood I needed to head downstairs now. I was halfway down when he yelled again, this time cursing loudly and threatening to come up to room if I didn't appear immediately.

I ran down the second half of the stairs, knocked on his huge oak doors and without waiting for him to answer, I entered.

'What the hell took you so long? Ya legs fall off or something?' he yelled. He was pacing up and down the length of his study. His huge frame and even bigger presence dominated the room as was always the case. I immediately felt like a scared kid in his presence.

'Sit down, gal.' He flicked his hand toward the two oversize armchairs that stood facing his large mahogany desk.

'I been wanting to talk to you, where the hell have you been?' I quickly explained about the new resort and reminded him that he was the one who gave me the order and told me where I was going. Looking at him I saw his mind was focused on other things and his ears had shut down. He wasn't listening.

Finally, he stood up and before moving from behind his desk, he unlocked the top drawer and removed a large glossy photo of a young man,

'This, my gal, is your future husband. Good looking guy, good pedigree, well-educated, unattached and willing to take you on. I picked him myself. It will cost me, of course, but we can plan the wedding as soon as possible.

Oh yeah, his names Remington Tillerson-Proctor the third. Distantly related to Rex Tillerson of Exxon Mobil. Damn perfect match. Newton actually found the guy. Almost like he was lying around enjoying his wealthy life and waiting for a purpose. So, we found him a purpose: his purpose in life is marrying you.' Daddy finished with a look of satisfaction on his face as he continued pacing the floor.

I sat where I was holding the photo in my hand. Staring back at me was a young man with brown wavy hair, blue eyes that smiled as he was doing now, a square jaw and handsome face. He looked harmless and maybe even nice. But I was not looking to spend my life with a *nice* guy, they were a dime a dozen. I felt the color drain from my face as I took my eyes from the face on the photo and stared at the floor. Daddy had really done it; he had really done what he kept threatening to. It took me a few moments to compose myself. I was not going down without a fight. Holt's blue eyes danced before me. I didn't want to mention him yet, but I may have no choice.

I stood up and squared my shoulders, the same as I'd seen my father do; only I never realized I did it also. Daddy paced up and down never taking his eyes from my face. As he passed me again, I stood, I looked him square in the eyes, lifted the glossy twelve by twelve photo in my hands, then I ripped it down the middle before ripping it again in quarters and throwing it on his desk.

'I am not marrying that man. Not now, not ever. I am not marrying some stranger that you have chosen for me just to make you happy.' My eyes blazed as he stopped in front of me and said in a very controlled voice,

'I don't give a damn if you marry him or not, but I want an heir. For the sake of your unborn baby, I urge you to marry him. I want you to do it right, Lyme. I never asked anything of you except this, and I intend to have my way on this matter alone.'

'Daddy, you have *your way* on all matters. But it's my life and I'm not marrying whatever his name is. On this matter I intend to get my way.' I knew my cheeks were flushed and my eyes were blazing dangerously as I faced him. He continued to pace until he stopped in front of me and spoke again.

'Lyme, honey, I'm not getting any younger and I need to know my empire will have someone to continue it on. I know you will try to do so and you're proving to be a reasonably business woman, but when you get old, what happens then, is everything I've worked for my whole life going to mean nothing. I need the Lynch name to continue on. It's what your mother would have wanted and it's what I want. This cannot be a shock to you Lyme, I've told you my deadline for many years now. How can you pretend to be surprised?'

'Daddy, I'm not surprised, but I want to marry a man I love, someone who makes me feel the way Mom use to make you feel.'

'You don't know anything about how your mom made me feel – you've had no life experience in those matters, I have. Well gal, you've had a good many years to find this special man. Pan takes you to all the best places, you're known in society. You go out often with your friends and you travel. I'm sorry, but in another few years you won't be able to have a baby, let alone two; you'll be too damn old.'

'Daddy, I think you're being mean.' I hated his tone and underlying condescension. What I really wanted to do was to be left alone by everyone, so I can dream about my date this evening with Holt. I didn't want to mention him to Daddy as I'd only just met him, but every part of my body and mind told me he was the one for me. I hoped to keep him secret for a while longer, at least until after our date tonight. Although, I didn't like where this conversation was headed. I can already see the veins in Daddy's temples throbbing, and that was a sure sign he was about to lose his temper. I tried to keep my voice calm, although I was having trouble hiding my rising annoyance. He had seldom become involved in my life and never in such an intimate way as this.

'I'm not being mean in fact, gal, I'm being about as patient as you can expect any man to be, and I've heard enough of your resistance – this is what I want and to hell with you, you will give in to me, or else…!' he yelled moving way too close to my face as he screamed the last words at me. I saw his blazing blue eyes staring into mine; I saw his pupils' contract until they looked like tiny black granite points. I hated being in the same room as him, but having him in my space and inches from my face, was indeed a nasty experience. It was like looking into the eyes of the devil only I was convinced this devil was quite crazy. I stood my ground. I had decided to stand up several minutes ago, thinking I may need a quick exit from the room. I must not show fear; he lapped at people's fears like a cat with a saucer of cream.

'Or else what, Daddy, or else what?' I knew I was playing with fire, but I was not about to back down. He was still staring into my eyes when my cell began to ring. I was holding it in my hand, and I lifted it to check to see who was calling. I must mention I am not foolish enough to consider answering it, I thought it was on vibrate only; in a flash Daddy grabbed it and hurled it across the room. It crashed into a huge Ming vase that sat on a narrow pedestal. My phone smashed through the top half of the vase before hitting the wall and bouncing onto the floor.

Daddy's eyes hadn't moved from mine or mine from his. The sound of the ancient vase smashing made no impression on either of us. Inside I was trembling, but I had no intention of showing it. I was, after all my father's daughter. A loud knocking came from the door and Newton's deep voice called,

'Everything all right in there, Mr. Lyn, sir?'

'Leave us alone Newton,' my father immediately replied.

Gradually, I saw the color leave his cheeks and return to normal; neither of us moved until finally he quietly whispered,

'Or else my gal, I shall take all this away from you, everything that is rightfully yours, yes including the resorts you own, your cars, clothes and even your phone, don't think I won't. This is mine to give, and its mine to take away. And one more thing, never threaten me again, I wrote the book on threats, so be careful what you start.' His voice was like ice as he turned away from me. The silence in the room was deafening. I couldn't believe what he had just said. How could he threaten me, why would he threaten me?

One thing I now knew was that he was serious, serious about me giving him an heir. I stayed where I was, stunned at the hatred in his voice, the hardness in his eyes, and the small amount of caring he had shown me in the way of financial support – the only thing he had ever provided me with, and it was to be so easily withdrawn. I wasn't sure what to do, but I knew I must answer him and do so now, he was an impatient man, and he had no tolerance for fools. Whether he thought me a fool or not, I didn't know, but over the years he had led me to believe he did think of me as stupid, foolish and dumb.

I knew I must tell him about Holt, but first I decided to throw in his face some of my learning at his hands.

'As far as threats go, Daddy, I have learned from the best. And learned I have, yes, I am your daughter, and I have watched and listened to all you say and do, as I have all my life,' my answer didn't appear to anger him as I thought it might, but instead he grunted and moved slowly toward his huge desk before sitting in his oversize chair and turning away from me.

Behind his desk, under the large window, stood an ornate small mahogany drinks table; on it sat a silver tray, placed on the tray was a single jet-black bottle of 'Royal Salute' blended scotch whisky. This was the only place he ever kept a bottle of his favorite whisky. This whisky was the real stuff; the bottle was designed with four hundred and thirteen tiny diamonds, set in three symbols, the scepter, the sword and the crown. It was my father's salute to his Scottish grandmother, the woman he claims taught him all the hard life lessons he really needed to learn to succeed. I watched as slowly, he moved his chair toward the whisky, picked up one of the small crystal glasses and poured himself a dram. He swallowed it in one swig before he said,

'Lyme, cancel whatever you have planned for tonight, instead you shall meet Remington. I did not choose him as randomly as you may think. Both Newton and I have put a great deal of time and energy into making the right match, not only for you but for this family and its future generations.' I was astounded to hear him being so sentimental and shocked that he had been working on this without my knowledge for so long. Well, I was going to have to tell him where I was going tonight and with whom.

'Sorry, I cannot meet Remington tonight. I have a date. I am not cancelling it. I am going out with Holt Visser, the man I intend to marry.' Slowly he turned his chair toward me and got to his feet.

'And who the hell is Holt Visser? Some ball boy you met on the tennis court?'

'No, Daddy, he is not a ball boy.'

'Well, tell me about him. If he is to be part of this family, I need to know more, much more. I'll whip his arse into shape anyway, one way or the other.'

'I'm sure you will. But, Daddy, it's you who can tell me about him.' I was beginning to enjoy the game of cat and mouse we were playing, so far, I knew I held the trump card.

'How the hell can I tell you about him?'

'Easy, you can look him up on your computer.'

'To hell with you gal, you're testing my patience as you so often do. I am not goggling my future son-in-law when you're perfectly capable of telling me all I want to know.' At his words, I paused to think of the way I would answer, but before I could Daddy asked more questions.

'Does he hold a job? If so, what does he do? I suppose if he's unemployed we can find him something for a while before he lives off us and becomes a complete bum…' Daddy said the last words quietly to himself. I was enjoying the moment and wondering if there was any way I could get away without telling him more. Too late, he could not wait any longer; his impatience had boiled over.

'To hell with you, gal, stop trying to control the conversation and tell me what I need to know. If he has a job, where the hell does he work?' Daddy yelled, moving dangerously close to me again. I took a step backward as he took a step toward me, then I answered him. I was close enough to see the look of surprise flash in his piercing blue eyes and watch the reaction register on his face.

'Holt works for you Daddy, for Lynch Oil.' I saw the pupils of his eyes dilate dangerously. I saw his stare falter, and then he looked away.

'I don't know the name, are you sure?'

'I'm sure Daddy; he is about to start work with you next week. He is your new geophysicist. He gave me the first business card he has ever given out.' Slowly I extracted the business card from my pocket, and handed it to him; on the card the Lynch Oil logo blazed up at him, it was unmistakable.

For a moment, I had a win. Or at best I had bought myself some time. I turned and left the room, leaving my cell phone in pieces where it was as Daddy stared after me.

On my way up the stairs, I passed Cerise she was Daddy's latest love interest, but I wondered why she was wandering around the house during the day, and just why she was in the house at all? Daddy was usually most discreet with his woman, and Newton always escorted them home before sunrise. It was the second time I spied her here during the day, and she looked as though she was beginning to feel right at home. She had a smug look on her face as she passed by me on my way upstairs. I nodded at her as we passed and something inside told me I no longer had a win over Daddy.

I needed to talk to Fox; she kept me updated on everything happening in the house. Without her I'd know nothing. I remembered we had missed our usual cup of tea, and a chat on my return, as I was in a hurry to get ready for my date with Holt. Now, I knew that was a mistake.

Was Daddy about to replace me in the house with his latest floosy, Cerise? Cerise looked much too young for him; in fact, she looked about my age, or did she just have a good cosmetic surgeon? I didn't think she was his type, but then I knew I hadn't ever given much thought to just what his type, was. Was I so naive as to believed he would stay true to my mother's memory forever?

I paused at the top of the stairs and glanced down at Cerise. Her heels clicking on the marble floor as she crossed the entranceway. Her long, curly, flaming red hair swung to and fro across her back as she walked. She was tall and slim and very pretty. She was dressed elegantly, and I was instinctively aware she radiated a powerful sexuality. She soon disappeared into the room I had just vacated, and I heard Daddy's animated voice greet her enthusiastically before the door closed immediately behind her. My brief triumph over Daddy seemed to fade as I watched her, until my mind snapped back to Holt.

Upon entering my suite of rooms, I saw my hairstylist and makeup artist waiting for me. A jolt of excitement pulsed through my body at the thought of seeing Holt again. I knew I would surprise both these girls when I told them they could do whatever they wanted, with me.

'I just want to look stunning,' I told them and watched the shock pass across their faces, followed by disbelief, and then, was it excitement I saw? I knew they would enjoy the prospect of changing this ugly duckling into a swan.

Chapter 7
Madam Roderic ~ 2

Pan's telephone softly beeped on the bedside table. Pan sat waiting for her hairdresser to arrive. She looked the picture of prettiness on her huge pink bed in her large opulent pink bedroom. Her blonde hair cascaded down her back with hardly a curl out of place, although to Pan it needed attention. Her complexion was perfection; her skin glowed softly in the morning light from the tall windows. She wore no makeup and to anyone observing her for the first time, they would know there was not a need for any. Her apricot negligee cascaded around her, almost smothering her in the giant bed.

She lifted the handset of her antique French phone and her butlers voice announced the arrival of Madam Roderic.

'Send her up,' Pan responded giggling with delight at the unexpected arrival of her confidant, all thoughts of her hair dresser momentarily forgotten. Pan's blue eyes sparkled as she waited for the soft tap on the door,

'Oh, do come in, madam,' Pan called giggling as the door softly opened and madam stood looking into the room. She had been here many times before but the huge room commanded attention just like the girl in the bed.

'I see you had a need for your madam this morning, Miss Janice. You require to know what the day holds ahead, do you not? But there is no need to reply; the mere fact you are still in your boudoir is answer enough.' Madam Roderic finished in her deep monotone voice, while her black beady eyes never left those of her client. Rising from the chair where she had briefly sat she now moved smoothly toward the bed; her many layers of brightly colored clothes floating out around her. No outline of her body could be seen through the sheer fabric, even with the sun at her back. Pan briefly thought madam must be very thin before quickly forgetting her thoughts as she merely giggled, while her eyes locked on those of the older lady. Madam Roderic was only a few feet from the bed when she turned again and moved back toward the huge deep pink velvet covered chair that sat under the window to the side of the room. The moment she sat down, she bounced up again her arms spread wide. This time Pan sensed a change in energy of the room; her smile faded, and she too became instantly alert.

'Madam, what are you sensing?' Pan asked with only the slightest giggle.

'I sense it is your friend, the one with the auburn hair; she lives now in her new home. She is about to meet the man of her dreams, but I sense she doesn't recognize him. He wears a uniform; he is a man of the law. Not the type, she usually chases at all. Wait, wait, I see danger for her, I see her old boyfriend. He will bring danger into her home. She is in her elegant new home, he is in her new home also, and she has not allowed him entry, but he is there. I see a knife. Danger, he is very dangerous you must warn her. But wait, I see her new lover there also. Both men are in her home together with Brook. He wears a uniform. She is very distressed, she is maybe hurt that is all.' Madam Roderic collapses on the chair in a dead faint, and Pan claps her hands and giggles.

Pan would never think to check if madam Roderic is all right, nor does she heed her warning. Pan likes being entertained and to be the center of attention, and she is used to it being so. She only heeds madam's words when they are about her, and only her. Pan enjoys madam's entertainment, and for Pan this is entertainment of the best kind. Pan stays where she is and waits for Madam Roderic to continue. She stares eagerly at madam marveling at her ability to so easily create drama. Pan likes the way she includes her friends. This new vision, she presented was so unexpected, but fun anyway. What a unique way to begin her day.

Pan waits until Madam Roderic returns to the world of the living. Her pale face now has tiny droplets of sweat glistening on her brow. She stares at Pan, her beady eyes fixed on the pretty girl in front of her, finally she asks, 'So, you wish to know only about yourself, about your day. You pay me, and I tell you what I see, but you do not hear, or do you not understand?'

'I adore having you around, madam. I couldn't live without your advice and entertainment,' Pan replied, giggling as she sounded slightly more dramatic than usual.

Pan was trying to imitate Madam Roderic, but it was a poor imitation and was lost on all, but her.

'I shall tell you what you must wear and where you must go. Madam Roderic is never wrong. I shall tell you only once, before I depart,' madam Roderic spoke in her quiet deep voice as Pan again began to giggle her eyes sparkled with delight. This was the Madam she knew, and these were things important to her and her world. But before madam continued with the trivial things, Pan wished to know they were interrupted by the phone softly chiming again. Pan was informed that her hairdresser had arrived. Pan giggled, knowing all was well with her world.

Chapter 8
Feather Brookston

Brook was enjoying her new house; she had moved in over three months ago but as yet hadn't spent much time alone in her home. It was large by her standards, at over four thousand square feet, but by Pan and Lyme's standards, it was no more than a shack. Her new home boasted stainless steel everything; it had polished concrete floors, pale matt gray walls, huge windows, and a modern sleek square design that suited Brook perfectly. She wished, she hadn't allowed Ric to ever set foot in her new home, but thinking back she realized she hadn't even told him where she'd moved to, he had found out and pushed his way in. Brook shuddered at the thought. Since then, she'd installed a state-of-the-art security system, and now she felt slightly safer. Safe was something Brook needed to feel, it was her greatest fear being alone and vulnerable – hence her many boyfriends. This was her first real home; she had paid for it in full and owned it completely. No more renting. Brook had invested in the house all the money she earned from endorsement and appearances at parties, etc. with Lyme and Pan. She would continue to live modestly off her allowance and salary from the law firm. Even though it was generous, it was hardly enough to keep up with Pan.

Finally, she was here alone, and she had some time before she needed to be ready for her night out with Pan. Lyme wasn't joining them tonight, apparently, she had a hot date, Brook just received a text from her and would call her soon, but first she was savoring a few moments in her house, alone. She sat looking around the living room it was long and understated. White leather couches with shiny chrome legs, and oversize chairs in a modern square design added comfort, giving the light edgy room a surreal ambience. Brook adored the splashes of red she'd added, and knew they caught the eye as you entered. On the biggest wall, a large abstract canvass hung.

One of her favorite places in the house was at the far end of the room where more large red cushions beckoned from the floor in the corner close beside a unique, tall, abstract statue. She had splurged a little too much money on the statue, but she'd fallen in love with its clean lines and modern contemporary appeal. Brook still didn't know exactly what it was, but she knew over time it would challenge her intellect, and it could become anything she wanted it to be. Today, as the light played on its shape, she thought she saw several men locked together mysteriously. She pondered and looked closer from her seat on the couch. The statue stood about four feet tall on a small marble pedestal directly in front of the tall window.

Brook was disturbed by the sound of the intercom, and she sighed at losing her moment of alone time, so soon. Looking into the security monitor, Brook saw what looked like a police officer at her door, but she couldn't be sure, he had his face turned away from the security camera. Something about him gave her the shivers, or was it the way he stood, so close to the camera his face was shielded from view.

'Yes?' she asked again searching the color monitor for his face,

'Officer Edward Boobkin – Westlake Hills Police department. Am I speaking to Miss Feather Brookston?'

'What do you want?' Brook replied without directly answering his question.

'Please allow me entrance, we have reason to believe a serial killer is on the loose in your area, and I'd like to show you some photos and check you have adequate security. We're canvasing every house in your neighborhood in the hope someone may have seen or recognizes the man. I'd appreciate you opening the gate, and allowing me to talk to you, ma'am.' There was something about his voice, his words were slurred, and his speech was forced. He seemed to be trying very hard to sound coherent. Brook also wondered why his face was turned away from the monitor, something about him felt strangely familiar, and she shivered involuntarily again.

'Officer Boobkin, what is your badge number?'

'Ma'am, I just want a moment of your time?'

'I will verify who you are first, officer; please give me your badge number.'

Brook already had her cell phone in her hand and had dialed the Westlake Hills Police Department, she kept the Department on speed dial – just in case.

'Ma'am, just open the gate.'

'Officer Boobkin, I cannot see your face, please look into the camera,' Brook added, noting that he seemed to turn further away from the camera and made no effort to comply with her wishes to be identified,

'Yes, ma'am, what is your inquiry,' the officer on the end of the phone asked.

'Yes, I have an Officer Edward Boobkin outside my gate; he refuses to tell me his badge number. I am looking for verification of his identity before I allow him into my home.'

'You did the right thing to call, ma'am, one moment please.' Brook was placed on hold, she had been watching the officer on her security monitor, but now he'd disappeared.

'Ma'am, we are dispatching a unit to your home immediately, please deny this man access, repeat do not allow this man to enter your home. ETA of our officer's arrival time is approximately seven minutes.'

'I can't see him outside my gate, he seems to have vanished,' Brook told the officer. He repeated again that a unit would be with her shortly, to sit tight and wait. Weird, Brook thought; anyway, he seemed to have gone now. Brook disconnected the call and decided to call Lyme; she wanted to know what her short text meant. Lyme answered almost immediately.

'Lyme, what the hell do you mean you've met a man? Have you suddenly lost your mind, or changed it, and now you think you're in love with Clive? Why girlfriend I thought you said the feeling just wasn't there with him, although he was a fun guy. Have you become so desperate that you're now delusional?' Brook spoke in her usual hurried manner without taking a breath. Just when I thought she'd stopped speaking she quickly added, 'I almost forgot I've been doing some checking on Clive, I knew I remembered the name. I met him at a law function several years ago. I believe he's a lawyer or something. But Lyme, this maybe a shock to you but, I'm sure he was there with his wife!' I heard her words and I knew she was waiting for a reaction from me, but I merely said,

'Brook, it's not Clive, although we had fun. I wish it was, I really did like him,' I replied honestly.

'Well, if he's single make it him. Love is vastly over rated. I should know I'm always falling in and out of it. Speaking of love, I need to talk to you about something…' her tone changed as her voice trailed off.

'Is everything all right, Brook? You sound…'

Brook dropped her cell. There was a slight moment just outside her line of sight, a shadow, or something, or someone moving with sleuth. Then she felt rather than saw someone move up behind her.

The cold feel of the steel blade touched her throat.

'You've been avoiding me, bitch.' Brook knew the deep raspy voice, she knew it well. It was Ric. The blade of the sharp knife pressed slightly into her skin; she felt the uncontrollable tremors vibrate through his body and into hers.

'Ric, how did you get in?'

'Shut the fuck up, rich bitch, and if you do, I may let you live. I need money, money is the only thing that feeds my habit.' He swung her around to face to him. Brook was tall; she stood at eye level with him. She stared at the dead desperate roaming eyes; they seemed to move constantly in their hollow dark socket, she felt the hand that gripped her so hard shaking uncontrollably. Surely, she could over power him? But he held the knife? And he was crazy, crazy like a fox in a drug haze of withdrawal.

'Look, bitch, I'll make it up to you, I know you want to spend time with me, so we can be close again, but me skins crawlin' it feels like an army of ants is movin' under me skin. Give me all the money you have in the house. I been waitin' for you to come home, waitin' forever and watchin', you got to help me, you took way too long to get home. Money, bitch, money is all that will feed it and stop this horrible crawling feelin'.'

'Where did you get the uniform, Ric, where did you get it?' Brook tried to ask calmly, but the moment she spoke she saw the rage burn in his eyes as they came to life briefly with desperation and hatred. Again, he pressed the knife into her throat. She felt her own blood trickle warm and free down her neck and between her breasts. Then, he roughly swung her around, so they were face to face, again. Using the back of his hand, he smacked her hard across the face. Brook thought it was surprisingly hard considering how he was trembling. Now he grabbed her long auburn hair; it was tied into a ponytail. He wrapped it tightly around his hand making his grip solid. Brook was unable to move her head, the pain from her hair being held so tightly and the feel of the knife at her throat, made her tremble also. She was trying hard to remain in control and not to show Ric her fear.

'Get me your handbag, bitch, do it now OR I'LL KILL YOU – I've killed before, its easy. Hurry, I'm crawling, they're crawling under my skin, they're eating me alive.' He began twitching as he moved this way and that; Brook assumed he was trying to get away from his crawling demons. His hand that held the knife shook uncontrollably, making it impossible for him not to cut her again several times on the neck. He dragged her toward the kitchen where he knew she usually kept her handbag. It was on the chair where she'd thrown it.

He shoved her roughly toward it, still holding her hair, she felt the knife leave her throat, and wondered if this was the right time to fight back and try to overpower him. Brook knew she was young fit and strong. She knew several martial arts moves and could easily defend herself. But she was also very aware of how crazy Ric was and also how desperate. He was not rational at all and could easily kill her, with a flick of the knife. He had the upper hand. Brook thought of giving him a backward kick to the balls and then thought better of it.

She hoped another chance would present itself. Reaching into her handbag, she retrieved her wallet, and with Ric's darting eyes watching closely, she removed all the cash she had inside. She felt Ric twitching and sweating, and she could smell his foul body odor and rotten breath as he breathed heavily on the back of her neck, it was a sweet, rancid smell and one she would not soon forget. She only had several hundred dollars, and he grabbed it like a starving man before again placing the knife at her throat.

'More, bitch, this is not nearly enough, I'm a hungry boy. Don't worry, I'll pay you back. We'll be together again…' in her ear Ric's rasping voice was interrupted by the sound of sirens moving rapidly closer, followed closely by car doors slamming and the intercom buzzing. In every room the security monitors blazed into life, and Brook saw three officers standing looking into the camera. She immediately recognized they were wearing the same uniform as Ric. She wondered how he had got hold of a police uniform? He was more dangerous than she first thought; it had been a good move to leave him.

'Bitch.' Ric's rasping voice spat into her ear. He quickly touched the blade of his knife to her already cut throat before, with shaking hands, he roughly stuffed the notes into his pocket and bolted for the French doors, he seemed to instantly disappear. Brook was shaking as she pressed her hand to her bleeding throat. Trying to gain some control. She slowly moved toward the monitor and pressed the button under the screen that unlocked the gate. In the turmoil of her mind, Brook clearly knew her days dating bad boys were over – she had grown out of them and their dangerous immature ways. Brook grabbed a kitchen towel and wrapped it tightly around her neck, trying desperately not to faint. Focusing hard on what she must do she headed for the door, wondering again just how he had entered the place she called home; the place she thought, she was safe?

Three uniformed officers burst into the house the moment the door opened.

'Which way did he go?' the first one asked as she pointed toward the French doors that stood ajar. As he ran, Brook heard him speaking quickly into his police radio. The other officer called an ambulance, while the third escorted Brook to the couch.

'Miss, I'm Officer Morris Delaney, you're all right now, help is on the way.' Brook could see the officer looking at her blood-soaked t-shirt, or was he looking at her breasts? Then he moved his eyes again to hers.

He was tall and muscular with soft hazel eyes, a strong jaw and wavy light brown hair, and he looked deeply into Brook's eyes as he spoke. He was so close; she felt his breath on her cheek. Slowly, he unwrapped the soaked towel from her neck.

'I think, you'll be all right. Can I have your name please?' he softly asked. Brook felt his eyes penetrate her soul, but she couldn't look away.

'I'm Feather Brookston, my friends call me Brook.'

'Miss Brookston, can you tell me the name of your security company?' Brook responded with the information he requested, while he scrabbled in a small notebook with a short thick yellow pencil.

'Did you know this man?' he asked and Brook nodded wishing, she didn't know him.

'How did he gain entry, Miss Brookston?' he inquired as the other two officers joined him, and together they stood looking down at her. Brook's eyes were drawn to the eyes of Officer Morris Delaney, and try as she may to look at the other police officers; she seemed unable to look away. She felt mesmerized as if they were the only two people in the room. Brook was drawn to him like she'd never been drawn to another human being. He was a police officer, not her type at all, he had short hair, he was clean and well-educated, so why was she feeling this way? Then Brook understood, she must be in shock, yes that was it; she was in shock. With a huge effort, she pulled herself back to the questions they were asking her...

'...and your relationship to this man was...?'

'...he was an ex-boyfriend. Very X. I think he was waiting for me to return home. But I don't know how he got inside.'

'A key, perhaps?' one of the officers replied a slight jeer on his lips,

'Ric never had a key. I've only lived here recently, and we broke up some time ago.'

'Were you aware that he is maybe a serial killer, Miss Brookston?'

'No, I was not. I never had any reason to believe that he was a serial killer. A drug addict and a bad boy, perhaps, but I can't believe he is a serial killer,' Brook replied as his words sunk in for the first time.

'No, Ma'am, friends and loved ones seldom do,' the second officer replied jeering down at her again. Brook felt she was at a distinct disadvantage as she lay on the couch looking up at them. She could feel the clean towel Officer Delaney had placed around her neck quickly becoming soaked.

The wail of the ambulance siren cut through the still neighborhood, before abruptly stopping. One of the officers opened the gate from the security monitor and then the door. Two-uniformed paramedics, a male and female, moved swiftly into the room; a stretcher unfolded. Brook watched the activity as if it was happening to someone else. She remained half lying on couch holding tightly to the towel around her neck.

'I don't want to go to hospital, it's only a minor cut, nothing more.'

'We'll be the judge of that, ma'am,' the woman said bending down to unwrap the towel.

'Knife cut, or several I would say, looks clean enough, not very deep, you were lucky, Ma'am, very lucky. Once someone gets a knife and means to inflict harm, they seldom know how soft human flesh is.'

She opened her medical kit and began dressing the wound as again the security monitors came to life, this time a security guard asked for admission. Apparently, the whole break in, had been recorded, and they would have had someone here sooner, but all units were occupied elsewhere. He apologized for the time it took to attend. It was the smart mouthed officer who replied sarcastically and jeered his condescending smile. The security officer seemed not to notice. He moved toward Brook showed his ID, and gave her his card.

'I'm just going to check the point of entry and re-secure the perimeter and reset the monitor, Ma'am,' he said looking down at Brook.

'Take photos, Officer Delaney, and also some of the throat wound if you please before it's bandaged, then the usual routine photos of the premises.'

'Yes, sir,' Officer Delaney replied. Moments later, he was taking photos of Brook's throat along with several of her. As he was about to move away and photograph the rest of the house he bent down toward her and whispered.

'I'm so glad you're all right, may I check in on you later?'

'Officer Delaney, we don't have all day.'

'No, sir,' he replied before she could answer, but before he moved away, Brook gave him a slight nod and hoped he understood. In spite of her injured throat and the horrific ordeal she had endured at the hands of Ric, Brook felt a definite tingle ripple through her, she knew that feeling, and she understood it. But it still surprised her; he was not her type, not even close. She didn't feel any sexual attraction toward him, but she certainly felt something, something strong and real. But somehow, it was something new, something she had never felt before. It was the same feeling but different somehow. Brook had never been confused about the effect she had on men, but for the first time she was confused about the effect the handsome police officer had on her. Yes, she must be in shock! That was it; she was heavily in shock.

Chapter 9
The First Date

What an incredible surprise when I gazed in the mirror, the reflection looking back at me was more like looking at someone else. I looked sophisticated, and I felt beautiful; what an amazing job my makeup artist and hairstylist had done. For me, it had taken way too long, and I knew I had fidgeted throughout. Several times I thought of dismissing them, but on each occasion, I focused on Holt and the night ahead.

My hair was layered from my chin down; it was cut in around my face. It looked straight, shiny and sleek. The color was a deep chestnut with thin blonde highlights framing my face. It had movement and body but felt so light, I hardly felt it belonged to me. My makeup was just as tasteful. I had never before allowed a complete makeover as I felt it took too much time, and I couldn't really see the point. But looking at myself in the mirror, I knew that had been a huge error on my part. Sheer foundation had managed to even out my complexion; bronze highlights on my cheeks gave my face the appearance of being chiseled. Lash extensions that were barely there made my eyes look huge as they curled upward. My lashes looked nothing like the previous lash extensions I'd once tried, they had been thick and heavy, and I was aware of them the whole time they were on.

I felt and looked, amazing. I gave my hairstylist and makeup artist a generous tip as they hurried out the door. Moments before the door closed, I heard Cerise call to them from the floor below. I felt annoyed that she should want to use my people and jealous that she could. Fox almost danced into the room holding my sheer lace charcoal gray, off the shoulder dress across her outstretched arms. After depositing it carefully on my bed, she stopped and turned to me; her mouth open as she stared, finally she said, 'Wow – unbelievable. Turn around, slowly now. Oh my stars, Lyme, you look beautiful. You glow. I've never seen you look more beautiful. The hair, the makeup, it's all perfection. I hoped you tipped those girls generously; they have done a wonderful job.' Fox cooed still staring. I felt myself blush from her praise. I was not used to it, and I knew it was genuine. Looking at Fox, I saw admiration etched across her face.

'Yes, Fox they got a generous tip, of course, they did.' I replied, 'You do like what they'd done, don't you?' Fox added,

'Yes, of course; how could I not? It just takes some getting used to. It doesn't even look like me,' I replied again turning to stare into the mirror.

'Oh, but it does, Lyme, it looks like the best you. Let's get you dressed, and then I must take some photos,' Fox said moving forward and hugging me. It was an unexpected hug, and it took me a few seconds to respond. I felt beautiful, I was in love, and I wondered if my world could get any better.

I walked slowly down the long stairway before turning left and heading for the door that lead through to the garage. I couldn't decide which car I should drive tonight. I was leaning toward the Lotus Evora 400; it is supposedly the fastest car in the world. Daddy had only recently purchased the brand-new Lotus Evora, which now replaced the Lotus Exige S roadster. I loved speed, and I loved driving the Evora. Then, I remembered how tall Holt was and thought the SL65 AMG Mercedes sports hardtop was a better fit. It was slower than the Lotus, but for a tall guy, I knew it would be an eminently more comfortable ride.

Our garage currently held ten cars of various makes and sizes, but one thing I knew for sure, they were all top of the range and expensive. The garage was temperature controlled and had bright overhead lights and hidden lighting that remained on always. The moment I entered, the overhead lights immediately blazed into life. I opened the safe on the wall using my pass code and extracted the keys to the Mercedes.

It was early, and as I stood in the garage, I felt my nerves refuse to settle. I tried to move my mind from constantly thinking of the man I love. Yes, I knew I loved him already, and I also knew this is what it was supposed to feel like. I sat in the quiet of the garage trying to still my racing thoughts. Then, I leaned over and retrieved the owner's manual on the Mercedes from the glove compartment and briefly studied the information. Holt was an engineer and may ask questions about the car. After learning that the SL65 boasted a 5.5 liter V-8 engine, I decided I had read enough. I got out of the car and walked briefly around the huge garage, not noticing the many gleaming cars all around me and hearing my heels as they clicked on the polished concrete floor.

I was trying to settle my nerves, but it seems useless. I couldn't wait to see him, and I was completely unable to focus on anything but him. Then, I began doubting myself, maybe he wasn't as I remembered him, and maybe I had exaggerated just how wonderful and handsome he was? Maybe, he didn't really even exist? My demons were out in force and chasing all these negative thoughts around my head. I quickly tried to put them to rest. Wiping my sweaty palms on my lace dress, I slid into the soft cream leather seat and behind the wheel. The car instantly greeted me by name, and then asked where I was headed. The moment the engine throbbed into life, the garage doors rolled slowly open behind me. Before I moved, I spoke the address of the hotel into the navigation system.

I reversed the car out of the garage into the circular driveway and just as I was about to head out a movement in the full length window, caught my eye. Briefly I glanced sideways, and then quickly returned my attentions to my driving. I had seen Cerise and Daddy clearly through the huge open windows of his study. He was kissing her neck as she arched her supple body in delight; his large meaty fingers were fumbling with the tiny buttons down the front of her blouse. I saw it fall from her shoulders to the floor. Her bra was red lacy and barely there.

A shiver of repulsion rippled through me as I waited for the huge gates to silently swing fully open. I willed my mind to think of Holt and the evening ahead, but the vision of Cerise's skimpy red bra and my Daddy's huge hands covering her breasts, seemed scorched into my mind. I knew then a visit to Granny Harry was needed. She was my mom's mother, and the woman I ran to whenever I needed guidance, someone to talk to or just a warm and loving hug from a genuine old lady who wanted nothing in return.

I exited the freeway, and I was soon pulling up in front of Holt's hotel. Before it loomed into view in the busy downtown, my eyes began searching, searching intently for the tall blond man who had stolen my heart.

I couldn't see him. He wasn't there.

I'd always known this was a possibility. I had only managed to leave him a message on his cell phone and had never actually spoken to him since I saw him on the plane. My heart seemed to pound even harder if that was possible. The thought of never seeing him again made me feel like I was drowning. I slowed the car and pulled into the only space available in front of the hotel. The valet was beside me in seconds. I didn't know if I was going to be able to speak or not as the driver's window glided down.

'Can I park for you, Ms. Harrington-Lynch?' the young boy inquired clearly recognizing me. It was then I remembered the number plates on the car; all Daddy's number plates had the Lynch name and logo on them, my heart sunk. This was not the way I wanted him to find out who I was.

'I'm just meeting someone; do you mind if I just wait a while?' I asked almost in tears from Holt's absence. I took a twenty dollar note from my purse and handed it to the young boy who was bending down so close to my face.

'Certainly, Ms. Harrington-Lynch, is there anything else I can do for you?' he asked as I shook my head and closed the window. I was holding back the tears as I searched the crowd in the lobby.

Then, I saw him.

My breath caught in my throat as he moved slowly through the crowd. He was just as tall and handsome as I remembered. Every woman in his vicinity turned to look as he passed. He was tall, lean, tanned and his perfect wavy blond hair looked like it stayed wherever it was combed. His blue eyes sparkled as did his brief smile when he first saw me. He wore black wool trouser, highly polished shoes, that looked expensive and a teal and blue striped shirt, which also looked expensive. Over his arm, he carried a gray sports jacket. The valet quickly jumped forward and opened the door, and there he was sitting beside me.

'Hey, you're five minutes late. I'm not a man who's used to waiting.'

'Sorry, I've been waiting here for at least five minutes,' I responded, not expecting those to be the first words he uttered upon seeing me.

'How was I supposed to know it was you? You never mentioned the type of car you drive and you look way different from yesterday.'

'Sorry,' I said again. He hadn't complimented me on looking good, or my dress or anything. I was used to compliments from guys, even if they didn't mean it.

'So, where are you taking me?'

'There is a new seafood restaurant not far from here, I've met the owner, and the food is superb in his other restaurants.'

'That's the only reason you think this one will be good, because of his other restaurants or because you have met the owner?' Holt asked, his arrogance peeping through. He was obviously a man who liked to challenge.

'Both those reasons. I also like fresh local seafood, and I hope you do too?'

'So long as it *is* fresh?' Holt replied and there he was again challenging me.

'I know it will be. If you don't like the restaurant I've chosen, we can go somewhere else. Do you have a favorite?' I asked trying to give him what he wanted. Maybe, he was feeling intimidated by the car or me or not being given a choice. Somehow, he didn't sound like a man who would allow himself to be intimidated.

'Dumb question, I've just arrived in Texas. How could I have a favorite restaurant?'

'Maybe, you've been here before?' I answered not liking the fact he just called me dumb.

'Well, I haven't, first time here. Don't much care for it yet, although a stranger buying me dinner is something I hadn't expected.' I was again shocked that he called me a stranger, I hadn't stopped thinking about him all day, and he thought of me as a stranger. But then, I guess that's just what we were – strangers to each other.

'I expect, you have a lot of ladies who buy you dinner,' I responded thinking this would take the conversation onto a lighter note.

'Just what are you implying?' I realized the conversation had not taken a lighter note, and I was again being challenged. We drove on in silence; my mind in turmoil. What was the matter with him, didn't he feel as I felt? I noticed he played on his phone for most of the trip. I felt forgotten, neglected.

'This is a powerful machine, and you drive it like a tractor,' he said out of the blue.

'Sorry,' I replied almost in tears now,

'Stop saying that you're sorry, it's getting on my nerves.'

'Sorry, I mean okay…' I was holding back the tears now and taking several deep long breaths.

Finally, I swung the car into the circular entrance of the modern restaurant. The valet was smartly dressed and quickly approached the passenger's door, opening it a moment before Holt would have done so. Another valet approached me and recognized me instantly; I knew Holt was inside the restaurant and out of hearing as the young man addressed me by name. The Mercedes was a keyless car, so I searched my purse for the valet key – I had placed in there earlier.

We were shown to a superb table overlooking Galveston Bay and Tiki Island. It was a clear evening. Holt stood looking out the floor length windows at the view, while the server stood patiently holding his chair for him to be seated. He stood tall and proud, and oh so handsome, my heart skipped. I had forgiven his earlier bad behavior and hoped we could start over. I watched his back, running my eyes over everything, every part of him; memorizing it all. He stood with his large, well-manicured hands clasped lightly behind his back, his shoulders straight and legs slightly apart.

I stared at him drinking in the sight of the man I loved like a thirsty forgotten soul in the desert. I couldn't remove my eyes from his back. Again, I memorized every detail of his body, the way he stood, the evening sun made his blond hair glow around his head creating a halo of gold. I marveled at the way his wavy blond hair curled about his neck, and onto his smooth perfect skin. Then my eyes began searching his body all over again. I lingered on his hands, a man's hands are important and Holt had wonderful hands. Well-manicured and strong, the skin was smooth and well cared for, these were the hands of a man not used to doing manual work of any kind. Holt turned slightly more away from me as he observed Tiki Island in the distance. He moved one hand to shield his eyes as the last rays of the sun settled over the horizon for the night.

Then, my world collapsed. The evening sun that had made him appear a golden god earlier was almost gone, but as he lifted his hand to shield his eyes, the sun's rays flashed on the gold on his finger, and, there it was.

He was wearing a wedding ring. He was married!

Finally, the server's patience seemed to come to an end. Holt must have been standing looking out the window for at least five minutes maybe even ten; while I gazed at the wonder that was him.

'Sir, your seat if you please,' the server suggested softly. I expected Holt to turn and seat himself – instead he remained where he was.

'Wait,' Holt said to the server and then proceeded to remain standing and ask me about Tiki Island.

'It's a village and is part of Galveston, it has a population of around one thousand people and it's a popular holiday destination. Maybe, I could take you there sometime.'

'Why would you want to do that?' he asked as he waved the server away and finally took his seat opposite me at the table. Moments later, the smartly dressed drinks waiter approached with a large menu open in his hand. He tried discreetly to place it in front of Holt, who immediately waved him away until later. I decided to change the conversation as all the questions he challenged me with were starting to unnerve me.

'You look very handsome tonight,' I said expecting a compliment in return.

'Yes, my wife dresses me, she has good taste.' It was a statement rather than an answer and again his words threw me. My hands were shaking in my lap as I tried to regain control.

Well, there it is he freely admits it: He's married!

I couldn't stop thinking about it. I didn't hear what he said next, and when I ventured to look up again he was reading the drinks menu. I ordered a martini sour, and he asked me if I should be drinking when I'm driving. Again, I didn't answer, he was married, what am I to do? Then, I quieted my demons and told myself that if he was happily married he wouldn't be sitting across the table from me. Or would he? I would face this head on it was the only way and the way Daddy would attack the situation.

'Are you happily married?' I ventured, sounding more confident than I felt.

'So, you're talking again. I thought you were one of these sulky bitchy females that I had already managed to annoy.'

'Not at all. I don't sulk.'

'And I don't talk about my marriage, although yes, I am happily married. My wife is very competent and does everything for me, I'm a lucky man.' I almost froze at his words.

But I could attack also. 'So why are you sitting here with me?'

'A free meal, that is what you offered isn't it?' When I didn't respond immediately, he continued on, 'It's not like a date or anything. Or maybe that's what you think it is?' There it was; he had me cornered again. I must laugh this off. I couldn't bear the thought of him walking away. I calmed my muddled emotions quickly as I responded, 'It's always nice to have someone show you round a strange city, maybe I can show you Tiki Island.'

'Sure, why not. All I have to do is make the move into the company apartment, and I have several more days before I need to report for work.' His words made my heart flutter or rather it felt like it missed a beat altogether, all was not lost. The server arrived to present our dinner menus. With a wave of his hand, Holt told the man to leave them on our table, and we would look at them when we were ready.

Shortly after the menu was deposited on the table, the drinks waiter arrived, and my sour martini was set in front of me along with Holt's whisky. I sensed all the wait staff arriving at our table annoyed Holt, and I certain didn't enjoy the interruptions.

'Lyn, isn't it?' he asked retrieving the menu from the table and looking at me briefly.

'It's Lyme, actually.'

'Lyme, as in lime disease your named after a disease that can kill you. Maybe, your parents liked ticks? Either way it's a rather strange name for a girl.' I wondered if he ever said anything nice. I thought briefly about challenging him about his name, but some-how I knew that wouldn't go down well, so I didn't. But I didn't like constantly being on the defensive. It was not in my nature. However, for the moment, I would let it go.

So, I took a deep breath and merely replied, 'My parents chose it, and I have used it all my life. I am not named after a disease, maybe a fruit, but not lime disease, anyway I don't find it strange.' The waiter arrived again to tell us the specials of the evening, and Holt asked him.

'Do you enjoy interrupting our conversation, continually?'

'No, sir. Sorry, sir, shall I come back again, later?' the embarrassed server asked.

'And interrupt us again, I suppose, you will enjoy interrupting us then?' Holt harassed the young man who stood his ground in spite of turning very red in the face, he did not reply.

Holt stared him down until he finally said, 'Just tell us now or else you'll be coming and going all night,' Holt scolded. The young server quickly recited the specials. Holt said he would like the starter of lobster and bay shrimp and for the main he chose the fillet of soul, then turning to me he asked,

'I assume that's all right with you?' It took a moment for me to realize he was ordering for us both. I nodded my acceptance feeling confused and the server left. I have never had a man order for me especially one I hardly knew; most men would at least have consulted me first. My surprise passed quickly and I decided to challenge Holt,

'I have never had a man order for me before.'

"Well, there is a first for everything. Or perhaps, you've only been out with boys before me?'

'I am quite use to going out with men, Holt. I'm also used to ordering my own meal.'

'You think, you know your own mind, but women seldom do. If you knew the best things to order for yourself you wouldn't be carrying a few extra pounds now, would you?'

He was rude, insolent and most unfeeling before I knew what I was doing I had pick up my water glass and tossed it into his face. Immediately, I felt sorry, and I was ready to apologize, but looking at him with water dripping off the end of his nose, his hair, and his chin, I saw barely a reaction. My face was burning with embarrassment as the other diners turned and stared then they began whispering to each other.

'So, you're the usual crazy, hysterical woman I see. No surprise there, you females are all the same. I shall go and dry off.' Holt got up from the table and walked arrogantly toward the men's room. The many eyes in the room watched him, but he didn't seem to notice, or if he did he didn't care. He seemed almost to enjoy the attention. I felt the same eyes then move back to where I sat, until finally the buzz of chatter in the room returned. The evening was not going at all like I had imagined. He was sarcastic, arrogant, entitled and seemed to have a total disregard for anyone's feelings. However, he still made me feel weak at the knees when his eyes met mine, and all I really wanted to do was rip his clothes from his body and have him make love to me. Wow, I was surprised I had just admitted that to myself. But now, I had, I knew it was absolutely true.

A large party had just entered the restaurant, there were very few tables available, and I saw the manager scramble to accommodate them. I was watching the door to the men's room, and finally Holt came out; no one looked at him this time. It was then I felt an arm go around me from behind as exotic perfume filled the air; Pan's voice giggled in my ear,

'Lyme, how divine, we've had a simply wonderful night, you should have been there. Brook didn't show up, but I can see about a dozen messages from her on my phone. She really doesn't give up, does she?' Pan said giggling again as she sat daintily on the edge of the vacant chair at our table. Pan was amazed to see Holt take his seat opposite me. I had watched her eyes follow him from the men's room; her hungry, admiring eyes.

Now she giggled a little more and fixed her beautiful face on his gaze. I felt jealous until I realized every man in the place had their eyes fixed on Pan; it had always been that way. With her eyes still on his, Pan stood up from her chair and take two small steps toward him. I watched Holt's eyes rake her body, several times and then finally rest on her face. When she was nearly close enough to sit on his lap, she held out her well-manicured hand and said confidently but with feminine softness,

'Janice Pansy, and you are?' He took her hand and held it, and before I knew what I was saying I said,

'He's my date, Pan.'

'So, this is the man?' At my words, Holt looked at me sharply. Pan giggled and stared at me with admiration in her eyes, most unusual for Pan. Holt was still holding her hand; it should have been my hand he was holding; why wasn't it?

'I'm Holt Visser, Ms. Janice Pansy, and let me assure you, we are not on a date. Should you be sitting across the table from me I would say we would definitely be on a date. Won't you join us?' Holt asked still holding her hand and her gaze; and Pan was letting him. Pan looked quickly at me, I could see the confusion in her clear blue eyes and for once, she wasn't giggling.

The server hovered in the back ground with our starters. Finally, Pan found her tongue and replied, 'I am here for a party with friends, but I hope we shall meet another time.' Pan withdrew her hand, giggled and then over her shoulder, she said, 'I'm sure we will.'

'Excuse me, Ms. Harrington...' It was the manager, and before he could complete his sentence, I cut him short,

'Yes'

'You have an urgent phone call; apparently your cell is turned off. The caller asked for either yourself or Ms. Pansy.'

'Can Ms. Pansy take it?' I responded noticing Holt's eyes again on Pan.

'Here is the phone, miss, and sorry, for the intrusion on your meal.' He handed me the phone directly, so I had no choice but to take the call.

'Lyme, here, hello.' I had been expecting the call to be from Daddy. I'm not sure why as he'd never called me before. He is the only person who would be inpatient enough to have me tracked down. Newton was good at that. I couldn't imagine who else would know where to find me.

'Lyme, I'm hurt. I'm in Parkland Memorial. Please come. Is Pan there? I've been calling her all night.'

'Brook whatever happened? Are you all right?' I assumed it was Brook, her voice was different, it sounded like her inner strength was gone. Then I remembered Pan saying she had several calls from Brook.

'No, Lyme, I'm not, please come, I need you.' I could hear tears in her voice, and her strength quickly crumbling. I knew she was crying, and it broke my heart. I couldn't imagine what had happened, but I had to go. The evening was ruined anyway by Pan's arrival.

'I'm sorry, Holt, but I have to leave, it's an emergency.'

'Really, that's no way to treat your guest, make sure you pay the bill before you leave, remember you promised me dinner.' He was staring, his beautiful blue eyes on me. I felt my heart melt. I didn't want to leave, I wanted to stay with him, forever. In my mind, his earlier behavior was forgotten. I was in love with this handsome devil. Slowly I turned to go, I had to make a date to see him again. I couldn't just walk away, in his eyes I saw my future, I saw my children, I saw my life. I turned back to look at him, and noticed his eyes were already focused on Pan.

'Can I show you around Tiki Island tomorrow?' I blurted out, desperate to make another date. I was annoyed to see Pan approaching our table. I needed to tell her about Brook anyway. It took him a few seconds to tear his eyes from Pan and focus briefly on me; he appeared to have forgotten who I was, and then, remembering I had asked him a question, he gave me the merest of a smiles'.

'Sure, pick me up at eleven. I've got nothing else planned except moving into my apartment and that won't take long. I'll text you the new address and this time be on time.' With that last comment, he looked away and began eating his meal, Pan never looked up at me, but instead she reached for his hand and giggled at something he said, or maybe, knowing Pan, she just giggled at nothing at all. Just the way he looked at her made me feel horribly sick inside. I should have told her about Brook, but her focus was certainly not on me.

I turned several times to look at Holt as I headed for the door, but he never looked in my direction, his attentions were firmly elsewhere. Could Pan really do this to me? I couldn't believe she would take him from me. This had happened before, but the other times I really didn't care, and she was only playing with him anyway; nothing had come of it. Pan always had a guy on her arm and several hovering close by, but they were seldom serious.

I know Pan well, and she chooses her husband's wisely, somewhere under her blonde hair and sparkling blue eyes is a shrewd mind, calculating and cold. Pan works at being beautiful; she enjoys flirting, acting ditzy and playing the field. I was trying to convince myself she wouldn't take my guy, not this time. She knew from my text messages that this guy was something special. However, I was worried about what she might say, her words were often unfiltered and usually hollow. Pan could have any man she wanted, and I doubted if Holt had nearly enough money for her to seriously consider him as a future husband; besides he was already married.

My mind remained heavily on Holt as it had been since I first set eyes on him. I pulled slowly away from the curb once my car arrived. I slowed even further as I drove past the window. I looked into the cozy setting of the restaurant, the elegantly dressed diners and candle lit tables. Pan was leaning into Holt; he touched her cheek with the back of his hand. I inhaled sharply at what I was seeing. Then I saw Pan slowly leave his table as he answered his cell phone. I exhaled the breath I wasn't aware I was holding and release the steering wheel slightly. I had at some time began to grip it so tightly that my knuckles were white.

Pan was not going to take my man; I knew she wouldn't. I kept telling myself. I wished briefly I could return to the restaurant, to Holt. He was not at all what I expected. He didn't treat me like other men treated me. I had learned to expect to be treated a certain way, and I wondered why Holt was different? It was almost like he didn't like women, although he seemed to like Pan just fine. Maybe, he preferred blondes. I wondered what his wife was like; in fact, I had to know what his wife was like. I didn't believe he was happily married; he had said the words, but his eyes had not held the response.

I was now pulling into the parking lot of Parkland Memorial hospital before my mind returned to Brook. Suddenly, I realized Pan should be here with me, why hadn't I told her where I was going? Why wasn't she at my side? Brook had been calling Pan all night and not me, although my cell was turned off, so I really didn't know if she had or not. Finally, I managed to get Holt out of mind and focus on Brook; I assumed she had been in an accident. That must be it – I was scared at what I might see. I was expecting the worst.

Brook was in a private room at the end of a long sterile corridor where patients had obviously tried to make it more comfortable. There were small tables with flowers on them, artwork on the walls and several statues on pedestals.

Nearing the end of the corridor, I noticed a police officer standing guard outside a patient's door. As I drew nearer, I realized it was Brook's door. I moved toward the door and the police officer stepped in front of me blocking my way.

'Ma'am, I need your name and driver's license or other photo ID.'

It took me several seconds to understand what he required and several more to wonder just why he was asking for it. I handed him my driver's license, he looked closely at it and then at me. Before asking,

'Who do you wish to see?'

'Brook, Ms. Feather Brookston, she called me about forty minutes ago,' I replied.

'What is your relationship with Ms. Brookston?'

'We are best friends.'

'I'm sorry Ma'am, but I've been instructed that only close relatives can visit at this time.' I stood looking at the tall unyielding officer who remained on guard as he looked straight ahead.

Then I heard Brook's voice, 'Lyme. Is that you? Why aren't you coming in?' Her voice sounded weak and scratchy, but it was Brook. It took me a second to push past the officer who tried to grab my hand as I pushed the door open.

Brook immediately sat up and held her arms wide. I rushed to her and she sobbed, her whole body shaking. These were the kind of sobs you held inside until you were with someone safe and had to release them; the kind of sobs I use to cry after my mother died. The kind I'd let out when I was alone late at night in my darkened room.

I had seldom seen Brook cry. She held tightly to me and didn't let go until her sobs subsided. Then, with her body still trembling, I held her at arms-length and looked at her battered face and the heavy bandage around her throat. I was shocked. But it was Brook who spoke first, her usual fast speaking voice was replaced by a raspy wispy voice and she spoke much slower, each word appeared to hurt her.

'Wow, Lyme you look amazing, I've never seen you look so good, your hair, your makeup, you look hot! And you're glowing. Oh my god, Lyme, I do believe you're in love.' When she uttered the last words, I thought her voice already sounded stronger. At her request I turned around to show her all of me. Finally, I had to know what had happened to her.

'Whatever happened to you?'

Brook didn't seem to hear; instead, she gripped my arm, and in a low raspy whisper said, 'You gotta take me out of here, I didn't want to be here at all. They said I needed someone to take me home; they wouldn't discharge me otherwise. Please, Lyme, sign me out. Hospitals give me the creeps, and the police presence at the door they say it is for my own good, but he never even speaks to me. They say, I'm maybe, in danger; he may come back. Lyme, get me out.'

'Who Brook, who are you in danger from? Who did this to you?' I tried to sound calmer.

Brook was gripping my arm again; she was about to beg me to take her away from here when my cell rang, it was Pan, so I put her on speaker, 'Why did you leave in such a hurry, Lyme. I thought you liked this guy?'

'Brook is in trouble, she needs us; I'm at the hospital now. I'm going to sign her out.'

'Well, I didn't know, how could I?' Pan said the whine obvious in her voice as she defended herself rather than ask after Brook.

'I rang you all night, you were having too good a time to answer,' Brook added.

'Who on earth is that? Who are you with?' Pan questioned with only a slight giggle in her voice.

'I told you, Pan, I'm with Brook, she's been hurt.'

'Is that Brook, god she sounds like shit. I'm on my way. I'll take her home with me.' Before anyone could argue with her the line went dead.

'Brook, what happened, please tell me,' I begged, I really needed some answers.

'It was Ric, he had a knife, he hit me. I don't know how he got in,' Brook said again collapsing into sobs. I held her close again as I asked,

'How could he get in to your new home? You have state-of-the-art security. Or wasn't it on?'

Brook nodded and then said, 'Yes, the perimeter was secure, and I don't know how he got past it. If the police hadn't turned up…' Again, she began sobbing. I was shocked by her words; I knew Ric was a bad boy but this…

A commotion took my attention it was coming from outside the door.

'Excuse me, ma'am, there is a Morris Delaney here to see you. Do you know him?' The uniformed officer asked with the door slightly open. All I could see was a huge bouquet of flowers and the top of someone's head. I didn't think Brook knew this person, until I looked at her face and saw after several seconds passed how it lit up. Brook nodded and into the room walked a tall young man with a handsome face, warm brown eyes and brown wavy hair. I don't think he even noticed me sitting there. His eyes were on Brook and hers were on him. He sat close to her on the edge of the bed and took her hand tenderly in his. I didn't think he was her type of guy, and Brook definitely had a type. But one look at her face and something told me that maybe he was.

I felt awkward sitting there and tried not to listen to what they were saying. Until, I heard Brook say, 'Morris, you mean it, you'll really take me home and stay with me. I would so much prefer to be in my own home, oh that would be wonderful.'

'I've got three days off, Ms. Brookston.'

'Brook, please.' until suddenly Brook realized I was still in the room,

'This is my best friend, Lyme Harrington-Lynch, this is, Morris Delaney, he was one of my rescuers in every sense of the word.' Brook never took her eyes from him.

Morris looked at me briefly and extended his hand before asking, 'Are you the Lyme Harrington-Lynch?' to which I nodded. Morris was helping Brook out of bed, and I thought I should make a hasty retreat Brook obviously had everything she required. I hugged her tightly and told her to call anytime, and that I would check in with her in the morning,

'Oh, thank you, Lyme, I know I'll be quite safe now, and I really want to be in my own home.' Her voice sounded remarkably strong, and she now had a sort of glow about her that I had never seen before.

The last words I heard her say were, 'I never wanted you to see me like this....' I couldn't hear Morris's answer, but I know it was a positive one. He had a wonderful up beat personality, and he was so opposite to the usual type of guys Brook dated. I wondered what was going on.

As I walked out the front entrance of the hospital, Pan was just getting out of her pink limo, 'Pan, everything is fine, Brook is going home, you can talk to her tomorrow.'

'But I just left dinner, I want to see her now, pretty please.' Pan giggled, but for once her girly ways were lost on me. I gave her firm 'No.' I glided her firmly back into her limo. Without another word, I walked away to where my car was parked and headed home. But it was not Brook who occupied my thoughts; it was Holt, his eyes, the way he looked at me, the way he spoke... everything. The evening had gone so fast. It seemed like I'd waited my entire life for this evening, and then it was over. But I still had Tiki Island to look forward to in the morning.

For the first time that night, I did write in my dairy, the pages had been blank for too long. The thick leather-bound book was old, it was a childhood present from my mother, and I promised myself that when I had something to write, I would do so. Tonight, I had not only something to write but so much to write. Was my mother watching down on me from heaven, would she read these pages? Was she still with me wherever she was? Childish thoughts, I know, but I'd always held them close. They were all I had left now, and I wanted to believe she was still with me in some way.

Later that night, I lay in my darkened room with my eyes tightly closed as I searched for the solitary safety of the void inside me. I focused hard on the empty blank space. The place that was mine alone, this place was full of my desperate needs and wants, I never wanted to see it, but as I always did I could feel it all around. I was engulfed in my fear of loneliness and my desperation was so deep it had no end. But it was my friend. It was my place, and no one or nothing could take it from me. It was a place, I happily retreated to. Yes, it was empty and blank, but it was mine – my own solitary void of nothing.

I knew my life was like my empty diary, it was something I held close, and it was dear to me but upon opening it the pages were blank. Only now the pages weren't blank any more. There wasn't yet a whole book of my thoughts, feelings and emotions, but this was a beginning. I smiled to myself as I felt myself dropping soundlessly into the dark void of nothing. I felt my own need; desperation and fear wrap themselves around me. I smiled again knowing I had successfully blocked out the world and was now in my world alone and isolated. But wait, I looked deep into the void, and there I saw the eyes, blue and deep, the eyes of Holt waiting for me, lighting up my void with light, laughter and maybe even love.

Holt was in my void.

Chapter 10
Granny Harry

I like to think each of us has someone – someone, above all others who we can confide in. Someone who knows us completely, and someone we know will understand. Share our happiness and feel our sorrow. Someone special, who will hear what we say and know what we think. Someone we can trust to cherish our thoughts and words and never speak of them to another living soul.

My someone stood about five feet tall; she had a face like a well-used road map; her large lips were the only things without wrinkles. Her kind pale blue eyes sparkled with life and vitality, and when she laughed they danced with mischief and happiness. She was scary thin, and her skin looked like wax paper, you could see the veins. But she radiated the biggest spirit, full of love and happiness. She glowed with an abundance of love for her life, and I knew she lived each day to its fullest. She usually smelt of apple pie, cocoa or warm cookies just baked and fresh out of the oven. To me, these smells were the best smells in the world, they meant safety and love.

She was my, Granny Harry, my mother's mother, and I loved her like no other. Although she was nothing like my mother, I found her to be a wonderful woman and like everyone who knew her, they gravitated toward her and wanted to live in her presence.

Granny Harry was to me everything Daddy was not.

Over the years as my thoughts meandered backward into childhood, I began to understand the attraction my father must have had for my mother. They were so opposite. I saw my mother as goodness, laughter and happiness, while Daddy was strength, success, stubbornness and anger. Now, I understood how my perspective was that of a child and over the years had become greatly distorted. I knew my mother was not nearly as perfect as I imagined, while Daddy has proved to be the devil himself.

Granny Harry started her days at dawn or before. I know her days often began well before dawn as she liked to sit on her back deck and listen to the birdsong as they woke in the morning. She had a wonderful wooded area, which ran between her small house, and the other larger homes she couldn't see. My mother had purchased this house for her several years before she passed away, telling Granny Harry to sell her townhouse, invest the money, and live off it while she enjoyed her new home.

I'd hardly slept at all. Every time I closed my eyes, Holt's face danced before me, and even when I tried to recede to my deepest and most private black void, I found him there, waiting, laughing as he looked past me to stare at something beyond. I dreamed about him the few times, I slept lightly and even tried to talk to him, but each time he put his hand in my face which told me to stop talking. I awoke even more confused but soon admitted they were only dreams, and nothing more.

I had dressed carefully as I will go directly to Holt's new apartment once I leave Granny Harry's house. Holt was as good as his word and had texted me his new address after I arrived home at two-thirty a.m. that morning. Of course, I wondered why he was still awake and also, even though I tried not to, I wondered whom he was with.

My wide tires squeaked with the delight as I drove into the semi-circular driveway of Granny Harry's house and stopped directly in front of her double cherry-red front doors. I had only just closed my car door and was heading to the front door when it burst opened, and my tiny Granny Harry held her arms wide inviting my embrace. I breathed deeply of her homely baking smells, and together we held hands as she closed the door and headed toward the kitchen.

'My favorite girl. I just knew you'd call today; I could feel it in my bones. Let me look at you,' Granny Harry said holding me at arms lengths as she slowly turned me around. I had a big smile on my face. Just being here and feeling her love made me feel less confused and warmer inside.

'You look beautiful, how you've changed since you were here last a few weeks ago?' I didn't reply, I really wasn't sure what I could say, so I beamed a little wider. She busied herself warming up recently made scones and making fresh hot chocolate.

'Well, Apple, I can see you didn't sleep much last night; what's on your mind?' Granny Harry always calls me Apple, she hated the name, Lyme and refused to use it, so she calls me Apple, it was another way of showing her dislike for Daddy and also part of her wonderful humor.

'Well...' I began and realized I had no idea what I was going to say to this sweet little old lady, or how I was even going to begin.

The clock ticked on until finally she said kindly, 'Apple, I am here to listen and not judge.' She placed my hot chocolate with huge marshmallows and two warm lightly baked buttered scones in front of me. I wasn't at all hungry, even though I had missed dinner last night. I remember the gift I had for her; it was the same licorice all-sorts, I always brought. Granny Harry was English and had moved to Texas when she was twenty years old. I wouldn't say she had much of a sweet tooth, but she loved the licorice all-sorts from the shop in the city that sold things from Great Britain.

'Oh, you darling girl, you always remember your old Granny.' She quickly took the large packet of licorice all-sorts and popped them in the kitchen drawer just the way she always did.

'Apple, you're very quiet you came here with something on your mind, didn't you girl?' She could read me, she always had. I guessed it was something older people could just do. I felt the bite of scone I had just taken expand in my throat, and realized I didn't really want to discuss Holt with her. But I needed to talk to someone and there wasn't anyone else I could trust. Then for no reason at all the tears began flowing down my cheeks. I didn't know if it was from lack of sleep or my feelings for Holt, but I cried. The look of concern on Granny Harry's face made me feel guilty, but as she cradled me in her loving embrace; I didn't know what I wanted or expected from her, but I did know I needed her love. Several minutes later I took a long sip of hot chocolate and a deep breath. I wiped away my tears as Granny Harry took her seat opposite me at the table.

My eyes roved over the large, sunny kitchen. My mother had it painted a pale canary yellow, and with all Granny's favorite nick knacks around the shelves, and the old paintings of chubby cherubs on the walls it felt homely, and secure. I took a breath and the last piece of scone.

'Something or someone has played with your emotions, Apple. I'm taking a guess here and saying it's Lyn?' Granny Harry offered. Although it was a safe guess as Daddy always played with my emotions. But this time it wasn't what I needed to talk about.

'Are your friend's Pan and Brook all right, honey?'

'Brook just got out of hospital, she was attacked by a former boyfriend, the one I told you about, Ric, the drug addict.'

I saw the shock in Granny Harry's eyes, and I could see her thinking that she knew this would happen but she only said, 'Oh, that poor dear girl, I do hope she will recover, although emotional scars can run deep. Do send her my love, Apple, when next you see her.'

'Of course, I will Granny. Yes, she is at home now, and I think she is happily recovering. She seems to have a new man in her life, and he is nothing like her usual needy, nasty mean boys. I can feel this time it's different, but I only met him briefly when he came to see her in hospital. She had a policeman guarding the door, Granny, so they must think Ric is very dangerous and will try to hurt her again.'

'You know she could have come here, should she need to hide. I could have looked after her.'

'I have a feeling she's in good hands, and right where she wants to be, but I'll pass on your invite.' I noticed Granny was looking at me very intently, I knew this look, her blue eyes seem to look into my soul.

'Apple honey, what about you?' she asked kindly, she cleared the table and was again sitting opposite me with her full attention on my face. Just then out the corner of my eye, I saw Roam, Granny's fat tabby cat jump up onto the kitchen windowsill; his large green eyes fixed on Granny conveying his demands to be let in. She quickly opened the window, and he leaped on the kitchen bench before jumping down and rubbing my legs continuously, then he leaped onto my lap and placed his huge front paws on my chest and continued rubbing me from my chest to my chin in a warm catlike greeting. Once he was convinced I had acknowledged him sufficiently, he slowly walked across the table and jumped down onto Granny's lap. Still purring loudly, he began to take his bath.

'Well, Apple, I know you've never had so much trouble talking to me before, so I'm guessing this is serious,' Granny said with her blue eyes still intently focused on me.

'Yes, Granny I think it is. You see I've met a man…' but before I could continue Granny face broke out in a large smile.

She raised her hands to the heavens and said, 'Hallelujah, praise the Lord; it's about time.'

'Oh, Granny, it's not that easy. I think its love, I just look at him, and I know. I can't stop thinking about him. He's so handsome, and he just looks at me and my knees go weak. But I don't think, he knows I exist.'

'Apple, I'm sure there's not a man alive that doesn't know you exist, you're beautiful, kind, smart and funny, what's there not to like?'

'Granny, you're my grandma you have to think like that and you also love me. I don't know whether he shares your enthusiasm where I'm concerned,' I replied dropping my head, so I didn't see her looking at me.

'How well does he know you?'

'We've only been on one date that was last night, and then Brook called from hospital, so I had to go to her. I left him with Pan, and they were into each other.'

'Oh you young people, what do you mean "into each other"?'

'Well, he couldn't take his eyes off her, Pan's very pretty, Granny.'

'I know she is, honey, but I don't believe Pan has much under the hood. Is that how you youngsters talk?'

'I know Granny, but he still looked at her more than he looked at me.'

'Why on earth did you invite her anyway, I can understand if it's a double date or even a blind date, but really, Apple, what were you thinking?'

'I didn't invite her she just happened to be there; it was embarrassing. Pan knows how to flirt and what to say and how to say it. She's much more experienced with men than I will ever be.'

'I know she is. Now does this man, whatever his name is? Want to settle down?'

'His name's Holt, Holt Visser.'

'Do you remember what I told your mother about finding a husband?'

'No, Granny, I may have been too young.'

'Yes, yes, Apple, of course, you were. Well, it worked for her, and it worked for me.'

'What, Granny? I'm not sure I understand.'

'Well, the key to a happy marriage is to find a man who loves you just a little bit more than you love him. That way you stay in control and every man needs to be slightly controlled to be happy and make a solid marriage. When the man stops chasing, however subtle, his eyes look elsewhere.'

'Okay, Granny, I will try and remember that although right now, I feel like I like Holt a whole lot more than he likes me.'

'Well, that's another reason to remember what I just told you.'

'I don't understand, Granny.'

'Honey, you must make a man want you, it is not so much about you wanting a man, because men are all fickle, visual creatures, if you put out the right bait a man will want you and chase you. If you're chasing the man, and he's looking in another direction you'll never get what your heart desires. Also, don't let him catch you too easily, men are like animals they like the fun of the chase.'

'I've never thought of it like that. Well, how do I know if he wants me and wants to get married? You know Daddy is pushing for me to marry.'

'I know honey, and its wrong, you know how I feel about that, don't be in too much of a hurry, and don't give too much away,' Granny said looking at me with meaning in her eyes. I guessed she was talking about sex.

'There's another thing about Holt, Granny.'

'Yes, I want to hear it all; I never thought I'd see my granddaughter in love.' Once she said this, I could hardly tell her what I knew I must say, but I was now committed to doing so.

'Well, Granny, Holt's married.' There I'd said it, silence followed, a long silence and Granny just sat their stroking Roam and looking deep into my eyes, several times she shook her head.

'I know it's wrong to want a married man, but I am in love with him, Granny. Granny, please, say something,' I begged as she just kept on staring at me. The silence stretched on, and I waited patiently unable to return her gaze; my eyes downcast, I was looking at the old worn wooden table. Mentally, I traced the scratches on it with my eyes, and I waited for her to say something. I knew she was about to scold me, and I was prepared.

She was the woman I loved most in the world. Fox was also important as were my best friends, but Granny Harry was the closest thing I had to a mother and her thoughts mattered. They mattered greatly. I peeked a look at her as the old grandfather clock in the hallway ticked loudly. The ticking of the clock made the minutes more real and time more obvious. As I looked slyly out the corner of my eye at Granny, I noticed she was no longer staring at me, but instead she too was looking at the table. She appeared deep in thought.

'Oh, Honey, I should have told you this many years ago,' she began, and I realized it didn't sound like the beginning of a scolding at all. Again, she paused as if choosing her words carefully.

'I know all about being in love with a married man.' I was shocked at her words, then surprised and then eager to hear what she was about to say. It was now me, who was staring at her.

'Apple, your grandfather was married to another when I met him. It was love at first sight. He consumed my waking hours, my thoughts, and my heart. I felt bold, guilty, desperate and alone. It was a long time until I learned he felt the same way. The only time we saw each other was in the company of others, and even though we seldom spoke our stolen glances said it all. Unfortunately, his looks were more obvious to everyone else than to me. Yes, it is wrong to love a man who is married to another woman but in my time; in the late 1920s it was shameless and sure to course a huge scandal.'

'Granny, I never knew. What happened? You and Gramps were so happy, so in love.' I noticed a flush rising in her cheeks as she spoke.

'We were so in love, and I think because it was forbidden it was all the more exciting. Gramp's wife wouldn't divorce him; she said she would never let him go. Divorce was unheard of in those days.'

'Well, how did you get together?' I enquired, my curiosity awakened, and my eyes firmly on the small old lady who sat opposite me.

'Well, Apple, it was a huge scandal, not by today's standards. But in England, in the small villages where we both lived, it was bigger than both of us. However, our love was much bigger than the scandal and all the heartache it coursed for our families and everyone around us, we hated it, but we knew we still had to be together. Neither of us could live apart.'

'Oh, Granny, how romantic. Did you run away and elope?' As I watched, I saw her cheeks positively blaze with color and then in a small voice she replied,

'No, Apple, we couldn't elope, he was still married, and everyone knew it, almost the whole of England knew it. You see he was a nobleman with a title, and he gave it all up for me. So, we ran away together.'

'Oh, Granny, how exciting. Where did you go? To London?'

'No, even in London, everyone knew. He was a well-known and well-respected gentleman. No, we ran all the way to USA – right here to Texas. It was a scary and unheard of thing to do. But Alexander said that if we were to have any chance of a happy life together, we must start over, in some place far away. We both left everything behind. Our families, our friends, and the country we loved. But neither Alexander nor I, ever regretted what we'd chosen to do, not for a second.'

'I never knew you had such a sense of adventure. Does Daddy know?' I asked not really knowing why it mattered.

'I don't think so, and I doubt if your mother would have told him. If she had, he would have said something sarcastic to me and used it against me, you know what he's like.' I nodded wanting to hear more, but realizing she needed to be prompted.

'Granny, I think this is the most exciting story ever. What happened then?'

'Apple, do you really want to know?'

'Yes, I really want to know,' I said eagerly searching her face. I saw her with different eyes now. My Granny Harry was the trailblazer of her error, she was a pioneer and adventurer, and I'd never known.

'Well, honey, I got pregnant on the ship that took us from England to the new country of America. It was inevitable we couldn't keep our hands off each other. We were both like thirsty drowning people, so great was our need for each other. We used a different name on the boat and everyone assumed we were newly-weds and that suited us fine.'

It took me a while to understand all, she was saying then I asked, 'So, my mother was conceived on the ship that bought you here?' I watched Granny slowly shake her head before she answered.

'It was a long voyage; we encountered some very rough weather. It was wintertime and it often got very cold and windy. We didn't have the right clothes for the crossing. We spent days on end in our cabin; the seasickness often seemed to want to consume us. I felt so ill, I just wanted to die, and I know Alexander did also. But our love kept us alive, literarily.'

'So, Mom was born on the ship?'

'No, Apple, I was not pregnant with your mother. I had a little boy. Because of my frail state and ill-health, he was born under nourished, and I was unable to breast-feed him. He lived only a couple of weeks. We buried him at sea, days before the ship berthed in the harbor. We were both heart broken and took it as a sign that we were being punished for our sins.'

'Granny, you weren't being punished.'

'We were living a lie, unwed and living together. It doesn't sound much by today's standards as you young people do anything and everything goes, but in those times things were different.'

'But Mom always said you had a wonderful life.'

'And we did, as soon as we reached America and regained our strength, we decided that nothing and no one was going to bring us down. Everyone was to regard us as a happily married couple and that's just what happened. Your mother was born several years after our arrival, and by that time we were settled in a nice house, and Alexander had arranged for us to have the financial funds to live a good life. That was before he decided to go into politics you understand. Anyway, we were madly in love still and very happy. But we didn't officially wed for another twenty years until his wife died, by that time we no longer wanted to return to England to the narrow-minded villages where we'd been born.' Granny finally seemed to come back to the present; she gently put Roam on the table and got to her feet to switch the kettle on. It was then I heard the old grandfather clock strike the half hour and looking at my watch, I saw with disbelief it was already eleven-thirty a.m. I said I'd pick up Holt outside his apartment building at eleven a.m. and here I sat.

'Oh, Granny, I am supposed to be picking up Holt right now and taking him to Tiki Island for the day. I'm sorry, I have to go.'

'I was just making a cup of tea, Apple, must you leave? I see you so seldom these days, and I miss you.'

'I'm sorry, Granny, I miss you too, and I will try and call more often. Holt hates being kept waiting, and I am already late.' I hugged her tightly and kissed her on her soft warm wrinkled cheek before racing out the door.

'Drive carefully, honey…' I heard her call as I shut the door behind me.

Once in the car I called Holt as I drove off, 'Well, no surprise there, you're thirty minutes late already. I should have guessed it,' Holt drooled, his annoyance obvious in his voice.

'I'm really sorry, I was visiting my Granny and the time just got away. I'll be there in less than thirty minutes.'

'Visiting your Granny when you were supposed to be picking me up. Am I supposed to believe that? Is that really going to be your excuse?'

'It's the truth, and I'll see you soon.'

'Well, I may not wait, I am a busy man.' Holt said hanging up the phone. My heart pounded in my chest. I don't know whether it was from the sound of his voice or the fact he may not be waiting for me. My palms began to sweat, and I began driving much too fast. My cell rang, and I quickly answered it expecting Holt's voice to echo through the car as I drove, but it was Pan,

'Well, how is she?' Pan asked giggling.

'Who? Pan, I've just been visiting my Granny.' It took me a few minutes to get my head around the fact it was Pan on the phone and another few seconds to understand what she was asking.

'Brook, silly. Who do you think, I'm asking about the man in the moon?' Pan giggled.

'Oh, I haven't checked in with her yet, but I have a feeling she already feels much better,' I replied as I slowed my speed and relaxed slightly into the conversation.

'Madam Roderic is on her way here; so I'll ask her, she will probably know more than you anyway.'

'If you believe all she says.'

'I do believe all she says, she has never been wrong.' Pan replied the giggle no longer in her voice, 'Are you in your car?'

'Yes, Pan. I'm on my way to pick up Holt. You seemed to get on well with him last night?'

Instead of answering she giggled and asked, 'Oh, Holt is your new guy the one you're in love with, Lyme. That Holt?' she giggled. Was Pan playing with me? Didn't she know? How many guys called Holt did I know? Or did she know?

'Yes, that Holt,' I replied flippantly.

'Wow, I wouldn't have thought he was your type, he's hot, Lyme, too hot for you.' Pan giggled. I felt my face blush, exactly what did she mean by that remark.

I wasn't going to let her get away with it, but before I could challenge her further, she said, 'Sorry, Lyme, Madam Roderic is here, gotta go. Have fun, kisses.' And she was gone.

Chapter 11
The Date
'Even Fat Girls' Need Lovin'

Once Pan disconnected, I pushed my car forward and it obeyed smoothly and immediately. Moments later Holt's apartment building came into sight, and I pulled into the driveway.

However, Holt did not come into sight, he was nowhere to be seen, and my heart sunk. I checked the time; I was fifty minutes late. My mind was in turmoil.

My palms sweated, and my hands started to shake. I could hear my heart beating out of my chest. Where was he? Was I ever going to see him again?

I had to swallow the panic. Clear my mind and call his cell. But first I needed to calm myself. Granny's words came back to me about remaining in control, and I needed to appear I was doing just that. The valet knocked on my window, and I physically jumped at the unexpected sound. 'Shall I park your car, Miss Harrington-Lynch?' the youthful looking man asked.

I had to think for a moment my mind was so focused on Holt, 'No, I won't be staying, I'll only be here a moment.' The man nodded and began to move away when I decided to call him back.

'Excuse me. A friend of mine, Holt Visser moved in this morning, I believe he is in one of the Lynch Oil apartments, do you know if he's in?' I enquired trying to keep the shaking out of my voice.

'No, Ma'am, he walked out of here about thirty minutes ago, he asked the way to the department stores and went in that direction. Guess you've come to pick him up for work?' I didn't answer and replaced the ten-dollar tip I had in my hand, back in my pocket. His answer surprised me, why would I be taking Holt to work? Then I realized how he had so easily made that assumption. I closed the window and called Holt's cell phone. There was no answer. He was probably out with another woman. Again, the panic threatened to take control, and I had to swallow hard then close my eyes and take several deep breaths. Just then the valet tapped on my window again.

'Sorry, Ms. Harrington-Lynch, you'll have to move you're blocking the entranceway,' the young man scolded none too kindly this time. I looked in my mirror and noticed a long white stretch limousine waiting to take my place. I moved forward and parked to one side of the entrance. Then I called Holt again.

He answered on the fifth ring, but there was no kind greeting or words of welcome, 'So, you finally remembered me?'

'Holt, I'm sorry something came up.'

'Something more important than keeping me waiting, well, I can't wait to hear your lie this time.'

'Holt, I'm sorry. I'll make up for my tardiness.'

'Your words are getting tired, Lyme, and they sound like the same ones I heard before. What do you want?' he asked as an afterthought, sounding like a parent annoyed with their child.

'I am at your apartment building, and I would still like to take you to Tiki Island, if you'll let me.' I didn't want to sound as though I was begging, but I had my fingers crossed that he would still see me,

'I'm out shopping, spending some Lynch Oil money before I've even made it.' His sarcastic words dripped with annoyance, and I wondered briefly if he knew who he was speaking to. Maybe, he was playing with me.

'Shall I join you at the mall, Holt? Or maybe we can go to Tiki Island later or tomorrow?' I know my voice sounded timid, and I wished it didn't but that was just how it came out.

'You can join me at the mall if you pay for my purchases, but I must warn you I'm an expensive guy.' I couldn't believe he was asking me to pay for his shopping spree, he must know who I am, he must. Could he actually be that arrogant? I didn't know what to say or how to answer, he couldn't be serious about me paying. Maybe, he was just being cheeky yes, surely that was it.

'I'm getting bored with this conversation, and it's eating away my shopping time. I wouldn't even have answered the phone at all, except I felt sorry for you. I can tell you're one of these elite rich disorganized females who has no idea of time and has no purpose in life except to spend other people's money. Guess you were born with it?' There he went again, was he baiting me or just trying to make me angry. He was succeeding at both, but I was not going to let him know. I was in turmoil. I didn't know what to say or do. The only thing I knew was that I wanted to see him desperately! I knew he would disconnect if I didn't answer, and he would probably never talk to me again, so I said,

'Holt, I shall wait for you outside your apartment building until you are ready to go to Tiki Island.'

I heard what sounded like a brief laugh before he replied, 'My shopping will take a while. It's Marnie, my wife's birthday, so I have to get her something. Sure, you don't want to join me and pay the bill?' he enquired with no hint of humor in his voice. I was speechless at his words but finally added, 'Holt I'll wait, and I hope to see you soon.'

'That's your choice, Lyme,' he replied and hung up. I was annoyed at him, what he said and also how he said it. I was also ashamed of myself as my body tingled from just the sound of his voice, and I was unable to control it. My body and soul felt alive and vibrant while my mind remained in turmoil. I didn't know why he would mention his wife to me. Wasn't he aware it would upset and hurt me? Maybe, he really did love her? I had to know. I would ask him. Granny Harry's story of her romance with my grandfather returned to my thoughts, and somehow I saw the parallel with Holt and myself. This had to be fate it must history repeating itself. I easily visualized our life together, in love and idyllic, until I was reminded that Holt was shopping for his wife. I made my mind change to more pleasant things, and I imagined once I was married to Holt how my name would change, and I would sign it, Lyme Harrington-Visser.

A loud tapping on the car window jolted me back to reality. A strange man was smiling and waving for me to lower the window. My nerves were on edge as I lowered the window several inches.

'Hi, I'm Martin Sheldon, I'm a chemical engineer and about to start work with Lynch Oil on Monday. I saw the plate on your car and wondered if you were here to see me. Just been out for a walk,' the man named Martin Sheldon said, I looked closely at him, he had balding red hair and a round flushed red face and I could see he was sweating as he tried to speak to me through the open gap at the top of the window. I had no idea what he wanted or what he was going on about, so I looked at him some more as he looked expectantly back at me. Did he have me confused with someone else. Once I didn't reply he continued, 'Mr. Lynch was so aggressive in his pursuit of me; he stole me from Exxon after twenty-five-years of service with the same company, this is a big change for me. I assumed he'd sent someone to check that I was actually here, and perhaps, show me around Texas…' He said as his last words trailed off, and he saw the look on my face and knew without me saying a word he was mistaken.

I knew I had to say something, so I replied, 'Sorry, but you have me mistaken with someone else.'

I was about to wind up the window when he replied, 'Well, I saw the car and plate, and so I assumed you were Ms. Cerise, Mr. Lynch's…' but before I could hear any more I rolled up the window. I was fuming how could a new employee of Lynch Oil know about Cerise? Did everyone know about her? If so, how long had she been in Daddy's life?

I sat in the car looking straight ahead and seeing nothing as thoughts of Cerise in her lacey red bra and sheer matching panties, being held tightly in Daddy's arms, while he ran his huge meaty hands all over her slender body – what a hideous thought. What a hideous woman! She was probably no better than my father. I said 'probably' loosely as I really don't know her nor do I want to.

Just as my mind again focused on Holt, I became aware that just the thought of him put a smile back on my lips. It was then I saw a tall, elegantly dressed blond man walking slowly toward me. His strides were long, and as he drew closer I knew it was Holt. I would know him anywhere; he was so tall and handsome. Even from a distance his large blue eyes sparkled. He held shopping bags in both hands and lifted one slightly as he approached in what I assumed was a greeting. My heart physically skipped a beat or two as my silly grin got immediately wider.

Several large strides later, he was beside the car. I had been staring up at him as if in a trance, but I quickly leapt from the car and raced around to where he was standing. I felt so overjoyed to see him, I wanted to hug him, to touch him, but I drew back at the last minute knowing I couldn't. He quickly handed the valet his many shopping bags after he extracted a small box from one bag and handed the young man a ten dollar note. Then he climbed into the car and announced he was ready to go.

'Take me anywhere you like, but remember you owe me a meal, and I'm starving.'

'I thought we were off to Tiki Island, Holt?'

'Thought I'd kept you waiting too long for a day trip,' he commented casually.

'Yeah, you're right where would you like to go?'

'Well, you're the one who lives here. I've just arrived; how the hell should I know? Surprise me,' he responded with a half-smile on his lips. I was beginning to learn that perhaps he was a rather volatile human being and needed to be handled with care. Even though his words were somewhat casual, they held an edge that, should I answer wrongly, it could easily become an argument. This thought I dismissed quickly as I looked sideways at him and felt wonderfully blessed that this handsome man was sitting at my side. I was trying hard to think of somewhere to take him, but my mind wasn't responding, all I wanted to do was feel his arms about me, and his body close to mine.

'Seeing, you're so undecided, as usually, let's go somewhere by the ocean. Do you remember I like seafood?'

'Yes, Holt, I do remember,' I replied eyeing him out the corner of my eye, never knowing whether he's playing with me or annoyed with me. I still couldn't think where we should go. I wanted somewhere intimate and nice, and I'd seldom had to choose a restaurant in my life.

'Isn't there a Fisherman's Wharf or something by the ocean? There is in most cities,' he responded, and again I heard the annoyance beginning in his voice.

'There is a Fisherman's Wharf at Galveston. Like yesterday, it's about a five hour drive,' I advised.

'Well, we'll never get there unless we start moving. I guess you do know the way?' he asked sarcastically, and I nodded although I had to use the voice activated navigation system. I told him it was so I could find the fastest route to the restaurant when it was actually because I had never driven there before. Holt had settled into the drive quickly and began playing games on his phone, while I drove. This was most frustrating, and after several attempts to make conversation when he didn't respond, I gave up and concentrated on my driving, although my whole body was aware of him sitting so close to me.

It was after seven o'clock when we arrived. The sun was a golden orb in the evening sky as it began to settle over the horizon for the night. The light was magical, and it played on Holt's blond hair making him look more like a handsome surreal god than a flesh and blood human. I could barely take my eyes off him. I just wanted to stare and drink in his presence.

We were soon seated at a wonderful table in the old restaurant, it was in a corner overlooking the ocean and relatively quiet. We had a clear view of the beautiful sunset. It felt very romantic, but I was unsure if I should mention how I felt to Holt or not. He soon answered my question, 'We can move if the sun's bothering your eyes.'

Holt commented searching for a server before I could answer, 'No, it's a wonderful sunset, and the sun will soon be hidden behind the horizon. What a perfect evening, Holt?'

'You make this sound like a date or something, and I can assure you, it is not.' Holt replied firmly as he stared into my face. I kept my eyes on the menu and didn't reply, although I could feel the blood rush to my cheeks. Hopefully, I still had enough makeup on for him not to notice. I didn't answer and kept my focus firmly on the large menu. He really doesn't like me, I thought sadly, and it was all I could do to hold back the tears. The menu began to blur in front of my eyes until I took several deep breaths, blinked away the impending tears and tried to forget his words.

'Having trouble deciding, you really are a most indecisive person. Shall I order for you?' he asked. I was saved from answering by the arrival of our server. She focused her attention on Holt, as I would expect any woman to do, until she finally noticed me and asked to take my order.

I ordered the crab and lobster bisque because food was the last thing on my mind, and he ordered the Galveston trio. Then he surprised me, and handed me a small brown paper bag. My heart skipped; my whole body rejoiced; he did care. At that moment I felt so blessed. Again, my face blushed, more from my embarrassment at ever doubting him. How wrong I was. How does this man constantly make me blush?

'I saw this, while I was shopping and thought of you,' he said with a smile or maybe a smirk on his lips. I was very touched by his unexpected kindness. I felt tears prick the back of my eyes again, but blinked them back. Why was I so emotional around this man?

I was touched by his thoughtfulness; that is until I opened the package. Inside was a green cardboard box, and when I opened it there was a small chubby woman with bright red lips and a flowing yellow dress smiling up at me. She had a small clock where her belly should have been but the hands weren't moving so I guessed it needed a battery. The chubby woman with the bright red lips stood on a circular wooden stand and under the stand read the words "Even fat girls need lovin'", again I was speechless. I was unsure if it was his way of having a joke or was he just being mean?

I wore a size six and on occasions a size eight, I was not a big girl. Pan, of course, was a tiny size zero and Brook a size two. But I was not a fat girl. I had been given my father's build so to be any smaller was impossible with his bone structure. I knew I should be saying something but words didn't seem to come, and I was not one to be short of words, usually. I could merely look at Holt, and my mind went blank. So, I must say something I held the little figurine up to the light and turned it around trying to form a sentence in my head all the while. It was obviously a cheap trinket and not something I would ever purchase. I finally decided to call Holt out on his gift. It seemed I had nothing to lose.

'Is this your subtle way of telling me I'm fat, Holt?' I asked keeping my voice calm as I spoke.

'Damn woman, you always think everything is about you. I've never commented on your weight or the way you look. I have no subtlety, my wife constantly tells me that,' he responded too loudly, and I didn't reply as I continued waiting for an answer to my question.

Finally, he continued, 'Sure, you've taken me out twice now, so I thought you would like it, it kinda reminds me of you,' he added, and his last words stung again.

'So, you do see me as fat then, Holt, because this little figurine is certainly chubby.'

'I don't even see you as a woman, why should I?' Again, I felt his words sting, but when I looked into his blue eyes I saw no malice there. I could only nod, then he added,

'I thought it would help you become more punctual. You do see the small clock, don't you? And you do know how to tell the time? Although, you have already proven you don't, so silly question.' I wanted to keep challenging him, but his last words stung as I heard the venom in his voice. I was searching my mind for a reply, when our meals arrived along with the wine. Holt had ordered the wine some time ago and of course he berated the server for taking so long to bring it. The wine was poured, and Holt looked deep into my eyes and toasted Texas. I imagined he was toasting me, and it felt almost romantic. Then I was surprised that he went back to the topic of the figurine. 'I didn't just purchase it so you could tell the time, or because I'm such a nice guy. I also purchased it because I knew it would annoy you, Lyme. I believe you are teasing me or not being truthful. I have noticed the number plate on the car you drive. Today, you are driving a different car a brand new Audi R80 with a similar number plate. I assume you're married, which is fine with me, I am too, only you keep secrets, and I can't trust people who keep secrets. They are the ones who usually have a lot to hide.'

'Are you enjoying your meals?' our server asked appearing from nowhere, neither of us had touched a bite, and her sudden appearance startled me,

'No, yes thank you,' I replied, but she remained where she was.

'Can I pour you more wine?'

'No, you can leave us alone and stop interrupting our conversation,' Holt abruptly answered and the server moved quickly away, her face downcast.

'So, you purchased this ornament for me, not because you think me fat, but because you feel I have secrets I should share?' I asked, but quickly noticed Holt was staring at the retreating booty of our server. I was beginning to learn Holt's focus was short and easily shifted while his attention span was quickly lost, once his focus was elsewhere it was almost impossible to get him back on track.

However, the thought of him sitting next to me was enough to turn my world inside out and upside down. My head was spinning; and he made it hard for me to concentrate. I found him to be very direct with his questions. Maybe, it was time I told him a few truths. Or maybe I would lose him if I did? But he didn't belong to me, anyway. He was mine in my head only. The only thing I really knew for sure was that I wanted this man in my life forever, I wanted him more than I'd ever wanted anything.

Granny Harry was right – I was in love – or at the very least in lust. Deep inside, I hoped it was love, and at that moment I really believed it was.

Chapter 12
Madam Roderic ~ 3

'Madam Roderic sees the world on a movie screen. In color also, yes, always in color. Everything is clear to Madam Roderic.'

'What do you see clearly today, madam, tell me, tell me, quick,' Pan ordered mesmerized, as usual, by the clairvoyant. She sat staring inches, from Madam Roderic's pointed bony nose and into her huge eyes; they mirrored those of her own. She felt this remarkable woman was looking directly into her soul. She could see her own blue eyes reflected in those of Madam Roderic. Pan shivered with excitement, today was going to be an exciting reading, she could feel it.

As if reading her thoughts, Madam Roderic answered her, 'Exciting, maybe not, but interesting most certainly. It is what I see around you, that you will find interesting.' Madam Roderic said in her slow deep voice before closing her eyes as her trance like state took over.

'I do not want to know what's happening around me but to me, I don't care about anyone else,' Pan said the whining in her voice apparent.

'Madam must have quiet if she is to go to the other side, or your reading will be compromised.'

Pan's pretty face formed a pout as she sat and waited, patience was definitely not one of her virtues; she would not wait for long, somehow she knew Madam Roderic knew this.

'I see weddings, two of them, I see... Yes, yes, both beautiful women and handsome men.'

'Oh,' Pan said clapping her hands together, 'Who do I marry?' 'Madam, must have quiet no questions about other things.'

'I am not questioning you about other things, you are telling me of my next wedding,' Pan said annoyed. 'I am not speaking of your next wedding; you do not listen to Madam Roderic's words.'

The giggle was slowly going out of Pan's voice as she listened intently to Madam Roderic's. The fortune-teller was in an unusual mood today, and it was not one Pan enjoyed. Pan had seen many of her moods in the past and understood it was part of the older woman's magic, but slowly Pan was getting tired of her temperament, and the way she wasn't telling Pan about herself, but instead, about everyone else.

'Madam, please tell me about my future, tell me what you see ahead for me,' Pan asked even though she knew the woman needed quiet. Pan wanted to get her back on the subject of herself again, and didn't care if she annoyed her by doing so.

'Madam sees a girl, her name is a color; yes, yes, I see it, they call her Cerise...'

'No, no, no, Madam, this is not about me. I don't know this girl. I am Pan, you must remember me,' Pan said her voice a shade higher than usual. Her words were hardly spoken when Madam Roderic sprung to her feet, she was as nimble as a cat, she jumped into the air and Pan was sitting so close she almost knocked her to the floor; She sprung around in mid-air until she landed on the floor with her face several inches form Pan's huge shocked eyes. Pan leapt to her feet also moving backwards as she did so. She wanted to move away from this woman with the wild eyes.

'You want to hear what madam has to tell you, but you will not listen, always you whine, and complain if it is not about yourself. Perhaps, madam tells it in a way you do not like; perhaps her story is told without you being the main focus. If you do not like what madam says, maybe I should leave, and never return to your home again…' Madam Roderic said her eyes blazing and staring straight into Pan's, her body tense.

Pan suddenly felt panic, hearing madam's words; she didn't wish to lose the lady, she must calm her and fast. 'Please, madam, I value your words; I shall try and listen more carefully,' Pan said as she saw the fire in the older woman's eyes slowly diminish, and Madam Roderic's calm demeanor gradually return,

'Madam, can have no interruptions, you pull me from the other side, it drains madam of her life's energy, and I leave with a migraine. I do not like feeling in pain no matter how much you pay.'

'I understand, madam, I understand. I shall call down for some tea. I know you prefer herbal,' Pan said picking up her phone and asking the kitchen to send up tea. It was a huge effort for Pan to think of anyone other than herself, and Madam Roderic knew this and valued the small victory. It was over thirty minutes later when Madam again took her position, closed her eyes and began breathing deeply before her head rolled around, and she moaned several times. Pan knew her voice would be that of another when next she spoke. Pan let out a small giggle at the thought of hearing what Madam was about to say, and then realized perhaps she shouldn't have made a sound. It didn't seem to make any difference; Madam appeared to be far away in another place and time.

Then she began to speak, 'I see two weddings, both women are beautiful, both men are handsome, one is tall and blond, the other is short and darker, and the woman, your friend, is tall with long dark auburn hair. They are in love, yes, so in love. I do not know which of them loves the other more, maybe him, no maybe her, no I think it is equal.

They have a very happy marriage and their love still grows. She is surprised by who he is, but she loves who he is. They are married for as long as I can see. They will slowly drift out of your world, the man – he is too clever, he sees who you are, the woman – Brookston, I think you call her, has always known you. I hear you asking about yourself in your mind; you want to know why I persist in telling you of others. The reason is that you are the bridesmaid at this wedding, it is beautiful and very casual, it will not be long…'

Pan couldn't help interrupting again, 'Why are you telling me this, madam? Am I part of the other couple who are getting married?' Pan asked knowing she shouldn't.

Madam stayed in her trance as she answered, 'The other is not your marriage either, and you should be happy it is not. This wedding is very grand, very opulent, and you are also a bridesmaid. There are many hundreds of people at the reception amongst these people you will meet someone. The wedding is not immediate but sometime later. It is not a wedding made from love. It lasts only a few weeks and then, and then, oh no… this is not right… but I see it, oh no…' Pan watches as Madam Roderic's body begins shaking, her eyes flicker then they open, but they are blank, she screams and collapses on the floor.

'She promised me an exciting reading…' Pan thought. Then she began to feel annoyed at its abrupt ending. Pan briefly stares down at the still form of Madam Roderic lying like a heap of old clothes at her feet, before she calls her maid.

Chapter 13
Brook and Morris

They sat close, facing each other, their hands barely touching. They stared silently into the others eyes, into the depths of their souls, there they saw emotions, mirroring their own. Large brown eyes, alive, sparkling, smoldering with hidden love and desires that for so long had been locked tightly away. Hazel eyes, deep and openly loving, caring, giving and sharing. They sat silently and stared, words were forgotten; there was no need for speech, a sentence left unfinished, its meaning understood, as they remained forever lost in the moment.

A flicker, a slight blink as the other's eyes did the same. Mesmerized, locked in their world away from everyone and everything, nothing existed except the eyes and each other. Slowly they inched closer, the settee was large with deep seats and soft cushions, they faced each other, and now as they gradually moved closer, their knees began to touch. Their hands held the others more firmly but still with tenderness.

Neither had said they love each other. They both thought it was too soon. It had been only ten days, but they had stayed constantly with each other. It was right, there was no question. Brook had never thought a clean-cut police officer her type, never in a million years; she knew her type, knew it well. Bad boys, and she liked them as bad as they came. Morris had taken leave from the force, so he could protect her, he'd said, and Brook hadn't resisted in the least. She thought she would soon tire of him, but she hadn't, and now she knew she never would.

She was worried about him taking time off work; worried he wouldn't be able to pay his bills. But he told her he was independently wealthy, and his trust fund more than covered his simple life style. He was in the police force merely to prove a point to his family; the point he had to prove was that he could hold down a job and enjoy doing so while supporting himself. Lately, he'd become disillusioned, he expected more action, more excitement from the force.

Still staring deeply into Brook's eyes, he assured her she was by far the most exciting thing that had happened to him since he finished his training at the police academy five years ago.

How could he know that since entering her life, Brook was doing a lot of soul searching? For the first time in her life, she realized she didn't know or understand her heart. She questioned her feelings, and definitely the strength of her feelings, all of which were new to her. Brook could see the love Morris felt staring back at her. It was mirrored in her own eyes. Brook asked herself again if this was love...?

Their lips moved closer as two bodies came gently together. The merest touch of their lips, electric, like it always is. The sound of their breathing becoming shallow, the sound filled the air and echoed through the silence of the room; they were almost panting, holding hands, each felt the other's palms become moist.

The intercom chimed several times, rudely shattering the moment. It chimed again before Brook or Morris recognized and heard the intrusive sound. Slowly they withdrew from their world, and came again into the reality of the day. Again, the intercom chimed for attention.

'Someone is impatient,' Brook said, uncurling one foot from under her body and rising from the settee. Still on the settee, Morris tried to clear the fog of passion and desire from his head as he too slowly got to his feet, and followed Brook to the monitor, they wanted to see who was disturbing their moment. Morris had his arm around Brook, and his body molded into hers. She felt his sudden intake of breath as his body stiffened.

'Oh no,' was all Morris muttered as Brook stared into the screen at the stranger who was still persistently pressing the bell.

'Who is it? Do you know him?'

'Yes, Brook, it's Grandpa. Guess he tracked me down. You're in for a treat now!' Morris added sarcastically under his breath, and Brook wasn't sure if he was teasing her or not.

'Shall I let him in?'

'I guess so. Guess he couldn't wait for me to introduce you to the family. Typical,' Morris added as Brook pressed the button and heard the buzz as the gate released. Holding hands, they moved toward the front door.

'Let me,' Morris said moving forward and opening the door just seconds after a loud rapping echoed through the house.

'Grandpa, you found me,' Morris said embracing the older man. Brook stood behind the door and observed the old gentleman for the first time. He was stout and portly with an abundance of wavy salt and pepper hair, although it definitely had more salt than pepper. Under his bushy eyebrows that seemed to have a life of their own, he had dark brown eyes, not large, but they slanted up at the outside edges giving him the appearance of alertness and youth. His square jaw resembled that of his grandson and his generous mouth and moist red lips sat under a large chubby nose. Brook couldn't take her eyes off his huge thick busy dark brown moustache. It didn't seem to fit with the rest of him at all. It was parted neatly in the center and combed out on either side before curling up at the ends into a very fine point. Waxed, thought Brook; he waxes his moustache. She watched the prickly thing move animatedly as he talked to Morris, it seemed to twitch and flip about almost like it was a wild animal glued in place and trying to escape, it definitely had a life of its own.

'Well, Grandpa, you heard correctly, may I present the love of my life, Ms. Feather Brookston, or Brook to her friends?

'Brook, meet my grandpa, Major Lavender Bliss,' The Major took several steps toward Brook who was now standing firmly at Morris's side, and he grabbed her hand tightly before bowing very ceremoniously over it as he touched it with his lips, although all she felt was the itch from the prickly animal glued to his top lip.

'Charmed, I'm sure,' he uttered in a very proper English accent. Brook wasn't normally a giggler, but she did so now at the many oddities that presented themselves regarding the old gentleman. Brook thought him a collection of things that didn't appear to blend together. She looked over his dark green pinstriped suit, his navy shirt and giant tie with swirls of blue, green and orange that was tucked neatly into his tweed waistcoat. In his hand, he held a very ornate and expensive looking walking stick, it appeared to be made of solid silver, and it gleamed in the light from the windows.

'Please, come in, Major.'

'Jolly, ho, thought I wasn't going to be asked,' he replied, winking bluntly at Brook as he past.

'Sorry,' Brook said, leading the way to the living room which immediately felt overpowered by the stout gentleman. Instead of sitting, he walked slowly around the room, looking at everything in detail as he grunted something under his breath and moved onto the next object.

Brook and Morris stayed where they were and watched,

'He's acquainting himself with his surroundings. I think it's a military thing, Brook,' Morris whispered and then in an even quieter whisper he added, 'Queer old boy.'

The Major moved with his hands clasped behind his back as he browsed the room. Brook was unsure whether to laugh or ask him to leave. It was at that moment her cell phone announced a text from Lyme, she said she was ten minutes away and wanted to know if Brook was home. Brook replied quickly, 'Yes.'

'Well, girly, you have quite a collection. This tall statue is rather unique, but I must admit I have no idea what it is. Nice house too, guess you have a sugar daddy? Nothing wrong with that at all, nothing at all, you're an attractive lass. Why not, why indeed, I've been a sugar daddy to a few wenches myself in my day, indeed yes,' he said quietly as he chuckled, and the furry animal thing on his top lip wobbled up and down obviously wanting to be anywhere else but there, Brook thought. She was annoyed at his insinuation of a sugar daddy, and Morris felt her body tense at his words.

'Let it go, Brook, he means no harm.' Normally Brook would have challenged him, but Morris's words soothed her annoyance.

She merely replied, 'This is my house, and I paid for it all myself. I only moved in a while ago.'

'Very good then, some boy lives here with you, does he? I know all about sexual equality and the sexual revolution!' he replied sounding pleased with himself.

'Grandpa, please,' Morris scolded his cheeks slightly red with embarrassment, but the old man appeared not to hear as he walked toward the armchair before asking,

'May I?' Brook nodded and he took a seat, then he asked, 'Did you say tea was on offer, girly, I distinctly heard the words?'

'Yes, Grandpa I'll make us tea while you chat with Brook,' Morris replied before Brook could; then kissing her lightly on the cheek, he exited the room. Brook remained standing until she slowly moved toward the settee.

'Well, it's all rather cozy, yes, cozy indeed. I knew our boy had found someone special when he didn't return home for several days. And now I understand, yes indeed, I do. You're a fine-looking filly if I say so myself. Our boy's done well for himself. High time he made a choice. I know there's a lot on offer out there, but a man's got to sow his wild oats and make a choice sooner or later, indeed he does,' the Major continued with a smile on his lips.

'We haven't known each other very long, Major. Anyway, I expect Morris must return to work soon.'

'Never mind, girly, he'll not be a police officer for long. Morris is a boy who was born with a golden spoon in his mouth, doesn't need to work, and now he's found you, I bet he won't ever work again. He was only proving a point anyway, and we're all proud of him and glad he did. But his point is made, yes indeed it is, and now Morris must move onto the next phase of his life, and that's all about family, and he needs a good girly by his side to achieve that. Did he tell you how my father made us all rich? Did he?'

'Here's the tea, Grandpa, shall I pour? I know you have milk and two sugars,' Morris asked setting the tray on the coffee table before swirling the tea around inside the teapot. The Major nodded, and Morris began to pour. It was obvious, he had done this before Brook thought and wondered how Morris knew his way around the kitchen. Brook only had one kind of tea and that was tea bags, she also remembered there was only about four left in the box, so how did Morris manage to make a teapot full. He lifted the pot toward Brook, and she nodded yes, she would have a cup.

The intercom chimed, and at the sound, the Major almost dropped his cup of tea. 'Whatever is that noise? These new age homes, I'll never get used to them. Can't a person just knock, that always worked in my day,' he said mopping up the spilled tea with his crisp white handkerchief before again lifting the half empty cup to his lips. Brook noticed the fury animal on his top lips quiver and raise upward, obviously trying to get away from the hot beverage, and again she suppressed a laugh as she moved toward the intercom.

I waited patiently outside the gate listening for the click that would tell me the gate was released, and I could enter. I needed to talk to someone about Holt, and I was relieved Brook was home.

Brooked greeted me warmly at the front door with a hug, and immediately I sensed something different about Brook, she seemed to glow.

'You look great, Brook; so glad you're well again. I just have to talk to you,' but the moment, the words were out. Brook moved her fingers to her lips as if to hush me, then she took my arm, and we moved toward the living room. My heart sunk as I noticed two men sitting there having tea; they both stood as we entered. Brook was not one to offer anyone tea, she was a true Starbucks coffee girl, so my curiosity was aroused, and I briefly forgot Holt as the introductions began.

'Lyme, this is Morris Delaney,' Brook said addressing the younger of the two men.

'Hi, Lyme, I've heard a great deal about you, all good, of course,' Morris said, and I immediately liked him. However, I was concerned Brook had been discussing Holt and I with a stranger. Then I turned my attention to the other man in the room.

He seemed to be almost bristling with energy, and I felt he might leap from his chair at any moment. What an unusual looking man with his giant hairy moustache and slanting brown eye, as he stood, I noticed the formal way he dressed, and his extraordinary mop of thick wavy hair. He hardly seemed to place his teacup on the coffee table before he bounded from the chair and stood several feet in front of me.

'Another delightful young lady has joined our party, I see, delighted, my dear, delighted, indeed. Let me introduce myself as no one else has,' he said looking sideways as Morris shook his head with a wry smile at the old man, 'Major Lavender Bliss, at your service,' he said with a deep bow, before he unexpectedly grabbed my hand and touched it to his lips. All I felt was the prickly moustache, and a ripple of repulsion ran through my body. When I didn't reply, he quickly asked, 'And to whom am I addressing? May I ask, my dear girl?'

'I'm Lyme Harrington-Lynch,' I replied extracting my hand from his firm grip. He was still bending over me and staring into my eyes as he spoke.

'Well, now my dear, so you're named after a fruit, how very exotic. You see I have six sisters, and we are all flowers, yes, all of us. I am Lavender, as I have just said and very glad of it. I fear it could have been far worse, although hardly a manly name is it? Let me tell you I never liked it, and it's got me into a few fights over the years. Along with my last name, of course, which seems to encourage the fruity boys if you get my meaning.' He stopped and looked cheekily at his grandson before laughing heartily and continuing on, 'Much more suited to the sisters, than me, you see, they are all flowers also. The eldest is Azuela, then Primrose, Lilly, Daisy, Petunia, Gardenia, all flowers you see the lot of us, and I know our parents had even more names picked out, never worried about the gender, we each got the next name on the list.' He concluded chuckling as we sat and Morris handed me a cup of tea, which I really didn't want.

'Your parents liked gardening?' I asked knowing it sounded lame.

'Oh no, my dear, Lyme, quite the contrary. My mother is Morris's great grandmother, she was named Rose, and her second name was Petal, quite scandalous in those days you understand, my father loved her dearly, adored her in fact, always called her Petal and never Rose as everyone else did. He said he needed more flowers from his Petal and, of course, that was us children. Because we were so rich, no one ever minded really. My father, Bristow Bliss, was a rather talented and ingenious chap, made a lot of money, by keeping his ears open and his mouth shut, his words not mine.'

'Grandfather, surely you're not going to tell them the entire family history over tea, are you?' Morris gave Brook a disapproving sideways look as he spoke. I didn't know what I'd walked into but clearly this was not a space where I could have a girl talk with Brook about Holt and our relationships or anything else, really. I wanted a reason to exit Brook's home and get away from this eccentric Englishman and his stories. But I could hardly just get up and walk out. Morris also intrigued me, he didn't appear to be Brook's type at all, but here he sat and from the electricity I felt between them, they both appeared very into each other. Brook and Morris had a glow surrounding them. They sat very close with their legs touching. I could tell Brook really didn't care about the Major, and all she wanted was to be as close to Morris as she could. Clearly their relationship had advanced beyond that of Holt and me. I could feel their energy; they were already a couple in every sense of the word. I felt a jolt of jealousy. But Brook deserved it, she was my friend. I was pleased to see she had recovered from her attack. It amazed me how terrible situations often become wondrous ones and here was another example of that.

'Lyme, my dear girl, you look bored, should I stop my story or start over?' The Major's voice penetrated my thoughts; I had been caught off guard and worse than that he knew I hadn't been listening.

'Oh, please start over. Your story is intriguing, and I don't want to miss a single word,' I said trying my best to sound enthusiastic. I didn't know whether it was or not but I knew from experience that eccentric people often told colorful stories and looking at the Major, I knew he wouldn't disappoint. Anyway, I needed something to take my mind off Holt. The Major needed no more prompting than that. He got to his feet again and talked as he paced the floor, hand clasped behind his back, a faraway look in his eyes and a captive audience in his presence.

'Well, it was back in the early nineteenth century. My father was a young man, in his prime so to speak. Good looking, carefree and without fear. It all began when he was taking the place of a friend, it was a dare actually, us boys sometimes do these sorts of things, don't we, Morris?' The Major said winking at his grandson who shuffled uneasily in his chair adverted his eyes from those of the Major and didn't answer.

'Well, anyway you'll have to take my word. Now, where was I? Oh yes, my father when he was young and foolish and definitely a lad. He was taking the place of a friend of his and serving the gentlemen in an elite upper-class gentlemen's club, in the heart of London. His friends had dared him to last the night without losing his tongue to the pompous upstarts he was meant to serve.

At this particular table sat six dignitaries from various foreign lands and two Englishman, one of the men no more than a lad his own age. It was to this lad the older men's attention was focused. They all appeared to be intently listening to the lad, leaning forward and holding onto his every word. So, my father became curious and hid behind the heavy floor lengths drapes of the bay window. From there, he could observe the six men and hear clearly everything that was being said. He soon learned the speaker was none other than young Oswald Cornelius, the uncle of the very famous writer Roald Dahl.

'Grandfather, I doubt if Lyme and Brook know of the writer he's been dead for some years,' Morris added hoping to put a stop to the Major's bantering story. But the Major merely nodded; he was not to be put off. Soon he continued on, undeterred.

'Well, now Morris that is so and they shall have to take my word for it won't they. Anyway. Young Oswald was telling his attentive audience about his discovery of a powerful aphrodisiac that would allow them to have sex, pardon the word ladies, for simply hours. It would turn them into young stallions. He guaranteed this no matter their age. Well, the short of it is that he had enough for each of them to try, he had the tablets right there in his pocket, and he would sell each of them one tablet at the very low price of fifty pounds per tablet. If they wanted more it would be double that amount. He would soon be leaving to visit the source of the aphrodisiac to acquire more.' The Major stopped to make sure he had our full attention, and when he knew he did, he proceeded on.

'Well, my father thought this a bit of a joke, but he also saw each of the men hand over fifty pounds to young Oswald. He waited around until Oswald was about to leave; by this time, he had finished his shift, so his absence didn't arouse any suspicion. He was after all on holiday from his studies at Oxford, and he had learned from his eavesdropping that Oswald was also a second-year chemistry student there.

He waited until Oswald left the club, and he followed him to his lodgings, not far away. He then briefly went home, quietly went to his room and packed a small bag with most of his belongings and all his money. Then he sat in the street all night waiting to see if Oswald was telling the truth, and he really was going to acquire more of the stuff. He didn't have to wait long, at first light Oswald left his lodgings with a receptacle in hand and headed straight to the airport.

My father needed to use nearly half his money to purchase his ticket, but before long he was on a plane headed heavens knows where. Two days later, he was trekking toward the Sudan. There, Oswald met with several local chaps and acquired for a small amount of money a bag of powder. My father took his time and waited until the next day; by this time Oswald had left by the same route he had arrived. Then my father quickly approached the same man that Oswald had spoken to the day before. He was a young chap, you understand, and by this time he was simply bursting with curiosity. Finally, he got the local boy aside and inquired just what his friend had purchased?

At first, the man was suspicious; asked him if he had money and then, when he was assured them he did they proceeded to produce a small black beetle with green iridescent wings covering most of its back. Was this a joke? – he wondered. But as they spoke some more, he learned that it was indeed no joke, for this tiny blister beetle was in fact the very rare Sudanese blister beetle. And when dried and ground up this beetle became the most powerful aphasiac in the world. Several other men joined in the conversation, and in their rough English elaborated on the first man's story, telling him about the potency and remarkable powers of the beetle.

These men were simply ecstatic with stories of how any man, even a ninety-year-old could simply enjoy sex for hours and satisfy the youngest damsel after using just enough power that could fit on the head of a pin. To use any more than that would mean certain harm would come to the user. They said Spanish fly, which was also developed from a blister beetle was nothing on the Sudanese Blister beetle it was a hundred, no a thousand times more potent.' The Major paused again to make sure he had an attentive audience and he certainly did, then he continued on,

'Well, my father asked why wasn't everyone using the beetle? 'No, no,' they said 'it is a very, very, well-kept secret and most hard to obtain.'

'Why?' My father asked and they proceeded to tell him that the beetle only lives on a few very rare trees deep in the jungle; it is a most dangerous journey to obtain them.

Finally, they trusted my father enough to ask 'How much did he want?' The men spoke in very low voices, when they finally offered to sell him the white powder, it was hardly more than a whisper. My father said he would take what Oswald had taken; that is until he heard the price. Then he knew he couldn't afford it. He would have to barter as Oswald Cornelius had done, and so finally they agreed on a lesser amount of money and my father took the small bag. Again, they assured him, he only needed to give each man the amount of beetle powder that would fit on the head of a pin. In that case, he thought he had plenty to make his fortune. He now only had enough money to get back over land to the airport and home, with hardly anything left over.

And so, he arrived back in London, half starving, dirty and sunburnt. But he was in high spirits, for he knew he would soon make his fortune. Now Oswald Cornelius was a great deal wealthier than my father at this stage and also a chemistry student at Oxford. Oswald made the powder into small red tablets and packaged them elaborately before they were sold. However, my father was not a student of chemistry, nor did he have the money to package what he was selling. But he was an ingenious man nevertheless, and what he did have was the beetle power, and it was the same as Oswald in every way.

My father devised a way of selling a measured amount, the amount that would fit on the head of a pin and wrapping it in folded tissue paper. He didn't try and sell it for fifty pounds to begin with, as he didn't know too many rich people. But he knew he must mix with the right gentlemen if he was to make a lot of money. So, he gave up his studies at Oxford University and acquired a job at another very elite gentlemen's club in London, and gradually he selected several wealthy gentlemen and gave them a small sample of his powder and a card with his name and address printed on it, should they wish to order more.

He only gave out six samples that first day. But the word spread like wild fire, the very next morning, there was a selection of couriers, and manservants waiting for him outside his parents rather modest middle-class bungalow. Within the first year he had made nearly a million pounds, and he still had two thirds of the powder from the Sudan, available. With his newly acquired wealth, he purchased a new house for his parents in a very upscale area and then a house for himself. When he met my mother, Lady Rose Petal Pomney, he literally swept her off her feet. The he married her before taking her on an extended honeymoon around Europe. By this time, he was asking several hundred pounds for just one tissue of the powder, and he was getting it too. As they traveled word followed him, and he made more money in Europe than he had in England, he now had more money than he ever thought possible. By then, my mother was expecting my eldest sister Azuela, and the blister beetle powder was beginning to run low. However, he wasn't concerned.

With some guidance he managed to invest his vast wealth wisely. He knew it was the only way to make it last for generations; he had so much wealth, he knew he couldn't spend it in one lifetime. Once they returned to London, he sold his house, purchased a larger one in Kensington and never sold the powder again. He adored his Petal, and she in return adored him. Before you ask, I have no idea if the Beetle was responsible for any of his us children.' He said finally sitting on the edge of his chair and beaming from ear to ear. The room was silent; I must say it was one of the best stories I had ever heard. No one spoke, Morris poured the Major more tea and sat again as silence filled the room. With a flash of insight I wondered what Granny Harry would think of the Major. I knew she adored colorful personalities. Finally, the Major cleared his throat and said, 'Well, there is still plenty of money for several generations to come. My father was also a shrewd investor, so boys and girls how about you let this old man take you all out for dinner? I'm feeling rather peckish.' Still no one spoke. I was still thinking of his story, and I actually wished Morris had allowed him to tell the longer version.

'Will you be changing for dinner, my dear?' The Major asked addressing Brook, she nodded and got to her feet as he added, 'How about booking us all into the best restaurant you know. Of course, you'll join us Lyme?' slowly I became aware he was addressing me, so reluctantly I returned to reality. Immediately, I wondered what Holt was doing. I needed to be with him. Before I could decline the Major's offer, he spoke again, standing before me this time, 'No need to change, my dear girl, I think you will do nicely just as you are.' I looked up to see him standing directly in front of me. We were alone now as I noticed Morris also had left the room. 'Now, girly, no good saying you have a prior engagement, because if you did, you wouldn't be here, would you? I do so enjoy the company of the young, and I promise not to tell any more of my stories,' he said looking very solemn with his large pudgy hand placed over his heart. I nodded as I slowly looked up at him. I couldn't help liking him. He was old and rather eccentric and maybe he had too many stories to share, but he was oozing personality and charm in a rather over the top old fashioned kinda way. Finally, I found my tongue and replied.

'Delighted. I'd be delighted to join you for dinner, Major.' His eyes lit up at my words, and before I knew it he had grabbed my hand and lifted it to his lips, again I felt the prickly furry thing that lived there, touch my skin.

The evening flew by, and it was not dull. The Major told several more fascinating stories, each of which held our full attention long after they were finished. Morris, of course, had heard them all before and threatened the Major that he was to tell the short version only, otherwise he would leave. Again, I wished for the longer version, but I knew I must be happy with what I got. I had my cell phone on the table beside me, and I told everyone I was expecting a call. I hoped Holt would call me; I wished it so badly, my heart ached. But the only calls I received were from Amber Buxton regarding the decorating of one of the hotels and Padbury Prentice, Daddy's CEO. He was looking for Daddy and mumbled something about Cerise signing some papers, but the line was bad and as soon as I said Daddy wasn't with me, he rang off.

The night in the Major's company flew by, the conversation flowed, and the Major and Morris easily blended into our group. I hadn't had any time alone with Brook, so I couldn't get to speak to her. However, I was annoyed when Brooke suggested to the Major that maybe I would introduce him to my Granny Harry. At the mere thought of a new woman in his life, his eyes simply lit up when he looked eagerly in my direction. I was angry with Brook for suggesting the Major met my Granny, although I had briefly thought of it myself, but I felt she had no right to do so. Granny Harry was very special and most dear to me, and I thought of her as my own secret property. I now regretted introducing her to Brook and Pan.

'Well, now, girly, so you have a spunky Granny, do you? Just my type, I'm sure. It's all about the personality, now I'm getting on in years. I'm sure she's a wench worth meeting indeed I am, and I'm ready to do so. Why, can you believe it's been a few years now since I've had a good wench beside me at night or even one that excites me in my life, and a gentleman is always in need of the company of a good little woman? Looking forward to meeting her, indeed I am?' The Major responded a broad smile on his face as his moustache twitched, he moistened his lips and his eyes shone.

I couldn't imagine what Granny Harry would think of this eccentric gentleman, and if I have any say in it they shall never meet. I flashed Brook a look that said it all, and I knew she got my meaning by the way she averted my eyes from then on. When she suggested we go shooting on Saturday, I replied that I would let her know what my social calendar was looking like. Still Holt hadn't called. I checked my phone several times until the Major guessed it was a young man, I was waiting to hear from. Finally, once desert was served and before the cognac arrived, I made my excuses and left.

Chapter 14
Daddy Takes Charge

Upon entering my room, I noticed a huge bouquet of flowers, their fragrance filled the air. The many different flowers were in bright and happy colors. They stood in a tall crystal vase in the center of the room. Oh, Holt, he had remembered me. My heart sung. I raced to the tiny card and opened it quickly. But my heart almost broke when I saw it was not from Holt but someone named Remington Tillerson-Proctor, the third. He wanted to invite me to a cocktail party and asked me to call or text to confirm. Who was he? I remembered hearing the name somewhere, but I didn't know him. I didn't care anyway, he wasn't Holt; quickly I ripped the small card into sixteen tiny pieces before throwing it to the floor. I was breathing deeply so the tears wouldn't flow.

Later that night I lay alone in my huge bed safely in my bedroom in the dark, there was only me, and however much I imagined Holt's warm sexy body beside me, there remained only me alone by myself with my thoughts and dreams. Alone in the darkness with my raw desperation, solitude and fear; my fear was so deep, I never wanted to allow it out; I never wanted to meet it – to feel it. I felt utterly alone and abandoned. Didn't Holt know I loved him more than life. He must know it. He must feel it. These feelings were so new to me they felt raw. How could Holt not feel what I was feeling, know what I was thinking. The love I felt in my heart for Holt overwhelmed everything, my life, my thoughts, my dreams. Everything! So, I focused instead on the blank and empty solitude inside me, it was a familiar place. That place was my only true friend. A place I happily receded to. There was nothing there. It was an empty void. A deep, dark, heavy hole of nothing, but I guarded that place. It was precious to me, more precious than anything I processed. It was my deep, dark solitary void of nothing, and with it I could do whatever I wanted, create anything I wished, and in my world, I could be anyone I choose to be.

As I lay in my bed I felt secure, I felt safe, and it was a time that was mine, all mine, and I treasured every minute. But even in the darkness I felt the ache, a slow deep ache, a real physical pain; throbbing somewhere deep inside. Ever since my mother passed away I craved having someone of my own, beside me, to share the nights, to chase away my demons and challenge my fears. Now, finally I had found that someone, he was real not just a visit into my imagination in the dark, not merely a creation living in my void at night. But Holt is a real living breathing, flesh and blood, man. I never thought I'd find him, and I had. But I could dream all I liked in my empty void where each night was like a blank page in my dairy, a page with no words of life, because on that page no one and nothing lived. I knew when I woke in the morning, alone in my empty bed, and Holt was not beside me; that it would hurt even more than it does now because Holt still belongs to another.

I hadn't spoken to Brook, and I needed to, but I quickly understood she had her own life and challenges, although I doubt if at present she knew it. Granny Harry was always wonderful to be around, but instead of giving me solid advice, she had told me a love story so poignant that it lingered in my mind still and fueled my desire for Holt. I saw history repeating itself with Holt and I, instead of my granny and grandpa. Granny had not really given me the answers, I craved. Just more questions, but then what answers do I need? Just what was I expecting anyone to tell me? I had no idea, something that would blow my mind I guess, and something that would point me on a course of success with Holt. Surely, I already had all I needed – I loved him, wasn't that enough?

He hadn't called, why was I expecting him to? Did I think he was missing me? Our last dinner hadn't gone so well, I hadn't explained myself, and perhaps I should have. I did however tell him before he exited the car that I was not married or in any kind of a relationship, but I guess the moment had passed as all he said in reply was, 'like I care, why are you telling me about your personal life. It is your own business; I can't help you with it. Thanks for dinner.' He slammed the car door and walked away into the entrance of his apartment building without so much as a backward glance. I'd driven around and around for almost an hour, circling his apartment block, and each time I passed the front entrance I slowed and stared inside. Finally, the doorman appeared to be waiting for me, and he moved onto the sidewalk as if to stop me. His actions alone bought me back to reality.

What was I doing? As I pulled away, I saw Holt turn the corner, he was heading straight for his apartment building. I briefly wondered when and why he had left? I hadn't seen him leave. But he didn't see me as he had his arm around a girl. At first, I thought it must be his wife. I felt sick; I thought I would throw up. Then, as my headlights drew closer I clearly saw it was the air hostess from the plane. I don't know how I got home after that, but I had and I hadn't slept at all that night. I stayed in bed until late next morning, tried to call Pan, but she had that horrid Madam Roderic with her again so her mind was definitely taken up. It was Fox's day off, so I couldn't speak to her, so finally I went for a drive again and ended up driving by Holt's apartment building, but, of course, he was at work. So, I drove to Brook's house and you know the rest of the story. The evening with Brook and her friends was both colorful and interesting, but I still hadn't been able to talk to her or anyone.

Now, I knew it was morning, even though the heavy drapes had been drawn tightly by Fox the night before. I was not in a deep sleep, but gradually I sensed it was time to wake up, although my eyes and my brain remained hazy and wanted to continue sleeping. The sound of the door opening startled me in my half-awakened state. The rustling of a skirt told me it was Fox, but just why was she here without me calling her? Then light flooded the room, bright sunlight, it pierced my eyes as I slowly opened them and Fox said,

'Miss Lyme, you better be getting up and dressed Mister Lyn been asking for you, and he doesn't seem any too pleased.'

'What's my father want so early in the morning, Fox?'

'I don't rightly know, Miss Lyme, but he's been asking for you since he woke at six o'clock and its now almost eleven and he's getting madder than a cat in a hornet's nest, so I suggest you get up and dress. What clothes can I get you, Miss Lyme?' My mind was foggy and I didn't feel like facing Daddy or anyone else right now. In fact, had it been anyone else asking to see me, I would have refused. But to refuse Daddy was not an option, he was not a man to be told 'no' by anyone. I still hadn't answered Fox about my clothes when I heard the shower running and noticed she had put out my cream crepe trouser suit and pale green camisole. I really didn't care; it would do as well as anything else.

'Did Daddy send you up here, Fox?' I asked as I entered the shower, and she hovered close by.

'He told me earlier to come up, but I wanted you to get your sleep. I know you haven't had much lately, being in love and everything. I can tell by those black marks under your eyes, and I haven't seen them since your mother passed.'

'Thanks Fox, no I didn't sleep too well last night, either. It's all very confusing, Fox, all I know is that I love him, and I can't think of anything else,' I replied as the hot steamy water washed over my back and seemed to release my tense muscles.

'Miss Lyme its always the way with love, it kinda consumes you.'

'Yes,' I said and thought Fox was right, how on earth did she of all people understand, but that was exactly how I was feeling, consumed.

'Yes, Fox you're absolutely right.'

'Well, Miss Lyme, he's a lucky man and don't you forget it, and don't you let anyone or anything talk you out of following your heart. Now out you get, times a wasting.' Fox was holding a huge white fluffy towel open for me to step into. It felt slightly warm as she wrapped me in it, like she used to when I was a child. Then before I could say anything further, she left the room closing the door behind her. Maybe, I should have spoken to Fox after all; she certainly knew more about love than I could have guessed. But how? I'd only ever known her to have a couple of boyfriends and that was years ago.

It was my mother's words I heard in my head answering the question. "It's not about how often you fall in love, but how many times your heart is broken." Her voice was clear in my head, and it was almost like she was with me. I'd often thought she was still here in spirit. Granny Harry had confirmed these thoughts many times, but was she just trying to lessen my grief or did she really mean it. I was brushing my hair as my mind raced. I was thinking about many things and seemed unable to block the thoughts inside my head. Then I heard Fox's footsteps, hurried footsteps approach my door, she knocked lightly and entered. 'Mr. Lyn is getting mighty impatient, he's threatening to come up here and get you, says to tell you he doesn't have time to wait around while you snooze.' Fox sounded anxious, and I immediately returned to reality. I had been day dreaming and forgot Daddy was waiting for me down stairs. Quickly, I put on my under garments as Fox handed me the clothes she had previously put out for me to wear. I added a splash of lipstick and perfume and partly brushed my hair before reluctantly following her out the door and down stairs. I wondered if he was actually going to throw me out of the house, as he had threatened to do last time we met. Half way down, I heard Daddy's voice from below.

'LYME – WHERE THE HELL ARE YOU? CAN'T MY OWN DAUGHTER COME WHEN SHE'S CALLED? LYME. GET THE HELL DOWN HERE.' He bellowed, I looked at Fox and we both understood I needed to move faster down the stairs now. I was almost at the bottom of the long stairway when he yelled again, this time cursing loudly and threatening to come up to my room if I didn't appear immediately.

I ran down the remaining stairs two at a time, knocked on his huge oak doors and, without waiting for an answer, I entered.

'What the hell took you so long gal? Ya legs fall off or something?' he yelled. He was pacing up and down the length of his study. His huge frame and even bigger presence dominated the room as it always did. I immediately felt like a scared kid in his presence, just as I had in my childhood.

'Sit down, gal.' He flicked his hand toward two oversize buttoned leather armchairs opposite his large mahogany desk.

He turned away from me to pour himself a whisky from the silver tray sitting on a small table next to his huge desk. I could see or rather feel he was trying to compose himself before he turned around. Finally, he turned and instead of pacing the room he took a seat in his chair. I could tell he was deciding what to say or maybe how to say it.

'Lyme, honey I built my companies from the ground up. Hard work, some luck, then made some money which I re-invested in the company and with more hard work and a little more luck the company grew, very slowly, but it was solid I oversaw everything, from the mailroom boy to the engineers. I knew it would take time, and I also knew that just one mistake could cause me to lose it all.

All the while, I felt the big boys of the oil world waiting, watching and hoping I'd go bust so they could gobble me up like a frog eats a fly. That fly is a small unimportant insect and to them, a nuisance, it is nothing. But that tiny fly, has taken time and energy to grow, it has struggled to survive, and while it maybe, nothing to most everyone, to itself it is something. Once I stumble all I'd achieved would be lost, and I knew they would quickly swallow me up, forget about me and keep on going. Well,

I wanted to be something, and I wanted to be known as more than a pesky unseen fly fluttering around in their world. I wanted that more than the air I was breathing, I wanted to achieved greatness; I wanted them to feel my power, I wanted to take them down, so I would become the best.

In the beginning it was all about survival that was the only important thing. It took micro managing from me on every level twenty-four/seven. It was mine, and the more it grew the more I had to lose, and I knew it could be taken from me in the blink of an eye, overnight. Anything could topple me, bad press, drilling in the wrong place, a fake geologist report, a lawsuit or rouge employee, anything. The enemy appeared from many places and hides in many forms. I knew all the crap, all the powerful people said and the games they play. I've seen it all and turned it to my advantage more than once and won.

I didn't sleep most nights as the company grew so did the fear inside me, and I knew I had no friends; no protection and no one had my back. You see, Lyme, the more powerful I became, the more I isolated myself. I could trust no one. If they didn't want to see me fall for their own financial gain then they were jealous of all I had achieved. Lyme, I built it all with guts, determination, hard work and some luck along the way. But I didn't build it all to see it crumble, and I never want to see it crumble – what I have achieved is magnificent; a life's dream. More than any one man can hope to achieve in one lifetime, and I've done it all.

Then I married your mother and life was perfect. I could give her anything her heart desired, and I did and loved doing it. It made me proud seeing the happiness in her eyes. She taught me to let some of the control go and trust others even if only a little, but I still slept with one eye open, because now I knew I was truly blessed, and I had even more to lose. And when you were born, life couldn't have got any better. I wasn't a good husband, and I know I'm far from a good father. But no one has strength in everything they do and mine is in industry, and I have proven my strengths many times over, and I don't need to prove it to anyone anymore. I am the best.' He stopped and filled his glass again.

I was shocked. Daddy had never spoken to me like this before. This was in fact the most he had ever spoken to me in my entire life. But I still didn't know why I was here? It didn't sound like he wanted me to leave. We sat, the room was quiet, the walls were thick and silence creep around us like a cloak, shrouding us, hiding us in its depth. I didn't know if I should speak, I didn't know what to say. Daddy had shocked me in yet another way, so I sat and waited. I stared at his back. I could feel and see the tension there. The minutes ticked by, until there was no need for words, the time for words had passed, we shared the silence, and I knew it to be a thing that Daddy was unaccustomed to. Then, like a bolt of lightning he turned, leaped from his chair which crashed to the ground and began pacing the floor. I saw the veins in his temples throbbing as he paced. A loud knock came from the door, and I knew Newton, who was always lurking close by, had heard Daddy's chair fall,

'I'm fine, Newton,' Daddy answered, and I heard footsteps retreat from outside the door.

'So, what the hell is going on, gal?' he unexpectedly bellowed turning on me; his brilliant blue eyes blazing the pupils no more than tiny granite dots in the center, they were focused on me. I didn't know what to say, but there was no need to say anything, Daddy was seldom short on words.

'What the hell, Lyme? I called this Holt person to my office a few days ago. Tall guy, good looking too; thought I may as well get to know him if he's going to be part of the family, promote him, perhaps if he's any good, and definitely move him back to head office here in the city; instead of him flying in and out every two weeks, that way he can be close to you. I put the word out to report back to me on his work ethics and the managers did so. However, the word is they thought him arrogant, rude, volatile and unpredictable. Anyway,' Daddy raised his voice again as he moved closer to me and stopped pacing.

'What the hell, Lyme? He didn't even know who the hell you were for a while. He certainly didn't know I was your father. And he doesn't have any intention of marrying you. Why he's got a wife already? says he loves her too. Are you taunting me somehow, because if you are it's a poor effort, a very poor effort from my own daughter? So, I'll ask you again, what the hell, Lyme?' I thought I had told him Holt was married, but perhaps I'd forgotten to. I was certainly going to tell Holt about Daddy, but the time hadn't presented itself, and now Daddy had confronted Holt, how embarrassing for me. I may have lost him forever now. I knew Daddy could be daunting, arrogant and obnoxious at best, and I cannot imagine what Holt would have thought, no wonder I hadn't heard from him. I didn't know what to say, I hadn't lied to him, but I guess I hadn't told him everything, either. I was certainly understanding just how serious Daddy was about me giving him an heir. I sat there looking at my hands and saying nothing, not sure how to make it right.

'What the hell, Lyme?' Daddy bellowed again. Daddy paced and stopped every time he passed my chair and stared at my down turned face. I knew he hadn't seen me do this since I was a small girl. Then suddenly, I burst into tears. I don't know why, and I wished I hadn't. I hated it when Daddy sees me as weak. I knew he played on people's weaknesses; I knew he did. I wanted to present strength, control and confidence, so he would take me seriously as a person and his daughter. But too late I was sobbing into my hands wishing I had a tissue. He said nothing and then after what seemed like ages he spoke. He must have sat on the chair next to mine at some stage. Then, I felt his hand touch mine, immediately I pulled away, no one wants to be touched by the devil. But then he touched me again, and I didn't resist. Slowly, he put his hand under my chin and lifted my face, so I was looking directly into his eyes.

'Honey, I shall fix this.' It made his words sound like a statement. His voice was gruff but softer and quieter than usual. I was overcome by his kindness, something I had seldom if ever seen from him before. But then I remember the way he treated my mother with so much love and affection. Then I remembered she told me it was only when they were alone. I knew in his own way he had cared for her and respected her.

He rose from the chair and yelled, 'Newton'. I jumped from his sudden change in temperament and loud voice.

Newton hurriedly entered he was never far away.

'I want everything you can find on Holt Visser; he works for me. You remember I mentioned him to you a few days ago? I want a P.I. following him and his wife. I want to know all about her, what the neighbors know and think and, the same for Holt's work colleagues. Spare no expense, be discreet and start immediately,' Daddy ordered.

'Yes, sir, Mr. Lyn, I'm on it,' the big man bristled with energy as he left the room.

'Lyme, my gal, we are going to buy you a husband.'

'What, Daddy? you can't.'

'Why not, unless you've changed your mind again, gal?'

'No, Daddy, but…'

'Lyme, money can buy anything, and I'll bet it can buy you a husband.'

'But,' I said amazing and shocked at his words.

'Lyme, go and get on with your day and make yourself beautiful, you'll soon be a bride.' He said moving behind his big desk, in his mind the subject was already suitably dealt with, and I was dismissed. Slowly, I got up, and walked to the door. I stopped and looked back once not believing what had just happened. How can I buy a husband? How is it possible? But I could see by the smile playing on Daddy's lips that he thought it was the perfect solution to the problem and very possible indeed. To him I was almost walking down the aisle. I had seldom if ever seen him looking so happy, or maybe the word is contented.

How would Holt react? Would I ever see him again? Would he hold me in even greater contempt than he already does?

Daddy's world moves fast, too fast for me. I was about to get what I wanted at lightning speed. I was about to learn how to buy a husband!

Chapter 15
How to Buy a Husband – The Plan

I turned my cell on as I drove home from visiting Granny Harry. I had told her everything. She laughed when I told her what Daddy was planning to do. Then in a more serious voice, she said that knowing Lyn, maybe he would actually pull it off. She asked me several times if I was sure of what I was doing, and was I sure Holt was the man I wanted to spend my life with? I nodded, but couldn't look her in the eyes. I told her I felt like I'd already lost him because of Daddy intervening. I hadn't heard a word from Holt, no flowers, nothing. Then I mentioned the flowers I'd received from Remington Tillerson-Proctor, and Granny commented on what a perfect match that would be. I hated her for saying that, because she briefly sounded like Daddy!

I told her how Daddy thought the same thing. I told her I'd never met the guy and never wanted to. Holt was my world, and he is all I want.

My cell phone took my thoughts away from my conversation with Granny Harry and back to the present. It was Amber Buxton, 'Lyme, I've just cleared this with your father, but we need you down here on site, we have some interior design conflicts, and it's holding up the completion date,' her voice was brisk and business like.

She was the last person I wanted to hear, 'It's difficult getting away right now, Amber, can't you handle it?'

'Lyme, I could, but I won't make a decision of this magnitude; the resorts are your baby, and Mr. Lyn said you'd be on the first plane down. I have ordered the company jet2 to be on standby for you, and Fox has your bag packed. I've been trying to get hold of you for several hours, that's why I called your home.' Amber sounded annoyed. I knew arguing was pointless, she was a woman who knew her mind, and usually got what she wanted. I also knew if she had cleared it with Daddy then I had to go. I told her I'd see her later that afternoon and disconnected the call. I wanted to wait right here in Texas in case Holt called and maybe wanted to see me. But I had responsibilities, and they were calling me also. How was I going to keep my mind on the resorts, with Holt's face spinning around inside my head, and so many questions threatening my sanity?

I roared home, driving much too fast as I often did. Briefly I checked my side mirror for cops, but saw none. However, what I did see was a black Buick, it appeared several cars behind me. I recognized it as the same vehicle I had noticed outside Granny's place. At that time I took no notice, but now I was nearly home, and it was still following me. At the speed I was driving I felt sure this couldn't be a coincidence. I reached into the glove compartment and found the Ruger 9mm I kept there. It was my choice to have one hidden in the glove compartment of every car we owned. With one eye on the road, I checked it was fully loaded and it was. I tucked it out of sight close to my side, closed the glove compartment and drove. But now I kept one eye on the side mirror.

I decided to give the Buick a run for its money. I knew the neighborhood well; I knew all the side streets and the 'one way' streets also. I pressed the gas pedal slightly toward the floor and the car responded quickly and smoothly. I turned left then immediately left again into a leafy laneway that went a short distance before turning a hard right. I pulled the car around the sharp turn, and it responded instantly although I was almost on two wheels. There were many back entrances to houses and hidden driveways. I choose a large double driveway and nosed the car over into the trees at the side, before cutting the engine and rolling down the window.

I listened and waited, but not for long. I heard the roaring of the Buick's powerful engine as I slid down low behind the driver's seat. My heart raced in my chest as I tightly gripped the barrel of the gun at my side. But then it roared right passed me it hadn't seen the right turn I had taken. Slowly I sat up in the seat, my ears alert, trying to slow my heart. I waited and heard nothing more. The sound of my cell phone receiving a text startled me. I grabbed it, and read a text from Brook asking me if I was going with her to the rifle range. I replied 'no' nothing more. Her response came immediately that she would take Morris in my place. I smiled, and guessed he would have come with us anyway. I started the car knowing I had to get out of here fast as the Buick was probably circling and waiting for me to reappear. I remembered once getting lost in these laneways and also remembered finding a way out that took me a distance away from where I was. After a few wrong turns that took me out onto the main street I arrived at the rear of a strip mall. I knew I'd lost the shady black Buick, and I relaxed slightly. By now I was late, but I could still make it home and get to the airport to make the flight.

It was early evening when I touched down in L.A. The sun was just about to hide its head from the moon. I headed to the house in Newport Beach. Showered and changed before jumping in the red Lamborghini we kept garaged at the Newport Beach house, and heading to the Four Seasons Hotel to dine with Amber. I know Amber was not pleased having to wait for my arrival and then needing to brief me over dinner. Although dinner was her idea, not mine. I realized I was starving as I read the menu. I had hardly eaten, and Amber casually mentioned that I had lost weight. The moment the meal was over Amber asked for the table to be cleared, and she proceeded to spread out many plans, charts, and color swatches.

Once she explained the problem, I understood there was indeed a color conflict. It seemed our designer had changed one of my color choices for another without notifying either Amber or myself. Already the color was being used throughout the resort, and Amber said she'd noticed the change, although subtl,e the difference was immediately obvious, and she knew I wouldn't be pleased.

The discussion was all I needed to stop thinking of Holt for a few hours. Somehow it cleared my mind briefly. I was able to focus and sort out all we needed for the project to move forward. We worked until almost midnight, and I agreed to meet her early the next morning at the resort. She told me several times the amount of money it was costing for the workman to stand around waiting for my decision, and I knew she was not pleased. I hoped she hadn't told Daddy, but somehow, I guessed she had.

The valet bought my car and commenting with a broad smile on his young face, what a beauty it was. I agreed, gave him a generous tip, and drove away, my head spinning with all we had discussed and the many decisions I needed to make. Checking my mirror as I pulled out I observed a black car pulling out behind me several cars away. The hotel was a busy place at night, and I told myself not to be paranoid. Why would anyone be following me? However, the feeling that I was being followed, remained. I drove slower than usual and watched in the mirror and yes, the car stayed discreetly behind. I hoped to find a Ruger 9mm handgun hidden in the glove compartment of the Lamborghini. I reached into the glove compartment in the dark with one hand as I drove with the other. After my hand searched around for a while, I found the false compartment at the back of the glove compartment, I released the latch and withdrew the Ruger 9mm placing it closely by my side.

I spent the next four days in L.A., they were busy days, but finally the work at the resort continued on, and I could return home. Holt hadn't called although I had several missed calls on my phone from private numbers and wondered on each occasion if it may have been him. By the time I left, I knew for sure that I was being followed. Maybe, Holt had placed a tail on me; of course, he could, I guessed Daddy had been having him followed, also. It was what Daddy organized Newton to do all the time.

The company jet arrived back in Texas late, and I went home to bed feeling as though I had achieved much. But I hadn't had time to daydream about Holt as I loved doing. I felt sure he must have tried to contact me at home. I was delighted upon entering my room, I saw a huge bouquet of flowers awaiting me. My heart leaped, it must be from Holt, he did care, and he was thinking of me. I rushed forward and grabbed the card. I only saw the name Remington before I ripped it up into tiny pieces. Why the hell was someone called Remington sending me flowers? I had never even met him? Was this Daddy's doing? Was he meddling in my personal life, again? Remington was quickly forgotten as I wondered, yet again, why Holt hadn't called?

Early next morning, Fox woke me for a long overdue sleep. My mind the night before had many thoughts until finally I was able to let them go and recede into my dark, lonely void of nothing. But waiting for me was Holt's face dancing around in my void, and his face, like his touch remained just out of reach. How did he manage to invade the only sanctuary I had?

'Miss Lyme, Mr. Lyn is calling for you, so you best get up and make an appearance.'

'So early, Fox, what time is it?'

'It's just after eight, and I have a breakfast tray for you, if you want it?'

'No, Fox, just get me some clothes.' I instructed, rubbing the sleep from my eyes, walking into the bathroom and splashing water on my face, cleaning my teeth and brushing my hair.

'Is that all you're about to do before you see your father?' Fox asked, looking me up and down. I stared back at her before retreating again to the bathroom and adding pink lipstick and Chanel perfume.

I took the stairs two at a time, beyond the closed oak doors I could hear him bellowing my name. Why couldn't he use the intercom system like the rest of us did? Maybe, he needed to be heard? He always wanted everyone to know he was the center of attention, and he never cared how he achieved it. Hurriedly, I entered the room, noticing as I did, that Newton was standing discreetly in the far corner.

'Well, gal, you took your time.'

'Good morning, Daddy,' I replied sounding much happier and awake than I felt.

'Thought you'd be a lot more eager to hear what we know, and what we've discovered,' he boomed as my heart raced.

'I am eager, Daddy, I just got back from L.A. late last night.'

'I don't give a damn, but if you cannot take the responsibility of the resorts seriously and stop holding the workman up then maybe I should take over.'

'I take my responsibility very seriously, and I feel I'm doing a good job,' I replied standing my ground and looking him straight in the eye,

'You caused delays by your absence and delays, no matter how short, cost money, we paid the guys for standing around, productivity is down, and progress is nil. Don't let life get in the way of your commitments, my gal. Once the horse stops racing, and you're thrown to the ground, it takes time, however quickly you recover to get back on and ride again. Don't let the horse stop, my gal – its unproductive and unprofessional. I always kept the horse galloping as fast as I could; it's how I made my money. Hard work, pure drive and focus, remember that. It's what we all need to achieve, however big or small.' I listened to Daddy loudly rant and remembered him saying much the same at the last seminar of his I had been made to attend. The horse thing was getting tired also; I almost interjected something smart about the horse but thought better of it, and kept my mouth, shut. Although, I knew he was right. In a split second, he had changed direction, and began talking about Holt. Immediately he had my attention, as my heart skipped a beat at the mention of his name, and I began to sweat. I knew my cheeks were blazing, so I kept looking at the floor.

'Well, the P.I. Newton engaged seems to have done an awesome job, full report, photos etc. So now we know what we're up against, and the enemy doesn't seem so great. Once you identify your enemy you can work out the best way to attack.'

'Daddy, you make it sound like a military maneuver,' I commented quietly still looking at the floor as I tried to gain control. Daddy was one person that valued strength, and I didn't want him to see my weakness where Holt was concerned.

'Hell, this is almost a military maneuver. So, listen carefully, if you don't, you won't get what you want.' Daddy bellowed as I nodded. Newton remained motionless in the corner of the room. I knew it was one of the many things Newton did best, standing motionless for long periods of time. Although, I had no idea just how he did it.

'I hope you appreciate, the fact that Holt is one of the few men on site who I allow to fly in fly out rather than keeping him on the site all the time. He has an apartment here in Texas, and he spends every second weekend here until he gets his leave to go home every eight weeks. He's a sharp business man not many men ask for leave every eight weeks, most go with the normal three weeks leave every three months. We only just noticed the clause he added when we looked over his contract again so we could change it to get him living in Texas every weekend. I hope you're making the most of his time here?' Daddy paused and asked his voice slightly quieter now. He briefly waited, and I felt his eye rest heavily on me. I didn't reply. I felt he had ruined my chances with Holt, but I kept my mouth shut.

'Anyway, we've spoken to his neighbors, and they gave our P.I. a lot of information. How much is true I don't know. But one thread that seems to come up over and over is the fact that Marnie Visser is not happily married to Holt, no matter what the fuck he says. None of the neighbors like Holt, they put up with him because they like his wife, but apparently, he is arrogant, rude and moody. Is this the man you want to spend your life with?' I was so busy listening it took me moment to realize there was a question in there directed at me.

'Yes, Daddy, it is,' I said completely unfazed by anything I was hearing against Holt. It was Newton who continued, it was rare for him to speak especially in Daddy's presence.

'Holt Visser lives in a relatively up market and affluent area of British Columbia, Canada. He owns outright his house and the valuation came in at approximately six million dollars. He has no children and doesn't want any.' I heard what Newton was saying but chose not to, and he continued, 'He has a big family in Toronto, that he hardly sees, but he speaks to his mom often. His dad passed away several years ago. Both his parents are Dutch and arrived here shortly after they were married. He believes he loves his wife, and she loves him. Apparently, he is a lazy man, and she does everything for him. He does nothing for her and seldom even calls her when he's away…' Daddy interrupted, 'Thanks to Newton we know all this and also know we can buy Holt from her if we offer her enough money. Which she will receive in two installments, one when she agrees to sign the divorce papers, and the other once the divorced is finalized.' Daddy paused, and then startled me by bellowing, 'You with me, gal – hell, I thought you'd at least show some excitement.'

'I am excited, Daddy – you and Newton have done a fine job. But what about Holt?'

'Wait until I finish telling you the plan. Firstly, you're flying to British Columbia this week to talk to Marnie Visser and make her an offer, she can't refuse. No more than twenty million, but I think you may get her for around seven, plus let her know she can keep the house… Happy wife, happy life.' I didn't hear anything beyond the fact that I am to fly to Canada and confront Holt's wife. I thought it would all be taken care of without my involvement. I was to go to this stranger's home who was married to the man I loved, and buy myself her husband – this was crazy. I could feel Daddy's eyes upon me, and I knew he was reading my mind.

'Now, my gal, you remember the first law of success in the Lynch Corporation?' I nodded that I did, but Daddy continued to repeat it to me anyway, as I knew he would,

'A desired outcome is achieved by the level of application.'

'Yes, Daddy, I remember.'

'Well, when you have a firm plan in place, it will be easier to avoid failure. Have a counter plan for every conceivable outcome, then you won't fail and failure will not be an option. Hell, I don't give a damn if you fail, he's your mother-fucker, and this is your life, but I've put a lot of my time and resources at your disposal so you can get what you want. And should you fail you SHALL marry Remington,' he concluded firmly, and I understood he meant it. If I failed I won't care anyway. I will concede to Daddy's suitor for me. I briefly remembered the flowers and realized they were from Remington. But I have no intention of failing. I nodded my agreement as I asked again the final and most obvious question,

'What about Holt?'

'I'll be handling that mother-fucker myself – and I'll enjoy doing so. Once this has been sorted, I shall get the best wedding planner in Texas, and we'll have ourselves the best ring dinger of a wedding this old town has ever seen. Your wedding shall be the social occasion of the year. Make no mistake; a Lynch wedding will not be forgotten easily for a very long time,' Daddy stopped briefly and thumped his fist hard on the desk. Whatever he was thinking, he seemed pleased with himself. He stopped pacing the floor, retreated around behind his desk, sat in his huge leather chair and turned away from me. Into the small crystal glass, he poured himself a dram of whisky from the bottle that stood on the silver tray. Newton nodded at me and discreetly left the room, closing the door silently behind him.

'Well, my gal, you gotta be happy with all I've done for you?' Daddy said, swiveling his chair around and facing me, a look of satisfaction on his face. I was, but I had a question, and it was one I knew might anger him,

'What happens if Holt doesn't agree?' I asked tentatively,

'Hell, my gal, no one and nothing is going to let that motherfucker turn me down. I'll make his life a living hell from here to eternity if he so much as suggests it. You leave him to me, my gal. I'm looking forward to the challenge.' I saw the spark blaze in blue eyes as they flashed into life, and I realized he would be enjoying every moment as he bends Holt's will to breaking point if he doesn't agree. Daddy was used to getting his own way, and he wasn't a man you say 'no' to.

'Daddy; do not call him a motherfucker, he maybe your son in law soon,' I instructed still trying to digest all he had told me.

'*Maybe*, my gal, you better fucking well mean *will be*. Hell, never doubt my ability at getting what I want, and I want an heir, and if this is how it must be done then what the hell. You always took the hard road, just like me. But you seem sure this is what you want, and you better not let me down on this.' He said coming around his desk and walking toward where I stood. His eyes focused completely on mine; he moved in two long strides and was in front of me at eye level. He was so close I could see the pupils in his blue eyes contract until they almost disappeared. He was challenging me, and I knew I must not show weakness. I stood and stared back.

'This is how to buy a husband.' He spoke triumphantly, never taking his eyes from mine.

As I was about to leave the room there was brief knock at the door. Cerise entered. I wondered why she was still around? This morning, she was dressed in tight fitting, low cut, deep pink dress, her red curly hair fell loose and bounced as she moved quickly into the room. Her heels clicked seductively on the marble floor at the entrance to Daddy's office. I noticed her makeup was perfection, complete with false lashes and shiny lip gloss. Daddy looked her up and down from head to toe and back again, as she entered, and I briefly saw annoyance flash across his face, until quickly it was replaced by something else, was it desire perhaps, because it surely couldn't be admiration! I nodded to her, turning briefly before leaving the room I saw his huge arms wrap themselves around her slender body as she moved forward into his embrace, and they kissed. Then I heard her speak to him softly, 'Good morning, Big Daddy.' she giggled in the voice of a little girl. Discreetly Newton moved forward and gently closed the door behind me. I could feel the vision pulling nausea from my stomach. As I passed Newton I asked, 'Why is Cerise always around?'

'It is Mr. Lyn's wish.' The big man simply replied as he stood guard outside the door. He never looked down at me, and he kept his eyes fixed straight ahead.

I headed back up the stairs to my rooms and wondered again, why Cerise was here in the house in the daytime? Apart from Daddy's money, I couldn't imagine what a girl like Cerise would see in an old man like my father. I knew she had no idea what she was dealing with. Had I liked her more? Although I had no reason not to like her, I would have talked with her and told her a few home truths about her Big Daddy. But something about her made my skin crawl. Was it because she was the first girl I'd seen around my father in a very long time? Or was it something deeper? Perhaps, a women's intuition?

Chapter 16
How to Buy a Husband

That night there was to be no deep dark void, and the familiar safety it offered me. I couldn't think of sleeping after all Daddy had arranged and told me. I needed to call Brook and Pan. Although on thinking of Pan, I decided to call Brook first. I wanted to talk to someone solid and focused and that would never be Pan. My mind was racing, and I gradually tried to calm it while I located my new cell. Brook's cell rang for some time, before her message came on. I asked her to call me. I thought of calling Pan, then again decided against it, but I knew I really needed to talk to someone. Pan answered almost immediately, 'Hi, Lyme.' She giggled her usual girly voice a whimsical sound in my ear,

'Guess what, Lyme, I am looking at bridesmaid dresses online. I want something stunning, over the top, gorgeous. I need a good social occasion I'm getting bored.' I was surprised by what she was doing, so I asked, not what I wanted to ask, but what I knew she wanted me to ask, 'Whose getting married, Pan?'

'Oh, Lyme, you need to use Madam Roderic too, she's just so wonderful I couldn't possibly survive without her.' She giggled,

'Pan, whose wedding are you going to?'

'Lyme, I'm going to be a bridesmaid. Madam just told me, it's not nearly a bride but almost.' She giggled again as I heard the computer clicking in front of her,

'Pan, whose wedding is it?'

'Lyme, it really is too exciting, it's not one wedding but two. I can hardly wait,' Pan said giggling.

I knew her mind was elsewhere, but I pushed on, 'Pan, who is getting married?' I asked again.

'Oh my god, this is gorgeous, it's Chanel, low back and scooped front, very flowing, and the color is to die for. It's only fifteen thousand. I think I shall get one in powder blue and the other in sunrise lemon, there, I've hit the button. It's mine, how divine. Don't you just love shopping online. These dresses are coming straight from the runways of Paris and Milan, and I can't wait.' Pan giggled with delight, and I wondered if I should ask again.

All thoughts of discussing my trip to Canada faded as I knew Pan would not be the one to talk to today. 'Pan, whose wedding are you going to be attending?'

'Oh, Lyme, I simply can't wait. I was just thinking why you could wear one dress, and I'll wear the other. I'm sure it can be let out a little, oh, how super, what a fabulous idea that is. Or perhaps, I'll just order the apricot one for you in a larger size, yes, I'll do it now.'

'Why would I want to wear the other dress, Pan?' I asked knowing I was getting nowhere. I could hear the computer keys clicking, and doubted if I would get an answer, so I waited.

Finally, she asked, 'What do you want to know, Lyme?' So again, I repeated the question, this time I knew she had heard me, but would she answer or was her mind elsewhere?

'Lyme, madam told me of two weddings, and I'm to be bridesmaid at both. It is almost as good as at being at my own wedding.'

'The other wedding is it one of your friends, that I don't know?' I asked thinking I knew most of her friends and feeling a little confused.

'Madam wasn't super clear on the second, but I'm sure the first one is Brook's, why she even said her name.' She giggled excitedly. Then added, 'Okay, I just ordered your dress, Lyme; I know you will love it. I can't wait to tell Brook,' Pan said giggling.

'Well, maybe you should wait a little perhaps, I bet she doesn't know she's to be married herself yet,' I replied trying to sound like the voice of reason.

'Yes, you're right. When she announces it, I'll surprise her by telling her we already have our dresses.' Pan giggled again.

'Who's is the other wedding, Pan?' I asked as I heard her cell beep with an incoming call.

'Why yours I think, Lyme, look I gotta go. Kisses.' And she was gone.

In a strange way she had given me confidence, and the answer I needed, if indeed the second wedding was to be mine. I wanted to call her back and ask more questions, but this was Pan, and I knew it would be just as stressful as that call had been. I lay on my huge bed and looked up at the ceiling seeing nothing. Many scenarios of tomorrow, and my meeting with Marnie went through my mind. I kept telling myself this was not a business meeting so it must be handled very carefully. But what would happen if she wouldn't even let me in or threw me out. Then, once she had seen my face, I would know her and she me.

It was in the early hours of the morning that I decided to approach Marnie without being me. I would make her an offer, and she would not know from whom it came. That way she wouldn't know my face. Then I decided she didn't even need to know there was another woman involved, just that Holt wanted a divorce, surely, she would be happy with that? Once I said his name, my mind couldn't keep him from my thoughts.

All the planning for tomorrow disappeared and Holt's handsome face floated before my eyes, it was so close I could almost touch him. Why hadn't he called? Why hadn't I heard from him? I fell into a deep fitful sleep where I was chasing Holt, and it was misty. I was running through ankle deep water, and he was always just out of reach. I yelled at him to stop and then woke myself. I sat up turned on the light; I felt the sweat on my face. The bed sheet was wrapped firmly around me, and it was also damp. Was it a dream, a vision or a nightmare? The room was light it was morning, when I looked at the time it was after eight. I heard a soft knock on the door. It slowly opened, and a huge bouquet of flowers entered the room followed by my maid.

'These just arrived for you, Miss Lyme, I thought I'd bring them straight up and ask what you want for breakfast. You haven't hardly touched breakfast the last five days.'

'I don't want breakfast just get my clothes out; my new pinstripe business suite, white blouse, and my gray pumps. Give me the card from the flowers and set them down on the bed.' I ordered my heart pounding out of my chest. Holt had remembered, he does love me. I felt like yelling, like jumping up and down on my bed like I did as a child when mommy promised us a day out together with Granny. But I didn't, instead I ripped open the card, the flowers where gorgeous all my favorites, lily's that smelled like heaven, roses, peonies and more. He must have asked someone what I liked. I pushed my nose deep into the blossoms and inhaled. Springtime encircled me. Then I tore the card from the holder. It took me a second to realized it was signed with Clive's name and not Holt's, surely there must be a mistake. Then I remembered the flowers he had sent me previously, and I knew there was no mistake. I held back the tears as I read the card. *To my petting zoo buddy, my tennis opponent and hopefully more. I miss you. You're not answering my calls. When can I see you again? Clive.* I tore the card into several pieces and flung it to the floor.

Time seemed to stand still as I sat in my bed. I know the maid spoke to me several times, but it was the phone ringing that finally bought me back to reality.

Apparently, the car had arrived and was waiting for me. My body felt heavy with disappointment as I slowly managed to climb out of bed. No shower, just a quick comb of my hair before I tied it up, and then I cleaned my teeth. I can put some makeup on in the plane. I felt listless as I dressed I barely checked my look in the mirror. Life was not fair – I loved Holt so much!

I relaxed slightly on Daddy's private jet as the hours fell away. I sat with my eyes closed, trying to steady my thoughts and focus on the task ahead. I couldn't fail for Daddy's sake but more for my own. Holt would be mine soon enough, and it was all up to me. As we headed over the mountains and the terrain changed beneath me, I felt a twinge of nervousness. We landed smoothly at YVR, and a limo and driver waited neatly on the tarmac for my exit. I had no luggage; just an expensive looking briefcase with papers; Newton had given me, along with many instructions, so I could get a signature. I also carried a small handbag. I hadn't yet put on makeup, but I knew I must do so now in the car. The driver told me it was a short drive to the address where he was instructed take me.

North West Marine drive, Point Gray, overlooked the ocean, and the many large mansions on the cliff side were discreetly tucked away behind high gates and tall trees. This was a different landscape, a different country. It was colder and greener and certainly lusher than Texas. Also, the trees were the tallest trees I'd ever seen. The ocean was a brownish blue, beyond the ocean the view extended to the mountains.

It wasn't long before we pulled into the driveway of a large home. It wasn't a mansion, but it was certainly more than your average house. Our way was blocked by two tall black wrought iron electric gates. The house sat some distance further back from the gates, tall and imposing. The driver sat in the front seat awaiting instruction. My mind had cleared since earlier that day, and I instructed him to reverse out of the drive and park down a side street, I would walk. I didn't want him to know what I was doing or what I would be saying.

Moments later, I was again in front of the gates only this time I was on foot. A small sign hung over the gate to the left it read; 'Holt's Haven' I knew I was at the right house, so I pressed the buzzer and waited for a voice, but nothing happened, so I pressed again, my nerves were now beginning to get the better of me. Nothing happened, just the occasional car passing on the street, the gentle breeze off the ocean and distance birdsong. But there was still no human voice asking me to enter. I pressed again and waited, moving from one leg to the other and then back again. I never thought, she wouldn't be home. It was mid-afternoon, where could she be? I couldn't stand here much longer. But I did. Then, as I turned to walk back to the limo, I saw a white BMW M5 approaching fast. It was moving too fast for me to run across the road to the other side safely, so I waited. Then, to my surprise, it slowed. It was a convertible hardtop M5, and I heard its powerful engine kick down as it reduced speed. Then it turned into the driveway.

All the ideas I had in my head, disappeared. I moved back toward the driveway as the car came to a fast stop, and the driver's window rolled down. I wasn't expecting to come to face with a willowy, attractive green-eyed woman with long curly red hair. Her smile was wide and revealed perfect white teeth.

'You must be the new Avon lady. I know I'm very late, so thank you for waiting. Come on in.' As she spoke the gate silently opened, and before I could answer she roared inside. The garage doors opened silently, and before I had walked up the drive, they had closed again along with the gate. This was not the image I had created in my mind at all, and I knew I should regroup before I entered her home. I was barely outside the black double doors when they were flung open, and she smiled again extending her hand, 'Marnie Visser, I'm so sorry again for keeping you waiting. You must have been outside for at least an hour. Come on in, I'll make tea.' She half pulled me inside as she shook my hand and pointed toward a beautifully decorated living area on the left off the entranceway. I turned to see her disappear down a hallway and out of sight. I stopped, and admired the house before I moved in to the large high ceiling elegant living room. I thought it reflected the lady perfectly. Sadly, I knew immediately I liked her. I felt as if I liked her very much. Minutes later, I settled in a large taupe leather armchair. I heard her heels click, and she moved swiftly toward me a huge tray in her hands. 'I need this also, been a busy day. Milk, sugar, cream?' she asked hurriedly.

'Just black, thank you.' I replied, it was the first time I had spoken.

'An American – but not exactly sure of the state, I can usually tell straight off, maybe Texas?' she said smiling and I nodded before she added

'I'm really good at this stuff.' She grinned again and set my cup on the coffee table in front of me, and offered me a shortbread. It was time I took the power back, but I did still like her. My plan would never work with her, she was too nice, neither would my back up plan.

'Mrs. Visser, please, let me introduced myself. I'm sorry to say I'm not your missing Avon lady. I'm Miss Harrington, and I'm here to offer you a divorce settlement on behalf of your husband.' I watched as many emotions played over her face, she sat slowly down and stared, until finally her composure returned.

'Call me, Marnie, please. Sorry, I'm just surprised. Holt said he would never divorce me, and he laughed each time I tried to discuss it. I cannot imagine what changed his mind, unless you're here to try and talk me out of getting a settlement. He has all my money, and that was the reason he married me in the first place. Forgive me, I'm talking too much, please, continue,' she said sipping her tea, her eyes never leaving mine. I took a long sip; I needed it; so far at least I knew I sounded professional.

'Holt, Mr. Visser wants a quick divorce, and he is prepared to listen to your settlement requirements.' I said taking her lead and hoping it wouldn't back fire on me, but I still liked her. I knew she was thinking and thinking hard, she was a smart lady, and I knew she had thought of this before, often.

Finally, she said. 'What I want is the house with everything in it, except his personal processions, of course. I would like the car and $5000 a month living expenses plus half of his retirement fund. And I don't think that's unreasonable.' She added quickly trying to talk me into it. I thought it was most reasonable, and I was surprised by her offer.

'I believe he will give you the house, car and possessions, but he would like a one-time monetary settlement of say…' I paused, hoping she would say something.

Finally, she added, 'I would like a million, but I know he can't afford that.' She was selling herself short. I hoped I wouldn't shock her.

'He is prepared to offer you twelve million if you sign the paper today. You shall get six million in your bank account now and another six after the divorce is complete,' I said, sounding more professional than I felt. I could feel myself shaking. Her mouth fell open, and she stared at me.

'Well, he must have got a very rich bitch pregnant or something,' she laughed a nervous laugh, and finally said,

'Sure, that will work for me. Can I have your business card?'

'I'm sorry, I forgot them I usually carry them in my briefcase, but I just got new ones printed, and I left them behind. I'll make sure one gets to you. I have the papers you need to sign here, if you would like to read them over before you sign,' I asked, just as I was feeling this was too easy.

She added, 'I think I should talk to Holt first, please, excuse me, if I quickly give him a call.' She got to her feet and went to the phone outside the door. I knew if he answered I was in trouble. I hardly breathed as I waited for the sound of her voice on the end of the phone. Finally, I heard her leave him a message and return to the room.

'He's not answering, he never does, especially when he sees it me,' she said sadly. I had the papers on the coffee table, and I was filling in the amounts and requirements in the places Newton marked. She began reading them over carefully. I said nothing and waited. Once she placed them back on the table I asked,

'Are you ready to sign now, Marnie? This is a good deal and a win, for you,' I said, sounding encouraging. I watched as she hesitated.

'Yes, I'll sign, but I'll need a copy for my lawyer to look over, if there's a problem I'll contact you. I also want to change the date of signature to Friday, that way you have time to deposit the money,' she said fully composed now, her mind working fast. I knew she was an intelligent, smart woman, and I admired her for it. I didn't know whether I should have agreed to her terms of changing the date, but I did, and she signed. As Daddy always said once the contract is signed say no more and leave. So that's just what I did. She escorted me to the door, we shook hands, and as we did, I noticed or rather felt we both had sweaty palms.

Moments later, I walked across the road to the limo, I turned at the sound of another car pulling into her driveway. I saw the small car had Avon written on the side, and I wondered if Marnie would feel like buying cosmetics after our brief meeting? Once inside my limo, we immediately glided from the curb. I wanted to scream with excitement. I patted my briefcase. I knew I was gripping it too tightly. Forty minutes later, I closed my eyes as the powerful jet left British Columbia and flew into the wide blue yonder and home. I still couldn't believe it.

I thought of Marnie Visser, she was a nice lady, and somehow, I didn't think she was too unhappy with the deal. I felt that somewhere deep inside she still loved Holt, in fact she probably loved him very much as she must if she had been putting up with him all these years. I wondered if I would be able to do the same? I was glad I'd offered her more than she needed, I somehow knew she deserved it. I felt she was a good person, and why shouldn't she have a good settlement and an easy divorce. Unlike me, she would have no trouble finding herself another husband. Although her methods, I'm sure, would not be as unorthodox as mine.

The blue sky stretched for miles as we broke through the clouds. I couldn't believe what just happened. It was almost too easy. I wanted to call Brook, but I thought this story needed to be told face to face. The smile on my face was huge I couldn't conceal it. My new life was beginning. I removed the contract Marnie had just signed, and read it over word by word.

I'd done it. I'd just bought myself a husband!

Chapter 17
Madam Roderic ~ 4

I reclined in the plush leather seat of Daddy's private jet as it wrapped me in comfort. Then my mind started to clear, and I really wondered what I had done. Should I have done it? Had I broken up a happy home? Did Holt really love her? And if so, could he ever turn that love on me? I wondered how Daddy had made out with Holt. I knew that no matter what Holt put in his path, Daddy would sweep it away with his usual heavy-handed determination and strength of will.

I wanted to tell the world that Holt was now mine, but I wasn't sure Brook would want to know until the deal was complete, and I felt Pan may laugh at me, so for some reason, I hesitated. I closed my eyes and thought of Holt as the plane moved swiftly homeward. I wondered what blackmail Daddy used to get Holt to agree to his terms.

My thoughts wondered to wedding dresses, romance, and how my life would be changing. I wanted Pan and Brook to be my bridesmaids and lots of flowers. I didn't know how Holt liked me to look, what perfume he preferred me to wear, or how he liked my hair, and just like that I realized I was marrying a stranger. After a wave of panic, the love I felt for him took hold and the warm feeling washed over me again. It was unusual for me to have any time to daydream, and I was enjoying it. Then, my cell began to vibrate.

'Lyme, where are you?' the girly voice said followed by a breathy giggle. It was Pan.

'On our plane headed home,' I replied.

'Where have you been? Anyway, it doesn't matter I'm here with Madam Roderick. Lyme, there are two weddings, and I can't decide what to wear. I wanted you to listen to Madam's words,' Pan instructed.

'Okay,' I replied feeling a tingle run down my spine how could this weird woman know I was getting married almost before I knew myself. Her deep masculine voice then came loudly on the line, and I put the phone on speaker, she had always creped me out. Her voice so close to my ear did not make me feel good.

'I am Madam Roderic, the famous mystic and teller of fortunes. I believe we are picking up on your future. I feel it is intertwined with that of Pan's. I see a huge wedding, but is it yours, I do not know? Although, Madam sees most things clearly, this she doesn't want to see, doesn't want to tell you that it is yours. Do you feel the power of Madam? Most do even over the phone, my vibrations are strong and clear.' Then her raspy deep voice which sounded the same all the time stopped, and waited, the only sound was Pan's giggling as she whispered 'Isn't she wonderful?'

I was about to reply when loudly Madam's voice came again on the line, 'Madam must have quiet, once you confuse the spirits, my connection is broken, please listen, and do not speak. Yes, here we are again at the wedding, there are two bridesmaids, and yes, Ms. Pan, I see you in a deep cerise pink, and the other bridesmaid a tall girl with long, dark hair, a happy spirit whose life is changing for the better, wears the same dress in a deep purple.'

'Oh, goody, now I know what to wear – can you tell me the designer, Madam, oh, please, try,' Pan said clapping her hands together with delight as she giggled. 'I must not be interrupted. Madam visions fade, and spirit become confused. You ask first for Madam to speak to your friend, and tell her what I see then you interrupt and ask again for fashion advise. What is it you want to know?'

'Sorry madam, I want you to read for Lyme because Lyme, I think this is about you,' she said to me and giggled. I didn't respond, I really wanted to cut the connection, but I knew to do so would only anger Madam Roderic, so I said nothing and waited on the line.

'Your friend remains silent she understands the ways of spirit. They get restless with confusion and interruption. Please stay quiet. Yes, I see again this wedding. The groom is tall, and blond very handsome but not so nice. The bride is shorter and dark haired, she loves him very much, but sadly I see no love in his soul. She is nothing to him. Now, I can see into their marriage, as they are two months later. Opulent setting, clear aqua water, a large swimming pool, perhaps. Another lady is sitting close to the tall blond man, intimately close, their knees and thighs touching. They are aware of only each other, there is no love, but a great lust in their souls. You, the girl on the phone is watching, you have been secretly watching for some time, they cannot see you they are not aware of anything but the closeness of the other; and still you watch, you are still in love and not understanding what you see. I sense a new life, it is stirring within you, and it is so new it remains your secret at this time. I see creation not from your husband maybe from a test tube. This is not how it should be; this is wrong.' Madam's voice went deeper and louder at the last words, and I thought she was finished. Pan didn't speak, so I stayed silent also, guessing Pan could see she was still in her trance. Then she continued, 'But slowly what they share and what you don't share with this man become clear. Behind you, a broad shouldered, powerful man quietly approaches. I feel his anger; he is a man to be feared. It is my warning that you proceed with caution. Oh no, oh no, no, please. There is a gun, it appears from nowhere. I feel it, I feel the pain, there are two shots and blood....' I can hear Madam collapse on the floor.

'Madam, wake up, it is not the time for a nap,' Pan says giggling, then she speaks to me, 'Lyme, I told you she was good, so entertaining, but always she stops at the best part. She has told me this story before, but she never tells me the ending so annoying. I can see it happening before she stops. First, she sweats, so unladylike and then her eyes kinda roll back. It's always at the best part. Don't you love her, Lyme? But she constantly wants to nap, most frustrating.'

'Sure, Pan, she's great,' I responded weakly, still shocked at what I'd heard, and also shocked at Pan's shallowness when she can't recognize that Madam has probably fainted from exhaustion. I could imagine Madam Roderic's body crumpled on the floor at Pan's feet, sweating profusely, while Pan continuing to berate her.

'So, now I know what to wear at the wedding, it must be yours, Lyme. When were you going to tell me?' Pan said giggling as she instructed her maid to bring Madam Roderic some water.

'Pan, I'll talk to you later we are about to land, gotta go.' I said relieved to have a reason to break the connection. Madam Roderic was a scary woman, but her words chilled me to the bone. However, I didn't really believe in mystics or Madam Roderic, or did I? This thought didn't last long as I spotted again the black SUV that I'd previously seen following me. It sat discreetly under the trees a short distance from the doors I was exiting. It may not have been the same vehicle, I may have been mistaken, but Granny Harry had always told me to listen to my gut and intuition, and my intuition told me it would follow us. And it did.

Chapter 18
The Soft Power of Conrad Lynch

While Lyme was in Vancouver visiting Marnie Visser, Conrad Lynch was not idle. In his world, things moved fast, and he was used to getting what he wanted, immediately. He expected complete success in all things, but if it took a little longer he would wait – never doubting he would achieve his desired outcome in the end.

Newton was due to arrive any minute, and he was escorting a reluctant, Holt Visser. He knew the man was arrogant, spoilt and reasonably intelligent. He also knew he would put up a fight; in fact, he was counting on it. Overcoming conflict made the victory all the sweeter.

A discrete knock on the door announced his arrival. Newton followed close behind, holding Holt's arms tightly behind his back; apparently Holt had not succumbed to the trip quietly.

'Just who the hell do you think you are? Dragging me out of the boardroom in front of everyone. You may own the company, but I see no reason why you should treat me like this, or why I should be summoned to your home. I also demand you return my cell phone, fucking immediately! I demand an explanation, now. Oh, yes, and by the way I quit, and I'll see you in court.' Newton had untied his hands and moved quietly in front of the door. He stood like a statue, eyes focused directly ahead at nothing, hands clasped behind his back with his feet slightly apart. Perhaps, Holt assumed Newton had left the room, or assumed he was standing anywhere but in front of the door. Holt's icy blue eyes hardly left those of Conrad's when he leapt from the chair; his tall frame and uncoordinated limbs knocked over the wrought iron and glass coffee table and it fell with a clatter to the floor, the glass remained intact.

Conrad stayed where he was standing behind his desk. Newton didn't move, his eyes never even blinked at the loud sound in the room. He continued blocking the door. Holt took several large steps toward the door and then seemed to charge directly for it. Had he not seen Newton? He crashed heavily into the solid man, his eyes blazing and fists swinging. Newton ducked slightly to avoid being hit in the jaw, and before he came up, he had Holt's wrists in a firm grip. Holding him tightly as he continued to fight for his freedom, he escorted or half dragged the younger man back to his chair.

'I suggest you sit quietly and show Mr. Lyn some respect. He requires your full attention,' Newton responded, his voice quiet and calm for a man of his size. He was almost a head shorter than Holt, but still stood over six feet tall; beneath his clothes, he was a solid mass of muscle and square bulky shoulders. He was a fighting machine, and he recognized Holt from the first, as no match.

'You've blackmailed me you fucking bastards, let me go, now,' he screamed, his face purple and contorted with rage, his eyes wild as he frantically searched his pockets for his cell phone. Upon remembering, it had already been taken from him, he grabbed the cell phone on Conrad's desk, he began urgently moving his fingers over the screen. Newton quietly moved up behind him and in one short motion took the cell phone from his hand. Holt roared out of the chair again and faced Newton square on. Newton locked eyes with his opponent as a small sigh escaped his lips. Conrad recognized the sound as a sign Newton was getting annoyed, and he was finding the situation boring. A slight smile played on Conrad's lips as he turned toward the small table in front of the window beside his desk. He reached for the jet-black glass bottle of Scotch and into a fine lead cut crystal glass, he slowly poured himself a dram.

'Sit down, Mr. Visser, and listen to what Mr. Lyn has to say. He prefers to have his guest's full attention when he speaks, and he is used to doing so,' Newton finished. Conrad stood with his back toward the two men; he was looking out the window and again a small smile played on his lips. Newton was a man of few words, and Conrad knew it annoyed him when he had to speak at all, he preferred to communicate in another ways, ways that caused pain. Conrad had instructed Newton to make sure Holt remained undamaged. Newton always obeyed his boss, but Holt Visser was beginning to annoy him.

Conrad heard no sound, no scuffle, but when he turned he saw Holt again in his chair only this time he was suitable restrained. His wrists were bound with plastic straps to the arms of the heavy Mahanoy chair, and his face was contorted and purple with rage. Conrad was enjoying the battle much more than he thought he would. With deliberate slowness, he savored the last of the scotch before he slowly swallowed and replaced the crystal glass onto the small table. He moved around the desk his blue eyes now firmly focused on Holt. Conrad appeared calm and in control.

'Welcome to my home, Holt, so glad you could join me at short notice. I would offer you refreshments, but you appear to be rather tied up at present,' Conrad briefly paused as Holt continued to thrash around in the chair. The heavy chair left the ground every few seconds as Holt tried to stand, then it thudded to the floor again as Holt collapsed into it. Conrad's eyes flicked a look at Newton his comment was entirely for his benefit. Newton seldom smiled, but a small smile now touched his top lip, then his reverted to his former stance. Conrad continued, 'I see from your behavior we cannot talk as adults.'

'You, rotten motherfucking bastard, let me go. I'll drag you through the courts with this, for years, and the press will be all over it – everyone hates you. I'll sue you for every cent you've got. No one has any respect for you, you're a fat, old rich man...' Holt sucked in the rest of his words when he saw Newton directly in front of him, his fist was raised, he was ready to strike.

He quietly said to Holt, 'Be respectful to Mr. Lyn.' Then he lowered his fist and moved silently back in front of the door.

'I do believe you've annoyed Newton. It takes a bit to annoy Newton. But, Holt, I for one would not want to be around when Newton gets annoyed. Do you need a moment to get yourself composed?' Conrad's words hung in the air as Holt gradually became still, his breathing slowed, and he knew there was no escape.

Finally, Holt spoke, 'Untie me, and I'll listen, but whatever you want I won't agree, and I'll see you in court.'

'I doubt that, we shall never meet in court and you will agree to what I am about to suggest. This is not a business meeting. I will untie you when you can act like a man, and not a rabid dog.'

'How dare you, you…' Holt's words were again cut short with the appearance of Newton directly in front of him.

'Should you want to be untied I can do so if you can act like a man. All relationships are built on trust, Holt, and I hope ours will be also.' This time Holt spat on the carpet, in a flash Newton slapped him on the side of the face. The large gold ring Newton wore connected, and a small cut broke his skin and blood flowed. Newton knew he was supposed to keep Holt unharmed, but apart from a brief glance from his employer, nothing further was said. The air hung heavy as everyone waited for Holt to again compose himself. Conrad was an impatient man, and he had been swallowing his impatience with Holt like foul tasting bile.

Conrad was about to speak when Holt quietly said, 'Untie me – I shall listen,' Newton slowly removed the restraints as Holt rubbed his wrists and wiped the blood from the side of his face with the back of his hand. Newton gave him a small cotton towel.

'Glad you can join us, Holt,' Conrad moved around from behind his desk. He was now standing just out of reach of the man in the chair. Newton presented Holt with a steaming mug of coffee, and for a moment Conrad thought Holt would knock it from his hand, but after he stared at him for a few seconds he took the mug, and gulped the hot liquid.

'What I'm about to offer you is a onetime offer, and it needs to commence immediately,' Conrad let the words hang in the air, and he could tell by the look on Holt's face, he was not listening, but instead he was considering how to escape.

'You have already taken up too much of my time, now I shall get right to the point. My daughter, Lyme, is – as you may know – is in love with you. Although I cannot imagine why, probably another poor choice…'

'Who?' Holt added, and by the look in his eyes Conrad really believed he had no idea who they were talking about. Conrad grabbed her photo from his book shelf and handed it to Holt. He stared at it for a sometime before he spoke.

'Oh, yes, the girl on the plane, dowdy, not my type. What about her? If she's in trouble it's not my fault,' Holt added, defensively.

'If she were in trouble, you would have put a ring on her finger by now, or the alternative would have happened to you,' Conrad added his eyes firmly focused on the younger man in the chair.

'Not, me, I'm a happily married man. I'll never put another ring on any other woman's finger than my wife, whom I love very much,' Holt added triumphantly. He was looking at Conrad as he noticed the small smile appear on his lips,

'Well, let me be the first to congratulate you on your divorce, Holt.'

'Are you fucking crazy, what is this some kind of a scam, a joke perhaps?' Newton retrieved his cell from high up on the book shelf, and handed it to Holt as Conrad continued, 'Probably, a text message or email by now, why don't you check?' Holt immediately noticed over twenty new messages, and ten texts along with several new emails. Conrad watched as his face crumpled, and he looked like he was about to cry. He flicked through several more text messages as he composed himself, however he was clearly shocked by what he read.

All he said was, 'What the hell. What's happening? How could you?' Newton removed his cell, and Conrad ignored his questions and continued on, 'So, this is my proposal. You will marry my daughter. If you wish to keep working I shall make you one of my directors. Should you choose not to work and spend more time with Lyme, you shall still receive one million dollars a year as your annual salary and your credit cards shall be paid up to a set amount each month…' Conrad was still talking when Holt leapt from his seat and lunged at him, they both fell backwards, missing the hard side of Conrad's desk by inches. Newton had Holt restrained and tied to the chair as helped his boss to his feet.

'You, fucking bastard,' he screamed as Newton again moved closer and stared down on him just wanting an excuse to inflict pain.

'Keep your mouth clean when you talk to my boss, Mr. Visser, or I have ways of cleaning it you may not like. So, let's get back to my proposal, was the salary not to your liking?'

'Since when do you think you can blackmail me into marrying your ugly daughter?'

'I don't think I can, I know I can, and blackmail is such a harsh word. However, call it what you like, it can be blackmail if you prefer, but it will happen and you will stay with her for a few years at least. In the meantime, you can live a life of pure luxury, and save every cent of your salary if you chose to do so. This is one hell of a deal; you will be a rich man.'

'I thought, I was happily married, when I find out what you've done to my wife, I swear I'll kill you,' Holt bellowed but remained restrained in his chair.

'We did nothing to your wife other than relieved her of a worthless loveless man who she has wanted to rid herself of for some time. I shall ensure you treat my daughter kinder than you have your wife. You shall be watched, Holt, I want only the best for her. I believed this whole charade is a mistake, but Lyme appears to be deeply in love with you, and my little girl deserves to get everything her heart desires,' Conrad finished almost in a whisper as he moved closer to Holt, and was now just inches from his face. Both men held their stare.

Until Holt's eyes broke away, and he added, 'How much is the signing bonus?'

Conrad laughed as he answered,

'Yes, so we see eye to eye at last. I see you have quickly forgotten the love you say you have for your wife. How fast the memory fades.' Conrad paused as he saw the anger again flicker across Holt's face, then he continued, 'Indeed, money talks, and I think nothing the less of you for asking. I would have done the same myself.'

'Well... what is it?' Holt asked, as Conrad appeared to consider this for a few minutes,

'How does three million sound, half when you sign your divorce papers, and the rest once the prenuptial is signed?'

'Three million, you gotta be fucking joking. Twenty million, and I shall take it in two installments if that is what you want.'

Conrad laughed in Holt's face, 'You are not worth half of that, you are already making a large salary, so take the three million, it is a gift and more than you deserve. In fact, in good faith, I shall make it five.'

'And I shall settle for nothing less than fifteen million.'

'You, Holt, are not in a position to barter with me.'

'I am in every position to barter with you and win. I have something you want, so all we need to do is agree on a settlement for this crazy scheme of yours to happen.'

'No, that is where you're wrong. You shall agree to my offer, and we move forward... otherwise.'

'Otherwise, what?' Holt challenged sarcastically, again trying to get free. Conrad was enjoying the moment. The time before the kill where he won the game was always the sweetest time of all. He was negotiating, and he had done so for many years for many different assets, and with many different types of people, but the common denominator with all of them was basically the same; money talks. Holt meant nothing to him, but his daughter did. If it weren't for Lyme, he would have walked away from this creep. He didn't like him, and he certainly didn't trust him. In fact, the thought of Holt walking around his home was physically nauseating; but he would address that issue later.

'Otherwise, you shall simply have no life, no employment, and no money.'

'So just how do you think you'll achieve that?' Holt asked, arrogance dripping from every word.

'I don't think I shall achieve it. I have already achieved it. It has happened.'

'How?' Holt asked not quite so confident now, but not backing down either.

'Your wife is divorcing you. I have frozen your bank accounts until you sign the divorce papers otherwise your wife receives everything. And just to be certain she goes ahead with the divorce we have sent her copies of these photos. Just a few of your late-night liaisons, I assume?' Newton handed him a pile of large glossy photos each one showed him in a compromising position with yet another beautiful blonde woman.

Holt was visibly shaken as Newton flipped through the photos, 'Where? How?'

'Neither of these questions matters. All that matters is, that this ceases once you marry my daughter.'

'Shall I continue telling you how your life will end should you not agree to my terms? Oh, and by the way a copy of these photos has been sent to every one of these women's husbands who are married. I notice your preference is for married woman, safer perhaps, or so you think.'

'You, bastard,' Holt yelled as his chair again lifting off the floor as he tried to free himself from his restraints.

'Language please,' Newton said calmly, cracking his knuckles with anticipation, 'May I suggest you decide on the option not to work for my company. Otherwise, you may be a sitting target for a jealous husband or two, some of these woman have high profile husbands, and I even know a couple of them myself, they can turn nasty real easy. You need protection, Holt, and as your father-in-law I shall, of course, provide it. Your secrets are safe from Lyme you can have a clean start, and this time play by the rules. If you don't, you won't live long enough to see tomorrow. Newton is an expert at making people disappear,' Conrad concluded with a smile. The pupils of his eyes were now mere points of black in his blazing blue eyes. Holt was heavily in thought.

'Okay, maybe, you have me, maybe, you don't. It will depend on the deal we cut,' Holt said confidently, too confidently for Conrad's liking. Either this man was a fool, had a trick or two up his sleeve, or he was as calculating as Conrad and that was a scary thought indeed.

'I thought we had, as you say, already cut a deal?'

'Three million as a signing bonus is laughable and is not a deal, it is not even pocket change; I want twenty or I'm out.'

'You are not in a position to just walk away, or hadn't you noticed? And for the record you will be dead before you receive twenty million from me.' Conrad added his voice slightly louder now. He waited, 'My last offer is fifteen and no prenup.'

'Go to hell. I do not barter with the likes of you or any man. There will be a prenup, and we shall agree on ten million, half when you sign the divorce papers, and the remainder after the prenup and marriage are complete. You will receive a salary of one million a year plus a moderate expense account. I am being more generous than you deserve, or than I should be. Your scum and the prenup will make sure you get nothing further.'

'Fifteen million or nothing, and I walk.'

'So, you are a fool, Holt. The only way you will be walking out of here is when you sign the papers.' Conrad watched as Holt again struggled to escape. Conrad was not staying around to argue with this man any longer.

'I shall leave you with Newton to consider your future, when you are ready Newton, will give you the necessary papers to sign, tell you the rules which you are to obey, and escort you to your room, a pleasure doing business with you.' Conrad turned toward the door and never looked at Holt again, although he knew Holt spat at his feet as he passed. He remained calm while inside he was boiling over with hatred for the man who would soon be his son-in-law.

Once he closed the heavy doors and had taken a few steps into the foyer, he stopped, stood still, closed his eyes and took several deep long breathes, he knew this helped him to steady his mind and slow the anger that had built up inside. As a younger man he used his anger as a tool, it was easy, he always found something to be angry about, and he liked seeing the fear in people's eyes; he realized they never knew what his mood would be or how to take him, so before he even spoke, he had their attention. He they would probably agree to whatever he wanted to keep him from attacking them.

As time went by and his fortune grew he used blackmail more and more, he had the resources to find out everyone's dirty little secrets, and they paid off, big time. The down side of blackmail, and Conrad knew there was always a down side, was that he had to keep his nose clean as everyone wanted to bring him down, he used discretion in many things and up until now his record was spotless. That is until the flame haired Cerise had entered in his life. He didn't love her, but she looked good on his arm. He no longer needed to call on Amber Buxton or Lyme to accompany him to important functions, and part of him was relieved about that. He knew Lyme needed to mix with people her age if she was ever to find a husband. That is until now. Now he had Cerise. She seems to genuinely to care for him or at least what he was able to provide her with. He was a generous man, and even though she had moved into the mansion a month ago, she was not intruding on his life, once she did, she would have to go.

Cerise lingered in his mind as he briefly thought of Holt, and shuddered at the thought of this man being the father to his grandchildren. Cerise was around thirty-two years old and had hinted several times that she would like to get married and have a family. At first, Conrad had been appalled by the thought, and his mind had immediately seen the beautiful face of the woman he knew to be the love of his life, Lyme's mother, Jennifer Harrington-Lynch.

Just the thought of his Jenny, melted away the years and he could clearly see her soft loving eyes gazing into his, the touch of her silky skin against his, the way her sensuous lips caressed his as they kissed, her slim perfect body; he must stop these thoughts she was gone, but his heart still ached. The worst time was at night because she was always there, always with him, and when her face drifted into his thoughts he couldn't sleep, he ached so badly. It was an ache that reached way down into his soul. She filled his heart; she held his heart, and he must keep her locked away in there forever. But as he often did now, he pushed his thoughts away lovingly deep down inside.

This time, for the first time, he began thinking of having a child with Cerise, this thought was a new one and had been gradually materializing from the depths of his mind. After his meeting with Holt, the thought of Cerise bearing his child seemed more appealing, however marrying her he couldn't yet come to terms with. But his thinking had come a full three-sixty degrees on Cerise.

The sound of movement in his study brought him immediately back to the present and with several long strides, he was at the staircase and heading up to his suite of rooms to get changed before he flew out to inspect one of his mine sites. He was already late; the meeting with Holt had taken much longer than he'd anticipated. He hoped Newton wouldn't be too much longer with Holt. Holt's face haunted his thoughts. The thing that haunted him most was the anger in Holt, the anger without fear. He understood anger, it was his friend, he knew and used it well. Holt was an interesting blend of emotions, and Conrad knew it was not a good blend, for a future son-in-law. Conrad did not have full control of Holt. He was certainly a loose cannon and a danger. Conrad was glad he would no longer be working in his company; he had too many bad character traits that Conrad recognized and didn't trust. A smile touched his lips; he knew, for now the battle continued…

Chapter 19
Holt Visser

Holt sat in the large overstuffed leather armchair. The sun brightened the deep colors of the room as it streamed brightly through the floor length windows. The windows overlooked the driveway and vast manicured gardens and lawns beyond.

Holt didn't know what was happening, or how this had happened. This morning it was just another workday, and now he was sitting here in this huge room, surrounded by his suitcases, nursing several bruises on his face. He had tried to call Marnie over and over, but each time his call went to voicemail, and he hadn't yet spoken to her. He had just received a message from her telling him to stop calling. But why would he? He loved her, she was his wife. Why had she consented to divorcing him so suddenly, and how did Conrad Lynch know? Holt swallowed hard at the thought of Conrad, he detested the man; he was forceful, mean and arrogant.

Holt's mind raced in circles as he tried to grasp the situation. But it proved hopeless; his thoughts were too muddled and mixed together. He didn't understand any of this, and it was all over a girl he'd met on a plane, and he couldn't even remember what she looked like. He assumed it was the same girl who had taken him to dinner several times, but of that he wasn't sure. There were so many girls; none of them meant anything to him. He only had their company because Marnie didn't like traveling with him, and he needed a warm body comforting him in his bed, so he was maybe, able to sleep at night and forget his demons. He didn't even enjoy the sex. He knew they expected it, but it was not what he wanted, or needed. Surely, Marnie understood? Why wouldn't she talk to him?

To begin with he had thought Conrad's offer was some kind of a joke until Newton slapped him. Even then, he still thought it a joke. What kind of father would pay someone to marry their daughter? It was sick, Conrad was sick. He had to escape, and get to Marnie or at least talk to her. Why wasn't she taking his calls? Was she really divorcing him? He sat where he was, his mind in turmoil as the anger inside gradually abated.

Until finally his mind turned to Lyme, weird name, he thought. He didn't love the girl she wasn't even his type; all he had done was accept a free meal, and now look where he was. He was about to marry the girl, a complete stranger. He didn't love her, and he never would. He wasn't even sure who she was, but she must be the girl from the plane. If so, he wasn't attracted to her she wasn't his type. The thought of her in his bed was frightening. No one could make him make love to her. He wouldn't do it, not ever. That was one aspect of his life Conrad Lynch couldn't control. But the money was good, maybe he'd stay for a couple of years, and then take the money, and find Marnie, yes that's what he'd do. But he needed to talk to her, his wife, she must know of his plan. He assumed she was still his wife? He had no idea how these things worked. He was still deep in thought when a soft knock came from the door. Probably, the maid wanting to unpack his things, about time!

'Come in,' he called expecting to see a young girl in uniform appear around the door.

'I'm Cerise Warren,' a seductive voice cooed. Holt almost fell out of his chair as a tall, slim woman with long, curly flame, red hair, sparkling eyes, full dewy rosebud lips, and a body to make angels weep, sauntered into the room. She wore a clinging green dress that left nothing to the imagination, high silver pumps and exotic perfume.

'Thought I'd introduce myself, you see everyone's out, so it's just you and me in this huge mansion. Didn't want you to feel neglected and lonely, all by yourself. I was hoping for some time alone with you handsome, so we can get to know each other, better.'

'Who are you?' Holt asked again slowly raising from his chair. He was hoping he had heard wrong, and this was actually Lyme Harrington-Lynch. If it was, maybe hell had just turned to heaven.

'Cerise Warren, I'm Big Daddy's live in lover, and I have a feeling that my dull, boring life here has just got a whole lot more interesting…'

Chapter 20
Engaged at Last

Within a week the engagement party was organized. Daddy had booked the very best and most expensive restaurant in town, and so far over two hundred guests had RSVP they were attending.

I had only seen Holt several times, although I knew he was here in the mansion and sleeping in the next room, although he kept the adjoining door locked, because I tried it often. I ached for him at night knowing he was so close, but didn't want me, and I often wondered just how I would get pregnant if he really didn't want anything to do with me. Last night I heard what I thought were lustful noises coming from his room late at night, although I knew that couldn't be so. Newton had been watching Holt like a hawk, and this alone made me understand that Holt was being a very reluctant bridegroom indeed.

On the night of our engagement party, I was nervous, I had spent the whole day getting pampered, massaged, primed and, painted and never before had I allowed so much attention to be performed on me. Fox hovered most of the time supervising, although I was glad she was there. I had even agreed to have my hair lightened a few shades, and some more blonde highlights to be placed around my face. Finally, I was almost ready, and I was very pleased with the result once I looked in the mirror, although who looked back at me I didn't know. It felt like me, but my reflection belonged to someone else. I was to wear a pale coffee colored sheer off the shoulder lace dress. It clung to my body to perfection. Pan had asked Madam Roderic what I should wear, and Pan had eagerly found the dress and sent it over, she was in her element. Bronze Jimmy Choos with a five-inch glass heel, I couldn't manage more, completed the look.

I now knew what Cinderella felt like, and I was ready for the ball. This would be a huge social event. Daddy would have it no other way. I knew a lot of Daddy's employees would be attending, but only Amber and Pradbury would be invited to the house for cocktails and drive with us to the restaurant. A soft knock announced the maid, and I assumed she would be taking me to Holt, so we could go downstairs together. But instead, she came in with a small bouquet of flowers, they were all blue forget me nots, and they had a note attached. I assumed they were from the man Daddy picked out as my suitor, Remington someone or other. But to my surprise they were from Clive Broadbench, the guy who liked tennis, and the one who scooped me up into his arms. I am looking forward to seeing my friends, Vaugh and Alvin, who must have told Clive I was to be married. His note was simply, unlike Clive it had no sugar coating it said: *Game, set and match, sorry, I wasn't the winner, congrats, Clive.*

I really had liked Clive, and his quirky ways, especially his zest for life, and his high energy, maybe I should have done as my mother, and Granny had suggested and married a guy who loved me more than I loved him. But I certainly wasn't doing that now, was I? Finally, the maid told me that Holt wished to see me in his room. My heart skipped, and I almost ran to him, however before I left my room, I tried again the adjoining door and was saddened to find it remained locked. I was seeing Holt, that's all that mattered. I needed to take several deep breaths and steady my nerves before entering his room.

'So, you're ready, don't like the color, but I guess it's the best you can do', he drawled.

'What color would you prefer I wear, Holt?' I asked delighted he had noticed and was taking an interest in my appearance at last.

'Why the hell ask me, like I care?' I almost cried at his words. He was sitting on his settee in his tux looking more handsome than ever. But instead of looking at me with admiration in his eyes, he was looking at the floor. The silence stretched on as I composed myself slightly and held in the tears.

Finally, I asked, 'Are you ready to go downstairs?'

'If I was I would have told you,' he replied arrogantly.

'I know most everyone has arrived, so maybe we should go down.'

'They can wait until I'm ready.'

'Okay, I guess I'll see you down there,' I said knowing his mood was dark as it so often was,

'Newton instructed me we had to stay together tonight, and you were to do most of the talking, seeing you're in love, and I'm not.'

'Yeah, maybe that's best,' I said trying not to annoy him further.

'Oh here, you better wear this.' Holt threw a small red velvet box at me, it said Tiffany, and I guessed he had purchased a present for me. Before I opened it, I remembered the last time he had purchased something for me, it was the fat plastic girl, and he had said she reminded him of me.

'Well open it, it's not like I'm going to put it on your finger. It's not like I even purchased it, hope it fits cause if it falls off I won't be getting you another.' I slowly opened the box and staring up at me was a huge solitaire diamond, it must have been around ten carats at the very least. It was set in a thin diamond encrusted band, and when I placed it on my finger it dazzled me. I wanted to hug Holt it was so beautiful, but he sat looking at the carpet, and not at me.

'Lyme, where are you?'

It was Brook, and I called to her telling her where I was. Soon Brook and Morris moved as one in to the room, they were joined at the hip as they had been since the start. I still wasn't used to seeing Brook so openly affectionate with someone, nor was I used to seeing her hold hands and cuddle so obviously. Once the prang of jealousy passed for what they had, and I didn't, I was genuinely pleased to see them. I knew Holt liked Morris and tolerated Brook.

'Wow, that's a dazzler, I almost need sunglasses,' Morris explained shielding his eyes from the mock brilliance of the huge stone.

'Yeah, it's gorgeous, Lyme, makes mine look rather small,' Brook said holding out her hand. She wore a five carat pink princess cut diamond, surrounded on each side by two large white diamonds.

'Darling, if you want a larger stone...?' Morris asked feigning hurt.

'No, I couldn't love it more. Just the fact you chose it all by yourself, makes it beyond special,' Brook said, and they looked deeply into each other's eyes and kissed.

'Okay, let's go,' Holt said springing unexpectedly to his feet and walking toward the door, then he added, 'Yeah, good choice, Morris, not too big and ostentatious.' Brook, Morris, and I exchanged looks and followed Holt out the door. His long legs took the stairs two at a time, and he waited impatiently for us at the bottom of the large staircase. Laughter and talking greeted our ears as we entered the large room we often used as a reception room. It was long and had floor to ceiling windows on both sides of the room. It looked over the circular driveway and fountain in the front and out the back to manicured gardens. There was around forty people present most of them I knew. Padbury Prentice, and his wife were the first to congratulate us, giving me a kiss and hug and Holt a handshake. Then Vaughn rushed over followed by Pan, who looked spectacular and immediately got Holt's attention. He gave her a tight hug and held her close just a little too long; again, I noticed the look that Morris and Brook gave me.

Amber Buxton was next, followed by Dr. Dan Bloussier, but I called him Dr. Dan and had always done so. I had known him forever, he was a personal friend of Granny Harry and my mother's and had been my personal physician all my life, but not Daddy's. Lastly, Daddy and Cerise, whom I must reluctantly say looked spectacular in a cobalt blue off the shoulder Chanel sheath; she held tightly to Daddy's arm. She also hugged Holt and I, briefly thought the hug seemed familiar, I wondered if Daddy noticed also? But then, I remembered he missed nothing, ever, that's one of the reasons he got to be where he was today.

All to soon we were off to the restaurant where a red carpet had been laid out for our arrival. The press hovered while crowds of onlookers and security guards jostled for space at the edge of the red carpet reducing our walking space to the restaurant entrance. I felt like royalty, and I knew everyone else did also, it was just the way Daddy liked it. The attention, the crowds, the press, all fitted Daddy's personality to a tee only. I now noticed how all the attention also suited Cerise as well. The evening flew by, and on occasions Holt was by my side, at those time the world seemed to fade away, just his nearness. When one of the photographers asked Holt to pose with his arm around me, I thought I should faint. His touch electrified me, and his nearness made my heart beat out of my chest. I knew he'd needed several stiff drinks to let down some of his walls in order to even touch me, but I didn't care, having him near was worth it all.

Much of the talk was now focused on Brook, and Morris's upcoming wedding it was to be the following weekend and apart from talking of my wedding in three weeks, Pan could talk of little else. She had organized all the dresses for both weddings, and my wedding dress was a dream. The evening passed in a whirl of laughter, fun, and friends, and even though I seldom saw Holt, I was happy just knowing he was there. He played his part as well as you could expect for him, although we had no conversations that consisted of more than three words. I noticed that Pan and him spent a lot of time talking in the corner and standing much too close. I couldn't believe she could do this to me? Wasn't she one of my best friends? As I asked myself these questions it almost made me cry, but then I remembered that it was I who was marrying Holt not her.

It was almost three a.m. the following morning when the last of the partygoers left the restaurant. We had all been dancing and having fun, except Holt, who said he didn't dance even though I had seen him on the dance floor with Pan earlier. Anyway, he did stay around until the end, and I was grateful for that. As we left I could tell he was rolling drunk, he needed to put his arm around me for support, not affection. His breath smelt like a fire hazard, and I hoped he'd make it home without collapsing as I certainly couldn't lift him. I had planned for a little romance after the party, but I knew that was never going to happen or not to night anyway.

Once Holt was safely in back seat of the limo we headed home. It was then I noticed again the black SUV some distance behind. I told myself there were many black SUVs in Texas. However, I knew I'd seen this one before. As I observed it out the back window of the limo I knew this one was definitely following us, and tonight it was not being so discreet.

Chapter 21
The Wedding of Brook and Morris

It was a perfect day for a wedding, the following Saturday, as Brook and Morris prepared to become husband and wife. It was early on Saturday morning as I sat in my huge bed and talked to Brook on the phone.

'Lyme, I just can't wait. I don't think I've ever been so excited about anything in my life. I mean who wouldn't love him…' her voice trailed off dreamily.

'Brook, he's certainly changed you,' I commented.

'No, he hasn't, you mean just because we don't go to the shooting range any longer or do other crazy things like we used to. We'll do all that again once we're settled.'

'No, Brook, that's not what I meant at all. You're a softer, more loving version of yourself, you care more about others, and the fact you've come up the hard way is less visible,' I replied hoping she wouldn't take it the wrong way and take offence.

'Yeah, well, thanks, I think. I wasn't aware I was so uncaring, and all those other things you said before.'

I was worried I'd said something wrong until she added, 'Morris brings out the best in me. He says we both make the other a better person. I agree with him, we do.

Anyway, wait till you see his families ranch, it's awesome and getting married as the sun sets will be amazing. Our photographer says it makes everyone look more beautiful, as it is the kindest part of the day.'

'I guess Pan knows that already.'

'I'm sure, she does, she knows everything she can do to make herself look more beautiful, if that's possible.' We both laughed as Brook added, 'Speak of the devil, she's on the other line. See you later, Lyme.'

'Yes, see you later, Misses Delaney.' We both giggled as she disconnected.

I lay in bed for a while longer, then a soft knock on the door announced my breakfast tray had arrived. I was smiling to myself thinking of the love Brook and Morris shared when I heard soft murmurings from the adjoining door. I know I shouldn't have, but I quietly got out of bed, and put my ear against the door. It was a solid door like the rest of the house. Holt was on the phone, his voice loud as usual. Apparently, Daddy had taken his cell away until after the wedding. So, he must be talking on the house phone. This is all I heard.

'Well, be patient honey…'

'No, I won't change my mind.'

'I've always loved you.'

'Just hold on, maybe a year.'

'All right, less then.'

'But we'll have each other and the money.'

'No, I've never so much as even kissed her, you know I only love you.'

I didn't want to hear anything more. I assumed he was talking to his ex-wife and making plans with the poor woman to reunite with her in a year's time. I liked Marnie, and she deserved better. She had a year to find someone else, and I had a year to make Holt love me. At present that seemed impossible. I needed to talk to Granny Harry. It was almost eleven a.m. when I hung up the phone from talking to Granny Harry, she always managed to put a smile on my face. I loved her dearly, and I promised to see her before my wedding day.

Again, I sat silently in my bed I knew that I should shower as the makeup and hair people along with my stylist would be arriving in less than an hour. Then I would have to sit still for absolutely ages, while they worked their magic, I hated it all. But, I would do it for Brook. Wasting time sitting around while strangers fiddled with my hair, and face was not my idea of fun. Pan would have loved it.

I'm not sure how long I lay in my cozy bed thinking. Until my thoughts were disturbed by a different noise close by. Softly, through the adjoining door, came the sounds of female moaning and whimpering with desire. Surely, it wasn't coming from Holt's room? Wasn't he just talking to his ex-wife, and telling her how much he loved her. I felt sick, how could he have another woman in his room when I was right next door. I hated him. I tried to close my eyes and block out the sounds. I knew I should stay where I was but my body seemed to move on its own. Slowly, I walked toward the adjoining door. I pressed my ear hard against it as my heart pounded in my chest, and I broke out in a sweat all over. I could hear two people talking and making love. I was only getting some words, but it was certainly two consenting adults enjoying whatever they were doing. But who was it in Holt's room, and how did they get in, how did they get passed Newton, or maybe Newton and Daddy were out. Then I heard two words that froze my soul.

'…not like Big Daddy and his sweaty meaty hands…' It couldn't possibly be Cerise could it?

Surely she couldn't be that stupid? Maybe, I'd heard wrong? Should I burst into the room and surprise them? No, it was two against one anyway, and neither of them liked me. I hoped I had heard wrong? If it was Cerise she was playing with fire and I wouldn't want to be in her place for anything. She clearly had no idea just who she was messing with, when it came to my father.

I moved away from the door and tried to stop clenching and unclenching my fists. I took several long slow deep breaths. Right, now I needed to calm down, I must have heard wrong anyway whoever was in Holt's room had left. Yes, I had not heard what I thought I'd heard. I headed for the shower.

The rest of the day was spent, getting brushed and combed, scrubbed and painted. I hardly looked at the end result. I moved like a robot giving each of my glam squad a huge tip. I couldn't wait for them to leave. In my head I was going over what I heard through the door, the moaning, the giggling, the words… oh no this would break Daddy's heart. So, what did I care if it did? Well, somewhere inside me I did care, and I knew, even if he wouldn't admit it, he would care also. Cerise was the only woman Daddy had allowed to get close in a long time, and she was just using him. Maybe, I should just tell Newton? Maybe, Newton already knew...

It was a small wedding by Texas standards. There were only a selected few invited probably around three hundred and fifty people, or so I guessed. The Delaney ranch was exquisite and suited Brook and Morris perfectly. Major Lavender Bliss was the first person I saw as I exited the car, I had decided to drive myself, I wanted to be alone. The guests had not yet started to arrive, but the place was a veritable hive of activity already. Wedding planners, caterers, security, relatives and many more, all ran around.

One of the horse paddocks had been made into an outside wedding chapel. Complete with fairy lights in the trees, bales of hay as seats covered in white velvet and neatly arranged in rows. White flowers everywhere, roses, jasmine, magnolias, peony, violets, and many more, but they were all white. It was quite a walk to the house where Brook was getting ready. The Major informed me Morris had taken over the large guest house, his usual quarters. He said the groomsmen, and Morris were having a wild time, and that he was going to join them.

The ranch was huge with many modern buildings, manicured gardens and beautifully tended flowerbeds everywhere. I walked into the main house, and Pan was the first to greet me. She was bubbling over with excitement, and looked beautiful in her deep pink dress that was similar to mine. It was low cut and feminine, and it billowed out behind her as she walked. She inspected my makeup and hair as she followed me into a huge room where Brook was being attended to.

'Lyme, I thought you'd never get here?' Brook said breaking away from the group and giving me a big hug, she then held me at arms-length and whistled under her breath, before she hugged me again, most unlike Brook. Still hugging me, quietly she whispered, 'Are you all right?' to which I shook my head and held back the tears as she was whisked back to the dressing table to get her hair taken out of curlers. This was her day, and I didn't want to ruin in it. Anyway, Pan was cooing enough for us both and micro-managing every little detail of Brook's look. I knew she was in heaven. I sat in the corner with a glass of champagne and tried to get myself in the mood for the wedding. There was a third bridesmaid who I didn't notice until she stood before me, it was Morris's sister, she wore a similar dress in a pale lemon, it was a very pretty color, and I would have liked to exchange it for my purple creation. Morris had just sent Brook a romantic note and pair of diamond stud earrings, everyone jumped for joy at the sight of them and then Brook read the note aloud, *'Brook my darling, don't read this note out loud it is only for your ears. You put the sparkle in my life and always will, these diamonds can never compare to all, you have given me. You complete me. You are my sparkling diamond now and forever. Your soon to be husband, Morris.'*

How lucky Brook was, although she deserved it. I envied her, even though I knew I would never get a note like that on my wedding day. Finally, the wedding dress was brought into the room, and we all stopped and gasped. No one spoke as Brook was helped into her dress. It was white satin, it was sheer on the top with a sweetheart neckline, and it fell straight to the floor, plain and elegant.

However, when Brook turned around the back of her wedding dress was an elegant party with many tiny covered satin buttons and deep plunging V. The skirt flared out dramatically and cascaded out behind her into a ten-foot train. The veil was sheer and fanned out behind her also and was longer than the train. Brook looked breathtaking, everyone stopped and stared once the veil was in place, and I thought I would cry as several other women were already doing, including Morris's mother. What is it about a wedding dress that makes women cry?

I couldn't wait for my wedding. My dress was nothing like Brook's, so I knew no one could draw a comparison between our two weddings. I understood now how it was more about marrying the man you love than the wedding. Brook had said she didn't care where or how they married just so long as Morris was the man sharing it with her. Slowly, I was coming to terms with the fact that Holt didn't love me, and probably never would. It had never occurred to me before that the person I loved would not necessarily love me back. It was a frightening thought, and one that I was realizing slowly and reluctantly. Once I was pregnant, I would tell Holt he could divorce me. Daddy didn't like him, although they were similar in many ways, and I knew that if his behavior didn't change, I wouldn't like him either in a few months.

All these thoughts went through my mind as I sat watching Brook. She radiated happiness, and she was a woman who was very loved, indeed. How Morris had changed her, in the short time he had known her, and she had changed for the best. They acted differently, she looked different, and I knew her life was different.

It was then I got a text message from Holt, apparently, he didn't feel like attending Brook's wedding, so he wouldn't be here. It said nothing more, it was blunt and to the point, no kindness, no love, no caring, no apology. I almost cried, but knew this wasn't the time to take the attention from Brook. So, I took several deep breaths and swallowed my tears as I so often did these days. Then it occurred to me that maybe Holt was going to leave while I was out. I began to shake at the thought. Quickly, I texted Newton, and within minutes he responded, saying he was watching Holt closely, and not to worry. Again, I took several slow deep breaths to steady my nerves.

The two tiny flower girls walked slowly down the aisle throwing red rose petals on the ground as they walked. The grass was a very dark green and candles lit the sides of the aisle. Followed by the littlest member of the wedding party, the ring bearer. Everyone laughed as he kept forgetting which way to walk and turned around in circles. Finally, the two flower girls walked up and guided him toward the makeshift altar under the arch of white baby's breath. Then the second bridesmaid, glided forward in her soft flowing yellow dress. Then, Pan who looked radiant and lastly, myself the maid of honor.

I hugged Brook tightly as she waited, 'Do you think Pan will forgive me for making you the maid of honor, and not her, Lyme?' Brook asked a slight cloud of doubt on her otherwise happy face.

'This is your day, Brook, yours, and Morris's, remember that. It is the first day of the rest of your life. He is a very lucky man, and this is your wedding, so I hope Pan realizes you can do whatever you like.' I hadn't really answered her question, as I knew Pan was as jealous as hell at not being the maid of honor, but so far, she had said nothing and appeared to be only helpful and happy for Brook.

'Lyme, thanks for being my best friend, and never judging me or telling me what to do,' Brook said as we realized there was a lull in the wedding procedure. It was my turn to walk, and I was holding everything up.

I quickly hugged her, and said, 'Love you, Brook.' And before she could reply, I began my slow walk down the aisle. I should have begun my walk when Pan was halfway as we had been instructed, so when I appeared everyone turned, and began clapping and cheering, I heard several comments about a runaway bridesmaid and not a runaway bride; I knew all eyes were on me.

The ceremony was simple, touching and very poignant. As Brook first read her vows to Morris, there was not a dry eye in the place and then Morris surprised everyone, and his vows were even more heart felt. No one could have a doubt that these two were very much in love. Their kiss was by far the longest kiss I had ever seen at a wedding, and it wasn't until everyone began to clap in time that the kiss finally ended; then we all cheered again, and as they walked back up the aisle. The sun was beginning to descend as the photos were being taken. Soon the wedding party moved to the banquet tables that were also set up in the paddock. The place was alive with fairy lights and fiber optics, the lighting technician did an incredible job. It was a true Texas feast, the speeches were taking place, each one more entertaining than the last. Until lastly, the Major, Morris's grandfather took the floor and everyone forgot about their meals. I had to admit that old man could really spin a tale.

I drank too many cocktails that night. I really wasn't hungry, and the cocktails seem to cheer me. We danced until late. I didn't need a partner everyone was dancing with anyone or by themselves. I was asked to dance with many young men and only danced by myself for one dance. Pan literally had suitors lining up to dance with her, so I knew she'd be pleased, she could take her pick, and she did. The evening was balmy although there were huge heaters on high poles around the paddock, and I noticed they were switched onto low.

The first rays of the sun were coming up over the horizon as Morris and Brook decided it was time to leave. They were headed to Hawaii and were due back the day before my wedding. Not many people had left, so they had a loud and long farewell. Once they left we all seemed to suddenly realized it was dawn, and the guests scattered until just a few bodies remained. Pan was doing a slow dance with a very handsome young man, even though there was no music. I had intended to talk to her, but she was far too involved to have time for me. There was nothing else to do other than try and avoid the Major and get to my car.

I drove home slowly as the sun began to rise, I noticed in my mirror the black SUV several cars behind mine, but I was too tired and too drunk to do anything. Although, I did take the gun from the compartment in the glove box and tuck it close beside me. I tried to search the windscreen for the faces inside the SUV, I thought there were two men, but the windows were darkened and I couldn't be sure. This time, they certainly were discreet. But who were they, and why were they following me?

Chapter 22
Madam Roderic ~ 5

'Where is she?' Pan asked the maid who stood looking at the floor and obviously feeling most uncomfortable.

'I not know, Miss. Pan.'

'Well go, go and find her,' Pan pouted as she yelled at the poor girl. The maid quietly left the room as Pan got to her feet and paced, back and forth. She was still dressed in her flowing nightgown and matching pink sheer overlay, as she moved it billowed around her perfect body. She then sat, and drummed her perfectly manicured fingers on the arm of the white leather chair. Pan did not like to be kept waiting, she thought Madam knew this. Why was she doing this?

Finally, after what seemed like ages to Pan, her phone rang. 'Ms. Pan, Madam Roderic is at the gate awaiting entrance.'

'Well, let her in immediately, you stupid girl. She knows the way to my room. Tell her I have been waiting and I'm not pleased.'

'Yes, Miss,' the young girl replied sounding close to tears. Again, to Pan it seemed like ages before she heard a soft knock on her bedroom door,

'Come in, Madam,' Pan called getting to her feet.

'Ms. Pan thinks Madam is tardy?' Madam stated the moment she entered the room. Pan had seen that look on Madam's face before, and she knew to back down. Madam's thin frame and birdlike face seemed to glide in to the room, she was dressed as always in her brightly colored flowing robes. Her long boney fingers with the long hawk like nails moving rapidly in the air as she spoke.

'I am just glad to see you, Madam. I have been waiting.'

'I understand Ms. Pan does not like to be kept waiting, but you are not the only person in the world.'

'But I am the only person who actually matters,' Pan replied then giggled as her face softened.

'You are spoilt and selfish and must one day learn to see the others who share your world.'

'I see them, Madam',

'You see nothing but what you want to see, and in your world there is only you. You are the only one who is important,' Madam continued her arms and hands simply flying around her as she emphasized her words. Pan giggled.

'You are right, Madam, you know me so well. This is what makes you special.' Pan giggled delightedly at Madam's words.

'Why do you always want to see me if you never listen to anything I say?'

'But I listen to all you say, and every word you speak,' Pan replied giggling.

'You listen only if it is about you. You do not care or hear anything else.'

'Oh, yes you're so right, you are always correct, how clever you are,' Pan exclaimed clapping her hands together lightly at the older woman's' words.

'So, why does Ms. Pan not listen to the warnings I give to her about her friends?' Madam was not to be put off this time, and Pan was beginning to see this, so she thought an honest answer was required, and then Madam could return to the subject of her.

'Because this is not what I pay you for. If they want to know what you have to say about them, then they can contact you, themselves.' Pan thought this a good answer and expected to not hear another word about it, but as she watched, Madam threw her arms in the air, and turned her blazing gaze toward Pan, she shook her head from side to side.

Pan giggled she loved the drama madam created, finally madam collapsed on the floor at her feet, her legs crossed. 'It is no good the words that madam speaks are not heard.'

'Oh, yes they are, Madam, I simply hang on your every word. No, please, return to me, and tell me about the young handsome man who stole my heart at Brook's wedding. I danced with him most of the evening in spite of the many others who wanted my attention. He was very mysterious, so please tell me all you know about him?' Pan asked excited that they were finally going to talk about her.

'The young man you speak of, is a pretty boy and not for you.'

'Have you forgotten all men are for me, Madam?'

'I have not forgotten this, but he is a pretty boy, and you should forget him.'

'I know he is a pretty boy, very handsome actually, so go into your trance, and tell me about him, I want to know?'

'Madam does not need a trance to tell you, he is only a pretty boy, and not for you, do you not hear what I am saying? Your pretty boy, Madam sees, he is gay?' Madam was staring hard at Pan as she waited for her words to be heard. Madam thought that after a few moments Pan understood, although when she spoke she wasn't sure.

'Oh, how much fun will he be, I am pretty also, do you not think so, Madam?' As Pan watched, Madam's huge eyes, narrowed, and she seemed to become angered by her words.

'You want to hear what Madam has to tell you, but you will not listen; always you whine and complain if it is not about yourself. Perhaps, Madam tells it in a way you do not like, perhaps her story is told without you being the main focus. If you do not like what Madam says, maybe I should leave and never return to your home again…'

'No, please, Madam, I value all you say and do most of what you suggest, please tell me what I should be hearing today.'

'A trance is draining to Madam, and should you interrupt, spirit gets confused. Madam loses her focus, and all is wasted. Madam can only tell you what she is told from spirit. Spirit must tell you what it needs you to hear.'

'Yes, I understand, Madam, I shall not interrupt.' Pan was getting impatient, she needed to start her day, today it was taking too long with Madam to get the answers she needs. But Madam was in a strange mood, and Pan knew to be wary, so as hard it was for Pan she said nothing and waited. Madam looked closely at her for some time before she closed her eyes, her body started to vibrate. Pan watched her eyes move rapidly under her closed eyelids. Then her body became rigid, and in a deep voice, and accent unlike her own, she spoke slowly at first then faster.

'Madam, sees it is after the wedding, some months after, the baby is not born, it does not yet know the person we think is the father doesn't love it. But maybe the father is not who we think him to be, there is confusion, only spirit knows. Spirit chooses not to tell at this time. Now I see the oil man, big and square. He and the girl are looking from a hiding place from a place they should not be. They see things they need not see. So much anger inside the man, so much hate. He is gone, then he returns to stand by the girl with the baby inside. But madam is confused, the woman he watches through the bushes also has a baby inside, she is with a man. Then the oil man, he has a gun, but he never gets to shoot…but yes, there is a gunshot, oh, no….no, no….no….' Madam screams a heart rending scream that ripples through the house. Pan claps her hands, and speaks as Madam crumples on the floor at her feet.

'You entertain me so, but I do not want children or babies; maybe this is not about me? Although I shall have a baby if you think I should, but please, Madam, do not sleep, you have not told me the baby's father, you have not told me enough about me, Pan, you remember me....' Pan looked down at the pile of colorful clothes at her feet. Her giggling stopped, and it was gradually being replaced by disgust, why did Madam persist in telling her about things she didn't want to hear or know?

A knock came from the door as Pan began pacing the room. This morning meeting with Madam had been a complete waste of her time.

'I heard a scream, Miss. Is everything all right?' the maid asked, then gasped as she saw the crumpled form of Madam Roderic on the carpet. Madam had always told Pan never to touch her, but today. Pan was annoyed; why should she pay to listen to things about others she didn't want to hear and didn't need to listen to? But if she dismissed Madam, who would run her life?

'Miss, can I get you anything?' The young maid's words broke into Pan's thoughts.

'Yes, tell the two young gardeners to come to my room, and make sure they remove their shoes.' Hearing Pan's words, the maid looked at her hard for several seconds, until Pan noticed she was staring at her and said, 'Go.' Pan flicked her perfect manicured hand at the girl. Pan knew one of Madam's rules was never to touch her, but she was sleeping on the carpet and in Pan's room. She seemed to sleep for longer each time she came here. Once the two young men arrived, they were startled to see what looked like a pile of colorful rags lying on the floor. Pan had seen one of the men before he was very short, less than five feet, and that was the only reason she recognized him. In contrast, the other man was tall, very tall, scruffy and lanky, they made quite a pair.

'I'm Jack, Miss, and this is Zeek, you sent for us?'

'Yes, move her out of my room?' Pan instructed pointing at Madam's still form lying on the floor. The two young men looked down at her, bewildered.

'But where shall we move her to, Miss.?' The older of the two men asked, the one named Jack, he spoke in a board southern accent.

'Why should I care? just take her out of here...' but still they hesitated, so Pan added, 'She is in my way, take her to the kitchen then.' Pan wanted Madam out, she had found the whole session tiresome this morning. So, if the young men needed to know where to take her then the kitchen it would have to be.

Pan watched as they gingerly moved toward the still form of Madam.

'Is she dead?' the other gardener asked.

'Come on, boy, I doubt she's dead, grab her legs,' Jack responded.

The tall one searched under the garments for her ankles and grabbed them holding them high. As he did so her many layers of clothes fell away. Pan saw his eyes open wide, he was staring down at Madam. Then she too saw Madam as her naked legs were now revealed, thin masculine hairy legs. On the end of her thin legs, she wore heavily muddied work boots. But now they were all staring together, as her clothes fell away further from the slim frame. Madam was wearing tight red men's jockey underwear. Pan stared. There was no mistaking. Madam Roderic was a man…!

Chapter 23
Lyme and Holt's Wedding Day

Granny Harry arrived early on the day of wedding. I was still in bed and sleeping, when my granny tiptoed in my bedroom. She didn't wake me but instead sat in the chair in the corner watching me sleep. She was an early riser, and I doubted if dawn had even broken before she was at my front door. I wasn't aware when, several hours later, the maid discreetly entered my room with a set breakfast tray for Granny. I hadn't slept much the night before. Doubts had begun entering my void. It had started when I first tried to remember when Holt had said something nice to me, and the closest I get was when he had given me the doll, for fat girls. The stress of having him in my life had caused me to lose a lot of weight, and with it I was feeling frail and vulnerable. My mother had always said to be true to who I am and love myself. I had to admit they were great words, and I had to love myself because at four-thirty a.m. this morning, I had come to the realization that Holt never would.

I was slowly coming to terms with the fact that I must let him go. I would tell him at some stage after the wedding, provided I was pregnant by then. Although I doubted I would tell him that. I knew how he felt about babies, and I knew he never wanted any. It would be best he didn't know, fewer complications, and easier if I never saw him again. After I made these two decisions, I slept easier, although the ache in my heart persisted, I knew I loved him, deeply, madly, truly, and I always would.

I finally awoke at ten-thirty a.m., and the first person I saw was Granny Harry, how delightful. She sat on my bed and gave me the biggest hug I had ever had, she then got into bed with me, and we talked. We talked of my mother, and how she would have enjoyed this day, we spoke of Grandpa, and how much she still missed him and much more, but not about Holt. I knew she wanted to know how I felt about him, but she never asked until finally, I felt strong enough to tell her what I had decided.

'Apple, this is for the best. I know you love him, but you deserve someone who loves you back. This marriage can only ever hurt you and take you into despair. Now, you have accepted what must happen, you will come to terms with it, I know, you are made of stronger stuff,' she concluded hugging me tightly as my maid knocked on the door and entered. She informed me it was time to get into the shower as my glam team would be here in less than thirty minutes. I declined breakfast knowing I wouldn't be able to eat. A tingle of excitement rippled over me; this was my wedding day.

The maid had just left, and I was headed to the shower when I heard a commotion through the wall from Holt's room. It was Daddy, and I think Newton. I put my ear to the wall and listened. Holt's said he wasn't going to walk down the aisle with me until the rest of the money that was promised him was in his bank account. Those were his terms, and Daddy could take it or leave it he didn't care. I was shocked, but once I thought about it I was not surprised, after all it was a mere business transaction for Holt nothing more. I was still listening at the wall when Brook and Pan burst into the room, followed by their dresses and assistants. Suddenly, the room was crowded. They hugged Granny first, followed by me,

'Lyme, why haven't you showered?' Pan questioned.

Before I could answer Brook asked, 'Do you want us in here with you, or shall we use another bedroom each?'

'Yes, the two across the hall are all ready for you both,' I replied.

'Lyme, get in the shower and order champagne, this is your wedding day, and the day I meet my next husband,' Pan replied giggling.

'How can you possibly know that?' Granny asked taking a seat in the corner out of the way of all the commotion,

'Oh, I have this simply divine, fortune teller, Madam Roderic, or I use to, I don't know whether I'll be using her any longer. Anyway, she told me that I would meet my future husband today, and she's always right.' Hearing Pan's words Brook, and I exchanged glances.

It was Brook who spoke first, 'What do you mean you may not use her any longer, Pan?'

'Well…' Pan began looking more serious than I had ever seen her, 'Madam has seen me in my bedroom in my nightie and in my undergarments when I get dressed, she has shared my most private and intimate thoughts, and now I find she is not who she says she is.'

'People seldom are dear,' Granny added.

'But, Granny, it's just horrid really it is, I thought I could trust her she said I could, she shared my whole world and then…' Pan looked at the floor, and I knew she was almost in tears.

'Pan, and then… what?' I asked, moving closer to her, she had our full attention now, and she was no longer giggling.

'Oh, it was so dreadful. I am still in shock. I still can't believe it, not, Madam, how could she…' Pan replied turning away from us, she knew that neither, Brook nor I had ever been a fan of Madam Roderic's.

'What is so dreadful, Pan?' Brook asked.

'I don't even want to say it, I am in total shock; I saw Madam nearly every day, and she scammed me in the worst possible way. I know neither of you liked her.'

'Pan, what on earth has she done?' I asked again, knowing the time was moving on, and today should be about me.

'She's a fraud, that's what…' Pan said, and she was more emotional than I'd ever seen her.

'There is a lot of them out there, Pan, and we often get taken for a ride, no matter how careful we are,' Granny added in her level calm voice.

It seemed to work for Pan as she calmed down and then quietly whispered, 'Madam Roderic is the biggest fraud of them all.'

'Why, Pan, why?' I asked again, knowing it must be something bad to give her a change of heart like this.

'Madam Roderic is one of the best-known fortune tellers in the world, but she is not Madam Roderic at all, she is not even a woman, she has been in my bedroom a hundred times, Madam Roderic is actually a man,' Pan said as a sob escaped her, then she added, 'And now she is suing me, because I know her secret. She's saying I harassed her, stalked her, and a whole lot more…' Pan said her head downcast, and I know she was about to cry. Brook, and I looked at each other, and then we both looked at Granny, sitting quietly in the corner. Then a knock came from the door, my glam squad had arrived, and I wasn't yet showered. Brook and Pan left to go to their own rooms where their glam squads had been setting up, while I headed for the shower.

The ceremony was to be a small affair with just my two friends, Granny and Daddy in attendance, although I knew Cerise, and Amber Buxton had invited themselves. Then at five we were due to enter the reception, a huge affair, with red carpet, the press, and almost a thousand people present. The cake I was told was almost six feet tall, and the focal point of the room. I no longer had any great expectations regarding Holt. If he could tolerate me, I would accept it. However, the thought of having to get pregnant by him confused me, and I wasn't sure how I could do this, he had rebuffed any, and all advances I had made to date, and he seemed to like me less as times went by. Should I get the opportunity, I would speak to Dr. Dan; I felt sure Granny had filled him in on the situation. These were my thoughts as I sat for what seemed like hours and it probably was, as my team worked their magic and transformed me into a princess. They told me I was getting the full wedding treatment, and I couldn't imagine it taking any longer than last time, but it did.

Finally, I was brushed, combed, sprayed and painted and the team cleared up their many things, and finally left. It was just Granny, and I. I let out a breath, I wasn't sure I was holding.

'My, beautiful Apple, you look so perfect, not like my girl, but perfectly beautiful as you've always been to me...' Her words were cut short by a loud knock on the door, I assumed it was the girls, but to my surprise it was Daddy who entered. His presence immediately dominated my room. He looked almost handsome in his navy -blue tuxedo; it had no doubt been made for him as it fitted him to perfection. He looked taller and slimmer.

'Well, girly...' he began, standing in the middle of the room and giving Granny only a quick nod of acknowledgment. 'This is your day, and already you look like a princess. I know it is not everything you had hoped, and I know you are doing a lot of this for me, and I'm damn proud of you. I wanted to give you these to wear. They belonged to your mother, I gave them to her on her wedding day.' Daddy handed me a velvet case, he almost appeared shy, and this was new to me.

I took it and held it in my hand as I asked, 'Is everything all right with you and Holt, I heard you, and him arguing this morning. He will be at the church, won't he?' This had been worrying me all day, I knew Holt was head strong and unpredictable. Daddy had a short fuse always and was easily angered and used to getting his own way. However, Holt, I was learning was unpredictable also.

'He won't let my princess down, it was nothing to concern yourself with, and nothing a little light persuasion couldn't fix.' We stood looking at each other, I wondered what he meant by light persuasion, I knew Holt didn't want to marry me, but I hoped Newton hadn't hurt him with his light persuasion. Anyway, why should I care Holt was getting paid very well, I knew it had taken some hard bargaining on his part, although to me it was all worth it. Daddy took a step forward, I thought he might hug me, but then looking awkward, he merely said, 'I'll come and get you in about forty minutes once you are dressed.' Then he turned, nodded again at Granny and left the room.

'Well, he hasn't improved with age,' Granny said chuckling, just as the door opened, and Pan and Brook floated in, they both looked spectacular and smelt even better.

'We saw Lyn in here, so we thought we'd wait,' Brook added as Pan nodded.

'Yeah, he gave me this, it belonged to my mother.'

'Oh, I almost forgot,' Brook said, turning to Granny, 'you have a gentle man admirer, and he wants to meet you one day.' I knew Brook was talking about the Major, and I didn't want to discuss him right now. Fortunately, I was saved by Fox entering the room with two maids; they held my dress over their arms. Everyone gasped, including me, it was exquisite, even more than when I had last had a fitting. It was covered in tiny diamantes, and it twinkled under the light as they moved. It was a very pale ice blue, so pale it appeared almost white. This had been Pan's idea, of course, she said it was the latest color on the runways of Paris and Milan, and that's where the dress was first seen by Pan. Vera Wang had designed it; it was her design, and I was to be the first to wear it.

The dress was a soft swirling mass of the finest, sheerest, layers of chiffon. And once it was on, I stood and stared. It was a princess dress with a sheer tight lace bodice that was barely there but covered me up to the chin and down to the waist. It had diamantes sequins strategically placed and lots of them. It fitted my diminishing waist to perfection. At my last fitting, it had been slightly too tight, but Pan had deemed that perfect. Then the skirt cascaded out around me in layers upon layers of dreamy chiffon, until when it hit the floor it created a huge circle of fabric. The train was at least ten feet and part of the circle of the skirt. As I moved the sequins sparkled. I knew each one of them was a genuine crystal and had been hand sewn on to my dress. The veil, like Brook's, was simply one layer of sheer fabric, but once it was covering my up-swept dark hair, it fell around me like an invisible cloak.

No one spoke as they all looked, my dress took up most of the room, and I noticed Granny wipe her eyes. This was a moment I would never forget; it was magical. Then Pan handed me the box Daddy had given me. I really didn't want anything from him, he had arranged this marriage, and that was all I needed, I was doing it for him anyway. But he had said my mother had worn them on her wedding day and that was enough for me. Inside the box was a pair of diamond drop earrings, a short matching diamond necklace, and two matching bracelets. Their design was not fancy but elegant in its simplicity. I wouldn't wear the necklace as my dress was more than enough, but I did wear the earrings and bracelets.

'Oh, Apple, I remember putting these on your mother, and it seemed like only yesterday. Right at this moment you look more like her than at any other time in your life.' Granny said getting up and carefully moving close enough through the fabric of my dress to hug me.

Then a tap came from the door, and Daddy entered, 'You better be dressed, girly, we're damn, well, already late, don't keep me waiting now...' he stopped talking as he entered the room, his mouth fell open, and he stared up and down my body; his eyes went, continued to go up and down. The he spoke in a whisper, I think I was the only one that heard, no one was used to Daddy being softly spoken, 'You look beautiful, you look just like your mother, Lyme, just like your mother, she would have been so proud. We had often spoken of this day.' I noticed his eyes were glistening as he presented me with his arm. The he boomed, 'You bridesmaids are supposed to keep the bride on time, what the hell, girls, what the hell. The evening hasn't even started and already you girls are lazy.' I could see Brook's jaw set, and I gave her sharp look, I knew she would have retaliated to Daddy's words and now was not the time.

'Where's that Granny of yours? I thought she of all people could tell the time.'

'I'm right here, Lyn, just had to get changed, and yes, I can tell the time, but this is my granddaughter's day, and time is not as important as letting her enjoy it.'

'Still got a fast mouth, time hasn't changed you,' Daddy replied, but this time he said it in a controlled manner as Pan and Brook exited the room. Then I heard another loud voice, and there was no mistaking who it belonged to.

'Leave, me, fucking alone; I'll leave when I'm ready. I don't need you watching and touching me. You're a fucking bully just like your master, so back off.'

Then I heard Newton's controlled voice, 'We should have left already; you are supposed to be there before the bride…'

'Like, I, fucking care.'

'You've had enough to drink, I believe, sir,' Newton replied.

'I could never have enough to drink to make me feel fucking comfortable marrying her.' I heard his words, and

I saw the way Pan and Brook looked sideways at me, but I wasn't going to cry. I made a decision last night which seemed to make me feel stronger and more prepared for the future. Before I exited my room, I grabbed my glass of champagne that was sitting untouched on the side table and swallowed it in one gulp. I felt Daddy tense at Holt's words, but he said nothing as we headed for the door. We exited my bedroom with great difficulty as my dress hardly fitted through the door. We saw Newton in the hallway, Daddy gave him a look, and Newton nodded briefly, it was hardly a movement at all, but they knew each other well. Holt was not in a good mood, again.

The marriage ceremony was brief and to the point, we both signed the papers, even though I had my doubts that Holt would. He was very drunk and Newton forced several cups of black coffee on him. I had expected him to object but somehow I felt Daddy had the upper hand and Holt understood that, but wasn't yet ready to accept it. Holt looked so handsome in his deep blue velvet tuxedo and pale blue evening shirt that matched my dress. I could hardly tear my eyes from him, and I knew many of the women, including Cerise, were mesmerized by his good looks.

I felt Daddy's pride as he walked me down the short aisle after Brook and Pan. Padbury Prentice was Holt's best man, as Holt didn't wish to have any of his family or friends involved. I knew, he was especially close to his mother, and I wondered if he had even told her? There were no vows written by either of us, nor was there any words of undying love, he placed the ring on my finger, without touching me, and as he wouldn't wear a ring himself the service was over quickly. Holt however did give me a kiss when it was requested. It wasn't on the lips, and I knew it was only for show, but the mere touch of his skin on mine sent shivers through me like I had never known. Then we had some photos taken, they were fun, and maybe it was because Holt was so drunk that he relaxed a little, or maybe he had just given in, but I somehow doubted it. I knew the photos would look awesome.

Then we were off to the reception, a huge affair; the likes of which Texas had never seen. There was over three thousand people invited, and it was by invitation only. Most of them were Daddy's work acquaintances, and I knew he was, as usual, showing off his wealth. So, I only knew a few of these people, and as the speeches began, I looked into the sea of strangers and at that moment I envied Brook's smaller intimate wedding. After the speeches and formal sit-down dinner, where I needed two chairs to accommodate the skirt of my dress. Pan, Brook, and I sneaked away and removed my huge skirt. Under the skirt the same bodice of the dress cascaded into a short cocktail dress in the wonderful ice blue flowing chiffon, sequins and style. It sat just above my knees and kicked out as I walked. I loved it, maybe even as much as I'd loved my wedding dress. I removed several of the pins from my hair, and as the hairdresser told me, the back of my hair fell loose.

I hoped with the shorter skirt that Holt would at least be able to get close enough to speak to me, as so far, he had not said any more than he needed to. The first dance was the father daughter dance, and Daddy, and I waltz around the floor with grace. Holt at some stage was supposed to cut in and that was to be the cue for the other guests to join us on the dance floor. But the dance was nearly over, and the second one had begun. I knew the band was confused, so they played another waltz. Daddy gave Newton a discreet nod as we whisked passed him, and I saw Newton speaking to Holt. To which Holt replied loudly, 'Fuck off.' I noticed a little subtle pressure was applied, and before long Holt reluctantly cut in on our dance. Soon everyone joined us.

'I hope you're enjoying this dance because it is the only time I will ever dance with you.' When I didn't reply he continued on with his negativity, '…and who the hell gets married in a blue dress. Like a wedding is fucking white, are you so dumb you don't even know that? You looked like a blue puffy meringue,' Holt's nasty words continued on, and I said nothing. I realized again he was not a nice human being and never would be. The moment the music ended and the next band arrived, I excused myself from Holt's arms. Even then, he made a scene, standing in the middle of the room and yelling, 'So that's how you treat your new husband? You just abandon me by walking off and leaving me in the middle of the fucking dance floor.' Holt had a very loud voice, and if he intended on embarrassing me, he'd succeeded. Brook and Morris gave me a very concerned look. I already knew how Morris felt about Holt, and it was nothing good. But I liked the fact that Morris cared about Pan, and I, in a brotherly way.

As the night wore on, I never sat down. I was wearing much higher heels than usual; I had meant to change them when I removed my skirt, but somehow as I chatted with Pan and Brook, I had forgotten to do so. Now I could barely feel my feet. Everyone wanted to dance with me. Most of these people I didn't know. They usually told me how they had met my father; a few knew my mother and then there was the endless list of cousins, which I had seldom seen. So, I danced the night away, my feet hurting more with each dance until, finally, I couldn't feel them at all. Daddy had flown in Elton John, Adam Levine, and his band Moroon 5, Steve Tyler and more. It was a night to remember, and the press had a field day. I knew my wedding would be in every paper in the USA by tomorrow.

It seemed like hours before we cut the huge cake, and it was handed around. Then more dancing began with yet another band. They soon had everyone jumping around on the dance floor. Later that night as the last band arrived, we all enjoyed the old rock 'n' roll songs. I assumed it was what Daddy requested. Everyone seemed to find their second wind after part taking of the late-night buffet, and soon the dance floor was full.

Finally, in the early hours of the morning, I noticed the crowd had thinned out, almost three quarters of the people had left, including Daddy and Holt. It was then a tall dark handsome stranger whisked me away from the older man I was dancing with. I looked into his hazel eyes, and my heart skipped. We moved slowly in each other's arms, then as my heart began to race faster, we moved closer. His eyes never left mine. Who was he? He was gorgeous and the chemistry between us was undeniable. Pan had been dancing with the same man all night, and I could tell she was smitten. I didn't know who the handsome stranger in my arms was, but I felt we looked good together. Brook and Morris both nodded at me, and Brook winked as they danced by, and even Pan noticed, so our chemistry must have been obvious.

As we danced past the balcony, he glided me outside. It was almost deserted, and the couple whom had been out there kissing, looked sheepishly at us and quickly disappeared. I was in a complete trance as he pulled me into his body and wrapped his arms snuggly around me. Our faces were so close that it seemed natural to kiss. It was a kiss like no other. It began softly as he searched my lips then gradually it got deeper until the passion running between us, swept over me. I felt like I would faint if he let me go. We seemed to kiss forever; I never wanted it to stop, and apparently, neither did he.

Finally, we drew slightly apart and looked again deeply in each other's eyes. I saw in his eyes, desire, need, and a depth of passion I thought only I could feel. Who is this tall dark handsome stranger, who has whisked me off my feet at my own, wedding? Doesn't he know I'm the bride? We stood looking at each other for what seemed like eternity as the noise from my wedding reception gradually dimmed, whether it was from people leaving or my complete focus on him, I didn't know or care.

Then he pulled back slightly but still holding both my hands in his, he spoke. 'I have wanted to do that from the moment I first laid eyes on you', he said as I blushed and looked away. Then he gently put his finger under my chin and lifted my face so I was again looking at him,

'You are the most beautiful girl I have ever seen. I dream of you. I have loved you for so long.'

'But...' I began, and he kissed me again, long and deeply, and my world spun out of control.

'You are even more beautiful in person than in your photos. You are the perfect woman.'

'But you don't know me?' I began, and again his lips brushed mine. It was then Brook and Morris found me, hugged me close and said goodnight.

'Pan and several others are looking for you, Lyme, Granny said to say goodnight she couldn't stay awake any longer.' And, just like that the spell was broken... for the moment, but he stayed by my side as I bid many of the guests' farewell.

Finally, when we were by ourselves by the door, he said, 'Come', I followed him like a lamb. I would have gone anywhere with him. And somehow, I knew I trusted him. Hand in hand we walked out of the reception area, and to the elevators, which lead to the penthouses. He stroked my back in the elevator and kissed my neck until I shivered with delight. The rest of the night or what was left of it was the best night of life. We made love, passionately, deeply, and longingly, we were both thirsty, like two lost souls who had finally found each other. I don't know how many times our bodies mounded together, but I do know that each time was better than the last. I had never experienced anything like it.

It was noon when we decided our lust was finally quenched. We lay back in the huge bed, naked and covered in sweat. He reached for my arm and softly kissed it until my cell interrupted me. As I answered it I looked into his face, it was a familiar face to me. I felt like I had seen him before; but maybe only in my dreams.

'Lyme, where are you? Mr. Lyn is asking for you…' I came back to reality with a crash.

'I'm on my way, Fox', at her words I jumped out of bed, it felt strange dressing in my fancy dress of the night before. It was still damp with sweat.

'No, Lyme, please, don't go. I have found you, and I want to be with you forever. I don't want to wake up and look at your photo beside my bed, I want you in the flesh, Lyme, please,' he said as I searched for my other shoe. It took me a while to get them on my swollen feet. I was amazed at his words.

'You have my photo beside your bed?' I couldn't believe anyone would have my photo beside their bed.

'Your beautiful face is the last thing I see at night before I close my eyes and sleep, and the first thing I see every morning. What better way to start the day?' I had both my shoes on as he said, 'When will I see you again?'

I didn't answer as I headed for the door. I had too much to think about, too much had happened and I was now a married lady.

I opened the door to leave and before I closed it I looked at him, so handsome and naked laying on the white crisp sheets, and I asked again, 'Who are you?'

'Don't you know?' he replied as I shook my head,

'I am Remington Tillerson-Proctor.' As the cab pulled away from the curb I noticed a black SUV with heavily tinted windows, also pull into the traffic. I no longer thought it a coincidence. I knew I was being followed. It had been my shadow for some time now. What I didn't know was what to do about it. Maybe, I should tell Newton? I also knew the black SUV sat outside our mansion, and I knew the occupants were watching. I had thought they were only watching me, but why I didn't know? However, I had observed lately that their focus was not on me when I was home. Was it perhaps Holt they were after? If it was him they wanted they could easily have taken him before the wedding?

In my mind, the name Remington Tillerson-Proctor, went over and over again…

Chapter 24
An Ending or just the Beginning?

I had no time to think; as I sat in the filthy cab my gorgeous dress, looking so out of place in the light of day. I had arrived at my wedding reception in a horse drawn carriage, and I was taking a cab home. I sneaked up the back stairs and quietly opened the door to my bedroom. Fox was standing in the middle of the room waiting for me.

She looked me up and down and said only, 'Into the shower and hurry,' I obeyed. In my head, I kept thinking, so that was Remington Tillerson-Proctor, the man Daddy had chosen for me. I couldn't believe it; I was in shock. Everyone could hear Daddy bellowing throughout the house as I descended the stairs two at a time.

'What the hell girl, just where the hell have you been? What the hell do you have to say for yourself?' he bellowed getting up from his chair from behind his desk and walking slowly toward me. I stood my ground and stared at him. Now I felt so loved it had given me strength, and I somehow felt more powerful also. I didn't need to answer him nor was I going to. I was thirty-five years old, and I didn't need to explain to him where I had been. Although, when he stopped in the middle of the floor and began pacing I understood this was not about me at all.

After the silence stretched on for some time, I ventured to say, 'Thank you for the wedding, Daddy, it was every girl's dream.'

'Yes, but was it your dream?'

'Yes, it was, of course, it was Daddy, you outdid yourself.'

'Well, what the hell girl this was all about me getting a grandchild, and I still expect you to produce. But things have changed, I know you married Holt because you love him, although I cannot imagine any one loving that motherfucker.'

'Daddy...' I replied, knowing I didn't sound at all convincing.

'Well, if you hadn't loved him perhaps there was no need for you to so hastily marry him.' I didn't understand what he meant, so I remained silent and waited.

'Just before you mentioned Holt to me, what was it two months, six weeks ago. I decided to ask Cerise to go off birth control. I'm not getting any younger, and you didn't seem to be seriously looking for a husband, or in any hurry to give me a grandchild and heir. You're a grown woman now, Lyme, and you must understand I am not getting any younger. I need to know my empire will be in the right hands after you're gone and for generations to come. So, it needs a blood relative, and I was beginning to get desperate...' I hadn't heard much after he said Cerise was off birth control. I was shocked, how could he think of having a baby with Cerise?

'Hell are you even listening, girly,' he bellowed taking several steps closer to me.

'Surely, you can at least congratulate us.' I hadn't heard what he was saying, and now I blurted out.

'For what?'

'What the hell girl! I just told you Cerise is going to have my child.' This time I heard, and I was lost for words. I felt like I would be sick, and again the image of Cerise in her lacy red bra with Daddy's huge meaty hands moving over her body, flashed into my mind. I swallowed hard. Then I saw Daddy glaring at me and tried to focus on him.

'This is not the reaction I would expect from my own daughter. I always support you girl, no matter how much I disagree. Is it the age difference that troubles you? Yes, she is a little younger than you. But I thought you'd be happy. I will not be alone any longer. I am amazed I can still make a baby, and so quickly also. This has made me feel like a young man again, only now I don't need to struggle, I have already made it, and now a baby. Hell, I really thought I was passed all this stuff. If I'd known about Holt sooner, I wouldn't even have contemplated having a baby, but when she asked, it seemed like a good idea at the time, and then Holt came into our lives. I don't like or trust the motherfucker, as you know. But I couldn't change my mind, you are strong willed like me. Cerise was so excited, and she has somehow managed to weave herself into my life both personal and business. So, can't you at least be happy for us?' This was a huge speech for my father to make without yelling or smashing anything so I needed to swallow my disgust hard for I knew I must say the right thing.

'Congratulations, Daddy, I am very happy for you if this is what you want.'

'I was reluctant to admit it, but she makes me feel young again…' he said wistfully. He moved back behind his desk and poured himself a dram of whisky into the small cut crystal whisky glass on the silver tray. He turned to look at me just as I was about to slip away.

'You shall, of course, be bridesmaid it is what we both want. We only found out the good news last night. She will still look fabulous in her dress. Hell, we have already started the preparations.'

'Me, a bridesmaid?' I said totally in shock.

'Well, of course, Cerise and I both agreed you would be her bridesmaid, or now you're married I guess you shall her matron of honor; is that the correct term? I never thought we would both be getting married within three months of each other.' He sounded wistful again as he turned his chair to look out the window. I quietly began to tiptoe toward the door and let myself out. But before I could, Daddy surprised me by saying one more thing.

'I hope you enjoyed your wedding night, whereever you and Holt decided to go.' I couldn't answer, I turned and walked to the door, he said nothing further, and I was unable to answer him. My cheeks burned with embarrassment about what I had done last night and also the envy and hatred I felt for Cerise. I knew I was about to cry. Cerise was pregnant, and Daddy was actually going to marry her. I walked passed Newton holding in the tears until I reached my bedroom. I lay on my bed and sobbed, deep racking sobs. I wasn't aware Fox had entered the room until I heard her softly put the tray beside my bed, then she sat on the bed and quietly rubbed my back. She said nothing. I must have fallen asleep then as when I awoke the shadows were drawing. The tea Fox had left for me was stone cold, but I drunk it and ate the griddlecakes that were also cold.

I rolled onto my back and became aware of the soft smell of jasmine. I turned to see a huge bouquet of flowers had been placed in my room while I slept. They were exquisite, all my favorites. I knew who had sent them, and I also knew that this time I wouldn't throw away the card. A slight smile played on my lips. I stayed where I was, staring at the ceiling as the last of the daylight played into the room and dusk covered the land. I was thinking of Remington, how could I not, he was after all the only pleasing thought I had. How could I have been so stupid as to not have agreed to meet with him. I was stubborn like Daddy; I knew that was the main reason. Although, would I have liked him if I had met him under different circumstances? The slamming of a door, close by, rudely interrupted my thoughts. It was the door to Holt's room. I then heard giggling, so I immediately jumped from my bed and listened at the adjoining door. This is what I heard; it was mainly Holt's voice.

'You, maybe excited, but I never wanted you to get pregnant.'

Then a pause as the girl muttered a replied, 'How do you know it's not his?' then another pause as the girl answered, I was now sure it was Cerise.

'Then don't speak of it, it's a fucking turn off to me, so shut up and use your mouth for...' then a moan, followed by sounds of heavy lovemaking. Why wasn't he making love to me? I had never felt his touch over my body, never had his kisses, nor had I felt his desire for me, only his cruel words. I felt like storming into his room, I was his legal wife after all, but I knew he would have locked the door. I moved away from our adjoining door that was never unlocked, and I collapsed on my bed, I lay there and placed my hands over my ears. I was, without a doubt, still very much in love in Holt, even more now that I had made delicious love to Remington. Had I fallen into the trap of wanting something just because I couldn't have it? I had usually gotten everything I wanted my whole life, so, yes, this was a new experience to me. And maybe all it is; is a case of wanting the unobtainable.

I wanted to get pregnant, but just how could I do this if Holt never touched me? Maybe, I would have to talk to Dr. Dan.

Another month went past, and it was only just over a week until Daddy and Cerise's wedding. I could not believe Daddy didn't know what was going on between Holt and Cerise. Although I observed, they were careful and always sure Daddy and Newton were out. I don't know if they ever thought I was worth checking on, but I guessed not. I noticed during that time once I began to pay more attention, that Cerise never left the mansion. Everyone she needed came to her. I also knew Holt was getting annoyed with her and had re-buffed her advances on several occasions. She had not been pleased and on these occasions instead of the moans of lust, it was Holt's loud annoyed voice, that came easily to my ears. I completely left him alone, and I noticed that gradually he began speaking to me, and we even went out to dinner on several occasions. Once with Pan, and her new man, Chester Lawson-Smyth and once with Brook, and Morris, although Holt's behavior was far from sociable on that occasion and the night ended badly.

It was about that time I decided to visit Dr. Dan. I knew he understood my predicament, and he did. He greeted me warmly with a hug as I entered his small but homely doctor's room.

'Lyme, my dear it is always a pleasure.'

'Thank you for seeing me, Dr. Dan; I want to talk to you about Holt.'

'My dear, I understand I had breakfast with your Granny and Roam just last week, and we again discussed your predicament.'

'Oh, so what can I do', I asked hating the thought that I had been discussed behind my back but then realizing it was making it easier for me.

'Well, let me ask you this. Is there any way of knowing if Holt's sperm are viable?'

'I don't understand. We have never…'

'What I mean, my dear, is, does he already have any children?'

'No,' I began and then added thinking of Cerise.

'Yes, maybe he does. Cerise is pregnant, and I am almost sure he is the father.'

'Cerise?' Dr. Dan asked confused.

'Sorry, Cerise is Daddy's young live in lover.'

'Oh, well, she could only be pregnant by Holt if she has been intimate with him.'

'Or my father, Dr. Dan.'

'Oh, no, my dear, that wouldn't be the case or it is unlikely to be the case, after you were born, your father had an accident in a mine which left him, well shall we say sterile and unable to do very much in the bedroom. I know your mother was devastated, and so was he, your dear mother wanted more children. We had hoped over time his injuries would heal, and they certainly may have. But how well they healed I wouldn't know he hasn't consulted me in years. The child maybe his, but if you think Holt has been intimate with this woman I would say it would more likely be his.'

'Oh,' I replied never having known any of this.

'I do hope I haven't said too much or spoken out of turn, it is not my desire to shock you, my dear.'

'No, no, thank you for sharing this with me.'

'So, now we know he is viable, all we need is his sperm.'

'But then what…?' I asked suddenly feeling very nauseated. I was never sick, and I guessed it must be from the thought of Holt's sperm. I quickly excused myself and headed for washroom. I threw up violently, once and then again. Never had I done this before. When I left the washroom Dr. Dan was standing directly outside.

Once back in his rooms he asked, 'Is there any chance you are already pregnant? I know Holt hasn't been near you but...' I was about to say no, and then I remembered Remington. I had been seeing rather a lot of Remington, and we made love several times on every occasion we were together.

'Well...' I said as Dr. Dan asked me to use the washroom again. I drunk a whole bottle of water straight down and waited. I knew, I was indeed pregnant. And I was....

I had bought myself a husband, and now I was going to have a child, only it wasn't his... I told Daddy the moment I entered the house, even though Cerise was in the room. I believe they both thought it was Holt's baby and that was okay with me. Daddy was overjoyed but the look on Cerise's face was priceless. As I left I asked Newton if I may have a word. He walked away from Daddy's door, and I mentioned to him that I thought, no, I was sure, Cerise and Holt were having an affair, behind Daddy's back. He raised an eyebrow and said he would take care of it. And I knew he would. Two days later, I received a note to joined Daddy at the pergola. This was a strange and unusual request. The pergola sat on a small hill beside our mansion and from there you could look over most of Daddy's domain. I knew my mother and him had often sat there in the summer time when I was a child. They would have cocktails, hold hands and giggle while I played somewhere close by. I remembered those as the perfect times of my childhood. I hadn't been there for years, and I didn't think Daddy had either. The note also said to come alone and to move very quietly. I was intrigued; this reminded me of some of the games Brook and I used to play before we were married.

I approached so quietly even Newton didn't know I had arrived. I was wearing green a good camouflage color. I thought both Cerise and Daddy were with the wedding planner making last minute plans for their wedding this Saturday. But I was obviously mistaken. Newton put his index finger to his lips telling me to stay quiet. Daddy was looking through high-powered binoculars. He was staring in the direction of the pool. I followed his gaze, and I could see Cerise and Holt lying in the sun and to my horror, Cerise was topless. They were lying very close to each other and as I watched she seemed to be arguing with him. We could hear them talking but not make out their words. Daddy's cheeks flushed crimson; I knew he was furious.

Then even from where I was standing I could see Cerise remove her bikini brief bottoms and straddle Holt as he lay on the lounger in the sun. I don't exactly know what happened next, but to me it happened in slow motion and it was a time I would never forget. First, Daddy dropped the binoculars and then from out of nowhere he produced an automatic rifle.

'Daddy, no,' I screamed, and when he turned to me his face was set, his eyes like steel and his pupils mere pinpoints in his head. I saw him slowly raise the small rifle. He held it in two hands, one hand supporting the underside. He looked through the sights, I was inches from him. He hadn't pulled the trigger as I raised my hand to grab the rifle but at that very second two loud shots rang through the air. I knew Daddy hadn't yet fired, but I knew he was going to. My eyes were so close to the trigger I was sure he hadn't fired. We heard a brief scream and saw, Cerise collapsed on top of Holt, there was blood everywhere. I turned to exit the pergola and in the distance on the hill of the road I saw a black SUV. A man was climbing off the roof and in his hand, I am sure, I saw a high-powered rifle. The SUV was the same one that had been watching me. Now it was they were silently speeding away. Had they meant to shoot me? But from that distance a good marksman would not have missed. I was much closer to the road than Cerise and Holt. Newton got to them first, and he told me to stand back which I did. One shot had missed while the other shot had entered Cerise and then passed through her going into Holt. Newton quickly pronounced them dead.

'I shall handle this from here, Mr. Lyn, Miss. Lyme.' Newton instructed and Daddy put his arm around me, and we both entered the house.

That was the last I ever saw of Holt or Cerise. Daddy locked himself in his room just like he had when my mother died.

Apparently according to Newton, Cerise was the target all along. Because Cerise never left the mansion, they decided to follow me so I would lead them to her. It turned out Cerise's real name was Fanny Smith, and she was the wife of a high profile Connecticut mobster. She was also the mother of four children; she had apparently cleaned out his bank account and disappeared several months ago after trying to poison him. I couldn't believe it. I didn't like her, but I had no idea she had a whole other life. I asked Newton if Daddy knew, and he replied that Mr. Lyn didn't want to hear anything bad said about Cerise. Maybe, Holt and Cerise were a good match after all.

I felt a deep sense of loss, but it was a loss at losing something I had never had. The funerals were held instead of Daddy's wedding. I knew he had taken it hard. Daddy never liked being taken or betrayed. I saw Holt's wife Marnie at his funeral, she was dressed in black and standing discreetly at the back. After the brief service I tried to go to her, she was visibly upset, but she walked toward a waiting limo got in and drove away without a backward look. Also, at the funeral was my darling Granny Harry, and to my surprise, on her arm was none other than Major Lavender Bliss. Now that was an extraordinary sight.

And so, I had bought myself a husband, loved him, married him and buried him. What was I thinking…

That evening I called, my old flame, Clive Broadbench.

'Well, it's not a lemon, it's a Lyme and what a nice surprised.'

'Yes, I was thinking of you.'

'Naughty thoughts, I heard you were married, shouldn't be thinking of another man unless it is my prowess as a tennis player and nothing more.' I laughed, he was fun, and I didn't know why I had called him, but I wanted to, so I did.

'Indeed, that is all, it is.'

'My world missed the fruity tang of your laughter for quite a while but not anymore. I have another doubles partner now, she may not be as fruity as you. She is Abigail my ex-wife and she is happy to return to my life and my bed. Sorry, Lyme. Guess we weren't meant to be together in this life time. Our timing sucks, you and I, but our tennis…. Well… But, as far as my favorite flavor of fruit is concerned I'm afraid it's too little, too late. I no longer have the smell of lime in my thoughts.'

I was surprised he had an ex-wife and also a little sad at his words, but happy he was no longer alone. I don't really know why I called him, I didn't really want to see him again, but I did want to hear his voice, he was fun, and I should have given him a chance.

'Clive, great news so glad you're happy. Maybe, we'll meet again sometime, and you can let me beat you at tennis again.' We both laughed and disconnected. I was truly glad he had found someone, as I had.

Daddy stayed in his room for two weeks after Cerise died. When he emerged, he was thinner and older and certainly much quieter. Remington and I announced we were to marry very soon. I told Daddy that his choice of a husband was right all along. All Daddy said was, 'The joining of the two biggest oil families in America, what more could I wish for in my lifetime, just perfect.' And he came forward and hugged us both.

Brook was happily married to Morris.

Pan would soon be engaged, again.

I turned to Remington who was holding my hand and standing close beside me. I looked into his eyes and saw my future gazing back at me. It was at that moment I felt for the first time the soft twitching of new life inside me, and I replied, 'Yes, Daddy, I agree, life is perfect.'

Once I found Remington, my need to visit my void at night gradually disappeared. It was something I thought I had valued, it was something I was glad to say was all mine, but I was learning that in life we often try and fulfil our need of being loved and wanted with something we make ourselves believe we value, something we want to believe is special. Well, I now understood my void was not special, and it had only been mine because I had nothing else.

Now each of my days and nights are filled with a love I have never known, from a man who believes in me, adores me and even thinks I'm beautiful both inside and out. With Remington I can be me, and I was learning *me* was someone I hardly knew. So, Remington and I discovered *me* together, each and every day and very slowly *me* got to know him, the person he was, the things he liked, and his heart, and the completeness of his soul.

No longer were the pages of my diary blank, but once I started writing I found there wasn't nearly enough space to accommodate all I had to say. I shared every little thought with my diary, my fears, hopes, dreams and desires. Somehow, I knew my mother was reading each page, as more and more I felt her love around me. Maybe, I had to be loved and know love to feel her presence. I didn't know, but I did know she was there beside me for every step of the way, like I had never known her to be, before. Now, with Remington beside me my dreams were all coming true. I didn't have to buy a man to love and marry me. I had thought the man I loved would automatically love me, but he didn't and never would. I knew Holt could never love anyone or anything. He was a horrible man who looked good, but inside he was mean, nasty and cruel. I would soon have a husband and son of my own. I no longer needed to learn how to buy a husband.

The End

<u>Other books by Mary Barr</u>

Mrs. Dolymauchers Daughters

The Grasshopper File

Wild Dog Canyon

A Rumble in the Attic

Hagar's Curse

Browning Amble – The Sect

Dahlia's Choice

<u>Plus</u>

A collection of short stories, Novella's, Young

Adults and Children's Books.

<u>WWW.Mary-Barr.com</u>